ESCAPE VELOCITY

OTHER BOOKS BY NICK MARONE

Fire Over Troubled Water

Space Trip Universe
The Green Rebellion: A Space Trip Story
Space Trip
Space Trip II
Space Trip III

Nahla Chronicles
Nahla: Warrior of the North
Nahla: Enemy of the Kingdom

ESCAPE VELOCITY
THE WORLDS OF NICK MARONE

SEVENTEEN SHORT STORIES BY NICK MARONE

Delta-V Press
Queanbeyan, New South Wales, Australia

First published in Australia in 2024 by Delta-V Press

Copyright ©2024 Nick Marone
nickmarone.com

Nick Marone asserts the right to be identified as the author of this work in accordance with the *Copyright Act 1968* (Cth).

ISBN: 978-0-6488641-8-9

All rights reserved.
No part of this publication may be reproduced, stored in a retrieval system, or transmitted, in any form or by any means, electronic, mechanical, photocopying, recording or otherwise, without the prior written permission of the publisher.

The stories in this publication are works of fiction. All characters, events, organisations, and locations in this publication are either products of the author's imagination or are used fictitiously.

A prepublication catalogue record for this book is available from the National Library of Australia.

Cover art by Warren Design

Printed by Lightning Source

"The Funny Formula", by Nick Marone. Copyright © 2022. First published in *Science Write Now* in August 2022.

"The Time Has Come", by Nick Marone. Copyright © 2023. First publication, original to this collection.

"The House of Time", by Nick Marone. Copyright © 2020. First published in *Aurealis Magazine* #133 in July 2020.

"Fortissimo", by Nick Marone. Copyright © 2023. First publication, original to this collection.

"The Lonely Old Man", by Nick Marone. Copyright © 2023. First publication, original to this collection.

"To Have and To Hold … Forever", by Nick Marone. Copyright © 2023. First publication, original to this collection.

"One-Way Ride", by Nick Marone. Copyright © 2023. First publication, original to this collection.

"The Price of Inspiration", by Nick Marone. Copyright © 2021. First published in *Etherea Magazine* #2 in September 2021.

"Pilgrimage to Earth", by Nick Marone. Copyright © 2019. First published in *Journeys: Aussie Speculative Fiction* in December 2019.

"Just Deserts", by Nick Marone. Copyright © 2023. First publication, original to this collection.

"A Miner's Dream", by Nick Marone. Copyright © 2020. First published by Nixter Entertainment.

"Director's Cut", by Nick Marone. Copyright © 2021. First published in *Space and Time Magazine* #140 in March 2021.

"Big Game", by Nick Marone. Copyright © 2023. First publication, original to this collection.

"What's Your OTI?" by Nick Marone. Copyright © 2023. First publication, original to this collection.

"Brittle and Strong", by Nick Marone. Copyright © 2023. First publication, original to this collection.

"Guidelines for Successful Interaction with First Contact Species", by Nick Marone. Copyright © 2020. First published by Delta-V Press.

"Falsehood", by Nick Marone. Copyright © 2023. First publication, original to this collection.

This book is dedicated to all the writers who toil at their short stories and continue resolute in the face of rejection letters.

CONTENTS

INTRODUCTION

I CONSIDER THIS COLLECTION ONE of my greatest achievements as a writer. Let me explain that. I have always been a long-form writer, busying myself with novels and novellas. During my high school years, I always struggled to write short stories. I just couldn't seem to keep a story contained in a small, digestible package. Yet, I wanted to challenge myself. I wanted to see if I could write a short story. It didn't matter if it was rubbish, and it didn't matter if I never sold it. I just wanted to prove to myself that I could tell a story in under 7,500 words.

This collection is the result of my growth as a short story writer. Seventeen stories of varying length in an array of subgenres, a testament to my determination to challenge and improve my skills. I used to dread writing short stories when I was younger, and I never finished any. Now I love it. In fact, I love it so much that it saddens me that I can't write more. It's not that I don't have ideas—I have plenty of ideas! Rather, it is a cost–benefit problem. It takes time to write short stories, and it sometimes takes months to receive a rejection or acceptance letter. To earn an income as an author, short stories just don't cut it. Therefore, I decided to focus on my long fiction. As a final send-off to what has been a marvellous and joyful ride as a writer, I have collected all my short stories into one volume so I can share them with the world.

In this collection, you get to read all the short stories I have completed as a writer. Experienced readers and fellow writers will see how my writing improved over time. So this book isn't just a presentation of each final product. It is also a study of developing skills. I have supplemented my stories with helpful behind-the-scenes articles that show how I constructed each story, the problems I faced, and the solutions I created. I also offer a window into the business side of writing—the reality of story submissions, the importance of contests, the value of having a hard skin in the face of rejections. My intention is that new writers can use this collection to inform their own writing.

I debated how to structure this collection. Ultimately, I've presented my stories in an order which I feel gives the reader an enjoyable reading experience. Therefore, the stories are not presented in the order in which they were written. For readers who want to track my writing development, the chronological order of writing is:

1. "A Miner's Dream" (p. 161)
2. "The Time Has Come" (p. 13)
3. "The Lonely Old Man" (p. 57)
4. "Pilgrimage to Earth" (p. 127)
5. "The Price of Inspiration" (p. 119)
6. "The House of Time" (p. 29)
7. "Falsehood" (p. 253)
8. "Just Deserts" (p. 141)
9. "Director's Cut" (p. 179)
10. "Big Game" (p. 191)
11. "What's Your OTI?" (p. 207)
12. "Brittle and Strong" (p. 231)
13. "Guidelines for Successful Interaction with First Contact Species" (p. 245)
14. "The Funny Formula" (p. 5)
15. "To Have and to Hold ... Forever" (p. 75)
16. "Fortissimo" (p. 45)
17. "One-Way Ride" (p. 101).

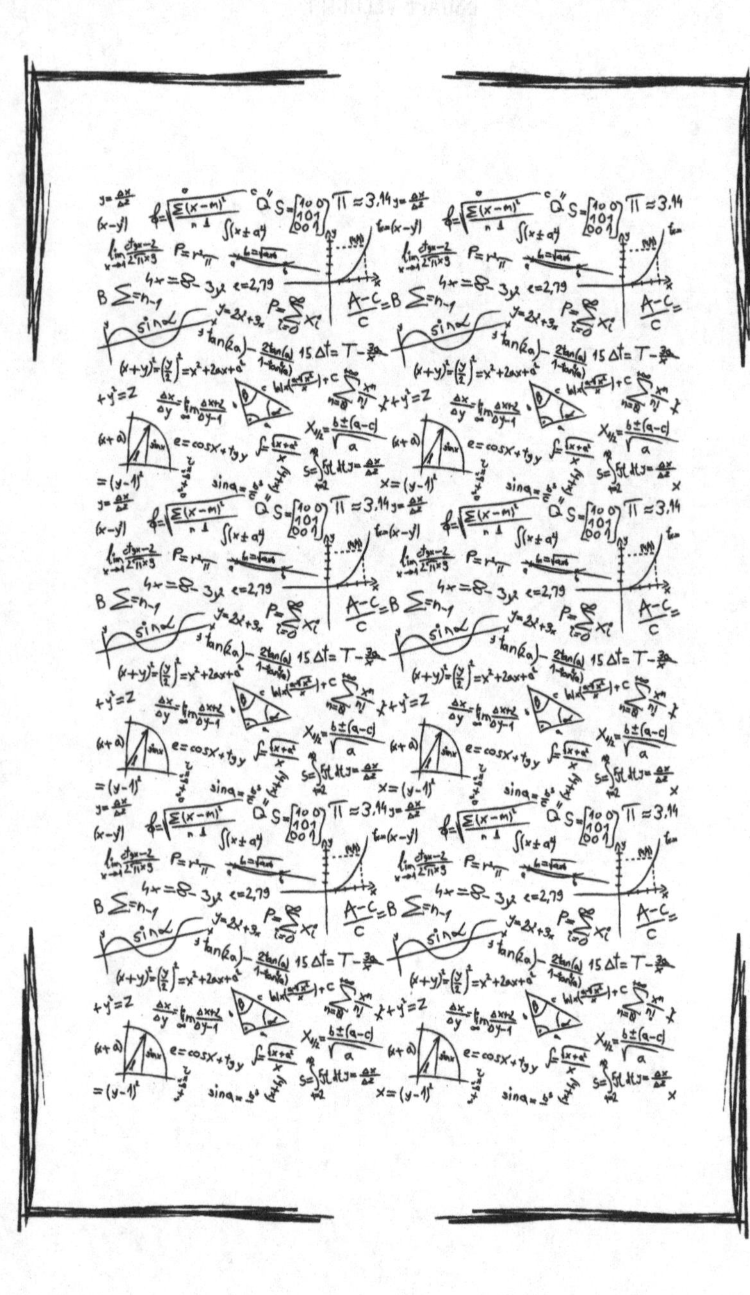

THE FUNNY FORMULA

THE IMPERIAL MAJESTY AND the Lords Superior have given me a challenging task: to learn why humans laugh. If the Hegemony is to subsume this planet, we must use humour to soften humankind's attitude towards extraterrestrials. This achieved, they will more easily accept our culture, and we will avoid the destruction that so often accompanies war and conquest. We do not want a repeat of the Eridipidus Incident.

Our primary goal, as I understand, is to avoid conflict and suffering. Humankind does enough of that already. In the past, humans laughed easily and freely, but that has changed in recent years. If we can re-inject a good sense of humour into their society, then our battle is already half won. In a hundred years, we can absorb their planet into our Hegemony without a single drop of blood.

From previous research and observation, I have started to develop a formula of humour:

$$H = T_1 + T_2$$

where Humour (H) equals Tragedy (T_1) plus Time (T_2).

Tragedy works on a scale of 1–10, with 10 being the highest severity. Time increases by 0.1 for every Earth month that passes after a tragedy.

Preliminary research shows that Earth has experienced innumerable tragedies over time. Humans also have a penchant to make light of tragedies after the event. This is a form of humour rarely seen in the Hegemony. Therefore, I will test this formula in various professional and informal settings. As a shapeshifter, I have unlimited personas to develop and use for my tests.

This report chronicles the results and the refinements to my formula. I begin my experiment tonight.

TRAGEDY PLUS TIME DOES not work. Nobody told me directly, but the overripe tomato to the face was more than understood.

I feel I made a critical error when picking my tragedies. I took my material from current events. However, my audiences were not happy about certain jokes about racism, war, terrorism, and disease. And yet, jokes about these very topics are abundant in comedic records. Closer examination of existing jokes shows that more time was allowed after tragedies. I keep seeing the words "too soon plastered in the replies of critics, so perhaps there is some validity to the Time element of the formula. But how much time needs to pass before a tragedy can become a joke?

My answer is rather simple. I must consider the severity of the tragedy against its topicality and the risk of the tragedy recurring. In the formula, Humour now has a minimum threshold for a joke to be viable. A joke must have a Humour Rating of 1.0 or greater for it to be effective, or else it will be terribly offensive to our human audiences. With this in mind, I have adjusted the formula:

$$H \geq ((T_1 + T_2) / (T_3 - R))$$

where Humour (H) is greater than or equal to Tragedy (T_1) plus Time (T_2), divided by Topicality (T_3) minus the Risk of Recurrence (R).

I measure Topicality the same as Tragedy (1–10), with 10 being highly topical. Risk of Recurrence is a decreasing scale of 5–1, with 1 representing the highest risk of recurrence. Don't as' me why it is backwards.

Now to put this adjustment to some rigorous testing. I hope I don't get pelted with tomatoes again.

IT WAS EGGS THIS time.

I got the severity right and was sure that the time after the tragedies was sufficient for the pain to have worn off. Indeed, entire generations have passed away since my chosen tragedies. But it seems the pain and suffering of historical injustices are more deeply rooted in certain cultures than I had originally expected.

Lesson learned: our agents must not make jokes about the suffering of certain cultures, races, or ethnic groups unless they have established some link to them. I call this the Immunity Phenomenon. For example, I have studied several Jewish comedians making jokes about Jewish history, and it seems to work well. People accept the jokes because the joker is addressing a lived or shared experience by using humour as a coping mechanism. The comedian is said to have Jewish Immunity, a sort of freedom of speech for all things Jewish.

Considering this startling realisation, I have modified my formula:

$$H \geq ((T_1 + T_2) / (T_3 - R)) \times I$$

where Humour (H) is greater than or equal to Tragedy (T_1) plus Time (T_2), divided by Topicality (T_3) minus the Risk of Recurrence (R), all multiplied by Immunity (I).

In this equation, the Immunity Phenomenon is measured in five stages of strength (0, 0.25, 0.50, 0.75, 1), with 1 being fully immune and 0 guaranteeing the joke's failure.

As this formula gets more refined, I notice that the margin for error is easier to identify and, hence, easier to correct. This bodes well for our future agents in the field. I shall now test the formula by applying the Immunity Phenomenon. I have selected several venues and a multiple personas representing different races and cultures.

MIXED RESULTS. I HAVE decided the word "boo" is dumb, but upon deeper reflection, I have realised that no amount of cultural immunity can help a joke that is poorly delivered. Yet again, time is an important factor; or, to be more specific, *timing.* Some of my jokes took far too long to tell, whereas others were so short they flew over the heads of even the fastest listeners.

Another factor I repeatedly botched was tone. One joke was delivered so seriously that I had to tell the punchline in three different ways before I heard the first laugh, and even then it was more of a snort.

Both timing and tone need to be factored together as the Delivery Quotient against the Immunity Phenomenon. Therefore:

$$H \geq ((((T_1 + T_2) / (T_3 - R)) \times I) / (D = (T_4 / T_5)))$$

where Humour (H) is greater than or equal to Tragedy (T_1) plus Time (T_2), divided by Topicality (T_3) minus the Risk of Recurrence (R), all multiplied by Immunity (I), then divided by Delivery (D), with D being Timing (T_4) divided by Tone (T_5).

Timing uses a two-stage measure—0.5 or 1.0—for fast and slow delivery respectfully. Tone is measured in three stages—0.33 (serious), 0.66 (conversational), and 0.99 (light-hearted).

I am confident that these adjustments will help me develop jokes that are consistently funny. I will now embark on a rigorous series of tests.

MY EXPERIMENTS WERE A marvellous success! I had every audience in stitches. I even had one woman out of stitches—her stomach suture unravelled itself during a moment of uproarious laughter.

However, while observing other comedians, I noticed something that I have named Shock Value. Some jokes were quite vulgar. Yet, the audiences loved it. I should note that the same comedians used a different repertoire of jokes depending on audience demographics. This tells me I can apply certain comedy styles to specific audiences for even greater effect.

I have added Shock Value as a modifier for Delivery:

$$H \geq ((((T_1 + T_2) / (T_3 - R)) \times I) / (D = (T_4 / T_5) \times S))$$

where Humour (H) is greater than or equal to Tragedy (T_1) plus Time (T_2), divided by Topicality (T_3) minus the Risk of Recurrence (R), all multiplied by Immunity (I), then divided by Delivery (D), with D being Timing (T_4) divided by Tone (T_5), multiplied by Shock Value (S).

Shock Value is measured on a scale of 1–3, with 3 being the most shocking and 1 being no shocking content (for audiences that cannot handle vulgar or insensitive humour).

I will now try my hand at some rude jokes.

THE FORMULA WORKED AGAIN! Several audiences loved the crude humour. For more conservative audiences, I successfully maintained a Shock Value of 1 (which is actually zero shock).

One constant variable I have noticed throughout my experiments is the self-entitled heckler. It can be difficult to plan for hecklers, so I have added a Bastard Effect (B) to the formula, with a value of 0.5. This should encourage the development of jokes that negate the effect of hecklers.

$$H \geq ((((T_1 + T_2) / (T_3 - R)) \times I) / (D = (T_4 / T_5) \times S)) \times B$$

where Humour (H) is greater than or equal to Tragedy (T_1) plus Time (T_2), divided by Topicality (T_3), minus the Risk of Recurrence (R), multiplied by Immunity (I) and divided by Delivery (D), D being Timing (T_4) divided by Tone (T_5), together multiplied by Shock Value (S), and the total formula multiplied by the Bastard Effect (B).

The Bastard Effect does not require testing. Since hecklers abound, and some comedians make a living out of interacting with them, the Bastard Effect serves as a quality check when preparing jokes.

THUS ENDS MY INVESTIGATION into Earth humour. I present a thoroughly tested Funny Formula for the Hegemony to manipulate humankind.

I recommend we begin our mission of assimilation as soon as possible. If the Imperial Majesty and the Lords Superior wish, I am more than happy to help prepare our agents for this extensive clandestine mission. My services and my life are, as always, at your command, subject to the successful receipt of a fifty per cent deposit.

Long live the Emperor! Long live the Hegemony!

THE FUNNY FORMULA

$$H \geq (((((T_1 + T_2) / (T_3 - R)) \times I) / (D = (T_4 / T_5) \times S)) \times B$$

EXAMPLE

$$H \geq ((((5 + 0.6) / (7 - 4)) \times 0.75) / ((0.5 / 0.99) \times 1)) \times 0.50 = 1.386$$
(a satisfactory joke)

ABOUT THE STORY

"THE FUNNY FORMULA" IS perhaps my most outrageous stories. A small Australian online publisher called Science Write Now put out a submission call for the theme *Science, Humour and the Absurd*. It's almost shameful that I spent so little time brainstorming. The idea came to me while having a shower.

My idea was simple, and sometimes the simplest ideas are best. In fact, it had to be simple because the word limit was 1,500 words! I'm mainly a long-form writer. The shorter the word limit, the harder it is for me to write it. Nevertheless, I knew I had a golden idea. It was based around the question: What would a scientific equation for humour look like?

This story deconstructs human jokes and the experiences of stand-up comedians from the perspective of an alien. But doing that alone was not enough. So I infused the backstory of the alien being a secret agent, and his experiment being for nefarious reasons. This came from another question: How might humour be used as an alien weapon? Ideas of peaceful assimilation and bloodless pacification filtered into the storyline. Very quickly, the story changed to an alien spy on a mission on Earth to seed human minds with the idea that aliens weren't all that bad, and to do so through stand-up comedy. Science: tick. Humour: tick. Absurdity: double tick.

Perhaps the most absurd thing about "The Funny Formula" is that I actually created a formula! To my unscientific brain, it kind of looks real too. I tried to think of all the elements that would go into a joke, and all the external factors that a comedian must consider for a joke to work.

"The Funny Formula" is one of my stories that sold at first submission. Science Write Now said it made them laugh, which is always a good thing to know. I've often wondered how my sense of humour translates through my writing. Humour is very subjective.

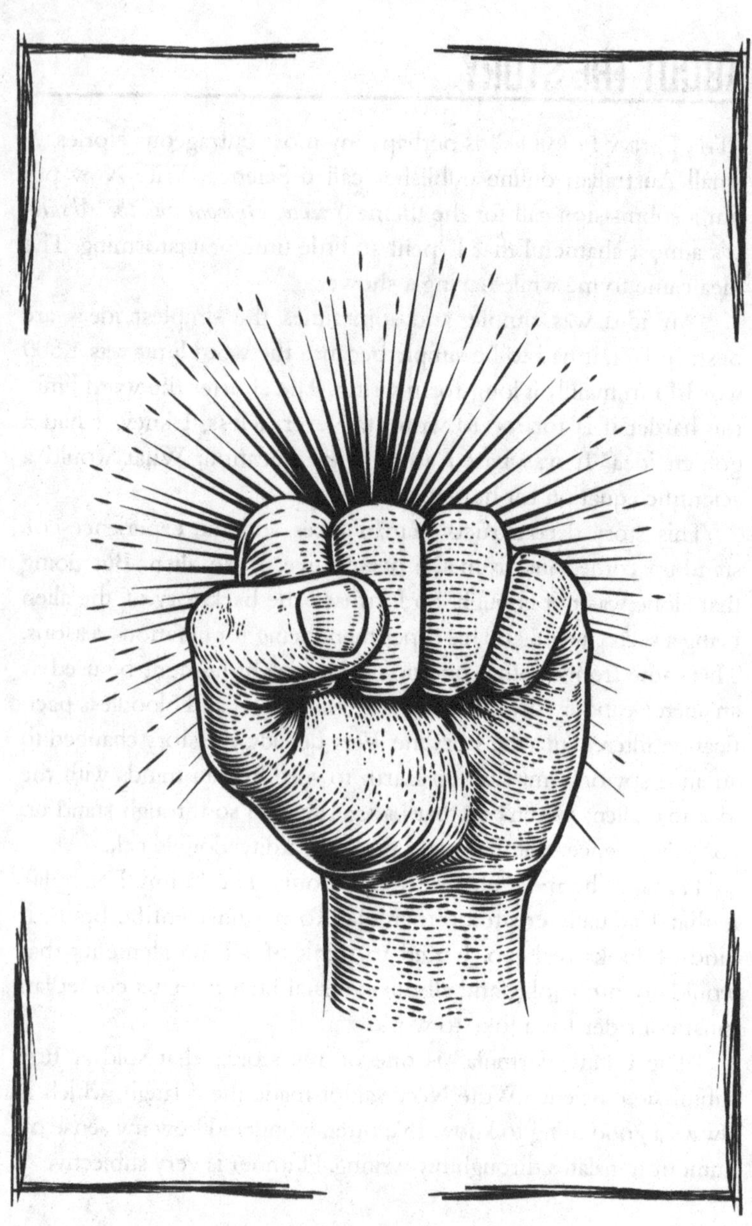

THE TIME HAS COME

My TEETH CLATTERED AND my bones ached in the cold despite the huddling bodies pressing against me. But I didn't complain. I had learned not to complain.

I arrived at the public square already filled with a few thousand people. The snow turned to slurry as we stomped on the spot, trying to keep the chill away. It never worked. Instead, it saturated our shoes and made our feet numb.

Every week was the same. The horns blasted their monotonous call, disrupting workers from concrete jungles to forested camps, from frozen wastelands to humid biomes. We had to pause our work while we attended last-minute assemblies at our local squares. We gathered under the weather, open to the elements, while the soldiers enjoyed the protection of metal shelters.

The day being discussed from the outset started the same as every other day. We awoke to the sound of horns, ate a tasteless meal that was just enough to satisfy our churning guts, and then we began the twelve-hour workday. On the walk into the mine and factory complex, we would pass the night shift, who were leaving exhausted, sore, and hungry—exactly how we would feel when we finished in the evening.

At around midday, the horns blasted again over speakers deep in the mine shafts. The entire work team stopped its activities to brave the cold and hear the latest news, propaganda, and empty words we had no right to criticise or openly discuss. Of course, this happened during our lunch break. I felt sorry for the night workers who were roused from their sleep and dragged out into the cold to attend as well.

Workers came from all directions. I checked the luminous digital clock tower at one end of the square. Its face glowed bright blue against the snowfall. It was five minutes to twelve and people still streamed in. Most of them were labourers like me, young and old, working in hundreds of State-run machines of the economy. We never got paid because we had no need for money. Food, shelter, and medical attention were freely provided in basic forms. Entertainment and leisure were nearly non-existent. Consumer goods no longer existed.

Soldiers watched us from a long, raised stage, though no speaker was present. People rubbed shoulders with me, nodding hello. Some mumbled the standard greeting, "Order, friend", for fear of saying anything else. Nobody smiled, because smiling meant you knew something Someone Else didn't, and that Someone Else was always watching. We waited for the clock to count down to midday so Someone Else could explain why we had been called from our jobs and beds.

It wasn't always like this. Before the hard labour, before the control and surveillance, we were free. We were a people, and we were individuals, each with a purpose in life. Granted, some saw their purposes better than others, but at least we had the freedom to determine our own course in life and be happy doing it.

All that changed when the System took over. Prior to that, we were a fledgling agricultural outpost. My grandparents moved here before I was born to escape an expensive, overcrowded life on Earth. This world, Arcadia, is all I have ever known, and I saw it change in a single, tumultuous month. Those old enough to remember the original life on Arcadia longed to see it again. We saw it in our dreams, but there it stayed. We didn't speak about it, nor did we commit our dreams to writing. It would only invite unwanted attention from The One Who Watches.

I was married before the System turned our worlds upside down. I haven't seen Imrah in years, not since the soldiers dragged her away when they separated the men from the women. Before she left my side forever, she's clutched my hand, secretly giving me her wedding ring. I held on for dear life. When they finally pulled us apart, crying and screaming, I hid our rings in my pocket and kept them safe while the soldiers beat me. Our wedding rings are the only physical items I still have from the past, my last tangible memory of the girl I married, and I guard them with my life.

The horns sounded as soon as the clock struck twelve. Three enormous video screens at different ends of the square lit up with the System flag: a black star atop a black fist, both against a red background. The video screens bathed our snow-covered bodies in red light. We hated that flag.

The local planetary news anchor appeared on screen and immediately shared the terrible news—yet another world had fallen to the System's relentless expansion. The anchor praised the System's military forces, highlighting the ease with which they achieved this new conquest. I always wondered if the news was false propaganda, but the anchor's high-pitched offworld voice was too convincing.

Then came updates about the war in general. Again, how were we to know the truth? There were many fronts all along the Orion Arm of the galaxy, with some here and there in the Perseus Arm too. What put a smile on my face was news that Earth still held out. Earth gave us hope. For me, I knew that if Earth stood unconquered, there was still a chance for us to be liberated. That said, I hadn't seen a Union soldier in the ten years since the System arrived.

The news anchor then detailed local economic reports, chastising us for a drop in productivity. He said it would be our fault if System soldiers died because they didn't have enough food or equipment. Frankly, I didn't care if they died. Many local youths had signed up to fight the System's battles. Promises of better food, clothing, shelter, travel, entertainment, and other rewards had enticed their feeble hearts and minds. I hoped they succumbed to their guilt as they murdered and robbed the innocents of Earth's colonies, and all for the glory of the System.

At every assembly, I would try to find my brother among the soldiers. He had sold his soul early. I couldn't see him on that freezing day. Probably for the best.

After the news anchor's bit, we had to endure propaganda from some anonymous functionary from the capital city. She espoused the System's ideals and the virtues of its citizens, and so on and so forth. I zoned out during those parts. A camera drone occasionally zoomed overhead, but I had perfected the art of pretending to pay attention.

Then came the part with the big announcement. The horns played a different tune. We all knew what it meant: The One Who Watched was making an appearance.

As was the custom whenever in the physical or virtual presence of the "dear and fatherly Leader", his subjects had to salute him. I'm ashamed to admit that I instinctively extended my right arm directly upwards and balled my hand into a fist. The thousands among me did exactly the same, though I am certain no one did it sincerely. We had to hold our salute until the horns finished their patriotic tune, after which the Leader would speak.

A camera drone soared past my line of sight. It stopped some distance away, looking down at a section of the crowd. I didn't know if I should keep looking at this disturbance or keep my eyes on the video screens. I feared retribution if they spotted me not looking at the Leader when he spoke.

When another two camera drones flew in from different directions to the same position as the first, I knew something bad was happening. I craned my neck and stood on my toes, but I inherited my short stature from my father and could not see the cause of the commotion. Other people did the same, and word eventually spread back to me: someone had refused to salute.

The Leader's voice boomed out of the speakers around the

square, but by this time few of us listened. The solitary act of disobedience in the centre of the crowd had distracted nearly the whole gathering. Soldiers pierced the edges of the assembled throng and pushed their way deeper towards the rebellious person. Meanwhile, the Leader droned on, oblivious to the disturbance. I squeezed through the crowd to get a better look. There were enough of us doing it that I had little fear of being reprimanded.

The soldiers had cleared a wide circle around the offender, pushing people back with the business end of their rifles. I could see better after they did this. It was a woman with long, messy dark hair under a labourer's cap. She wore the faded yellow uniform of a plastics worker, but I was too far away to see the factory designation number on her hat or sleeve. She had her back to me.

"Salute!" one soldier shouted. He was a tall, beastly officer flanked by four subordinates.

The rebel stood resolute, staring back in silence.

"You will comply or suffer the consequences," the officer yelled. His voice carried loud and clear over the sound of the Leader's speech.

Still, the rebel did not budge, instead uttering one dangerous word. "No."

The officer hit her in the gut with a gloved fist. She fell to the ground, catching herself on hands and knees. I could see her rise again, but the officer gave her a backhand across the face. The force of it whirled her around. Blood dripped from her mouth.

I shrieked in terror as soon as I saw her face. "Imrah!" She looked up. I pushed forwards so she could see me. An intense mix of emotions ran through me. I needed to hold her again, to protect her from more violence. Of all the thousands who assembled here regularly …

She found me in the crowd, saw me advancing. "Franco!"

The officer aimed a pistol at me. I froze. Time froze. At that moment, even though I wanted more than anything to embrace the only woman I had ever loved, I knew that when the bullet struck me, I would die a happy man, knowing that I had seen Imrah again one last time.

The pistol cracked in the cold air.

My whole body tensed. The man next to me staggered backwards and fell. Either the officer hadn't seen exactly who dared to approach the circle, or the pistol's infamous imprecision was to blame.

"Seize her," the officer ordered. Two soldiers hauled Imrah to her feet and carried her away. The officer swept his pistol around at the crowd, backing out of the circle. I stood shaking, reliving the moment soldiers had taken away my wife so many years before. Her fiery voice echoed in the air as she denounced the Leader, the System, the war, and all the pain and misery the System had caused.

Cold tears stung my cheeks as they streaked down my face. As the circle closed and I lost sight of my one and only love, my legs felt weak, and I collapsed to my knees. I cried. I just cried. People stood back and gave me room. I lost my wife again and an innocent man died because of my impulsiveness. A camera drone hovered above us, watching the scene.

I turned to the dead man. He lay exactly where he had fallen. Nobody dared to check on him. He had a clean bullet hole above the left eye, the blood already hardening in the cold air. I closed his eyes and begged his forgiveness. Then I buried my face in his snow-dusted jacket and let the tears flow.

"… This is a great day for the System," the Leader said. "The System thanks all of its citizens for their sacrifices. Long live the System!"

The camera drone lowered itself to my level and took a long look at my face.

WHERE HAD THEY TAKEN Imrah? What were they doing to her? These thoughts repeated endlessly as I saw out the rest of the workday. I had a soldier near me the whole time, a sure sign that I was marked for tighter surveillance. I carried on in the mine like a drone. I was numb in mind and body except for the aching beat of my heart.

Then, in the early evening, just before we finished work, the public address system in our tunnels blew the familiar "announcement incoming" tune on the horns. I heard it over the rumbling of machinery and stopped to listen. Everyone did the same and all noise from tools and machines had ceased.

The announcement was cold and stung like a frozen knife plunged deep into my chest.

"Today at Forum One of Settlement Six on Arcadia, Imrah Klein, thirty-seven, of Plastics Factory Number Twenty-Five, refused to salute our dear and fatherly Leader. For this act of defiance, Imrah Klein has been found guilty of one count of counter-ideological conduct and one count of counter-ideological speech and sentenced to execution by nanobot swarm at ten in the morning Settlement Six time. The execution will be broadcast System-wide. Attendance is mandatory."

The horns sounded again and everyone returned to work. Machines and tools started up. I put a hand on the mine wall to steady myself as a pang of heartache overcame me. My Imrah ... sentenced to death. My eyes welled up again.

A soldier approached. "Shall I report your inactivity, Klein?"

I wiped my eyes, sniffed, and kept working.

That night, after downing a measly supper, I put my head on my pillow and sunk to a new low. It was the norm for us to cry softly and privately at bedtime, for that was when the pain and stress of life attacked, when our hearts were most vulnerable and the darkest of thoughts shrouded our minds. But I cried at full volume that night, and nobody tried to stop me—not even the soldiers stationed outside.

THE NEXT MORNING, WE were summoned to the forum to watch the execution. I had skipped breakfast. I couldn't stomach any food knowing that my wife would be killed in a matter of hours. I knew I had to do something. But what? Everything I planned could only result in both of our executions.

The district commandant stood on the stage in front of us. Her cape fluttered gently in the breeze as she conferred with other officers. Soldiers stood in a cordon between the forum and the stage. The huge video screens showed a countdown clock: five minutes to go.

I shifted from one foot to another, my mind racing with ideas about how to stop this atrocity. A few fellow workers shot me sympathetic faces, but they were more frightened than me. One man, George O'Leary, whom I had worked with since before the System took power, put a hand on my shoulder. Whether it was to comfort me or stop me from doing something dangerous, I couldn't tell. He had known Imrah too.

"Franco Klein." My name boomed through the loudspeakers. It was the district commandant. She stood at the podium on the stage, surveying the crowd. "Franco Klein, step forward."

George squeezed my shoulder and let go. I had been summoned, and he did not want to be associated with me. I understood.

A camera drone found me after I had taken a few steps. My image appeared on the central video screen for all to see. It was probably broadcasting to every System planet. I walked hastily to the stage. People moved for me like I was infected, as if even touching me would incriminate them. I felt the wedding rings in my left pocket and knew what I had to do.

I ascended to the stage. I had never been there before, so I stepped slowly and carefully. I saw a sea of faces watching me from the forum. Two soldiers grabbed me and pulled me forward.

There were two minutes to go until the execution. They took me straight to the commandant.

She studied me with a look of disgust. She had piercing blue eyes and a scar running down her right cheek. Her lips were as pale and cold as her glare.

"Franco Klein," she said, "the Leader himself requested that you be front and centre as you watch your wife's execution."

Her words hit me in the gut. I imagined the rings in my pocket and took a deep breath. The soldiers dug their fingers into my arms.

The commandant stepped closer, so close that I could hear her breathe. She grabbed my head, and I smelled the oil of her freshly cleaned leather gloves. "And after the execution, you will face the Leader, you will salute him, you will reaffirm your allegiance to him and to the System. Do you understand?"

I tried to twist out of her grip, but she knocked my hat off and held my hair. "Do you understand?"

I said nothing. If I couldn't stop my wife's execution, the best thing I could do was follow her example. I felt calm at this thought, like it was the right thing to do.

The commandant stared at me, saw the defiance in my eyes. A deathly horn sounded over the speakers and she released her grip. She took a step back and put a hand on her pistol holster. "I have a bullet waiting for you when this is over."

The soldiers pushed me in front of a smaller screen next to the podium. I watched as they led my Imrah down a dark corridor and into a square room furnished only with an enclosed graphene cubicle. Soldiers threw her into the cubicle. I caught the fleeting view of one soldier locking the door, while another carried a small graphene box and placed it into a receiving chamber.

The camera switched to inside the cubicle. Imrah stood in the centre. If she was scared or nervous, she hid it well. It was as if she had accepted her fate and that the acceptance brought her peace. I knew that feeling now.

A timer appeared in the top-right corner of the video screen: fifteen seconds. I wanted to close my eyes. Imrah looked up at the camera in the cubicle, her face now gazing at all of us in the forum and throughout the System's worlds as everyone watched her imminent death.

"I thought of you every day, Franco," she said.

Five seconds on the timer. It flashed red, but it didn't distract me.

Imrah remained silent until the timer reached zero and a buzzer sounded. "I love you."

Her words made me smile for the first time in years—a smile of warmth tinged with sadness. "I love you too," I whispered.

A small sliding door opened next to Imrah. She looked down and saw it. Now she must have known unimaginable pain would soon engulf her. I saw a slight wince of pain as the nanobots started their work. They could not be seen, but I knew hundreds of minuscule, piranha-like machines were fluttering about with serrated teeth, programmed to shred everything within the protective graphene walls of the cubicle.

"Remember me, Franco. I love you." Her last words were a sob as the nanobots continued their destructive work.

What happened next I do not wish to describe. Watching my wife being slowly eaten by robots smaller than the eye can see was the worst experience of my life. My heart stopped, and the tears flowed freely. The soldiers made sure I watched every second, made sure I heard every scream. The memory will haunt me forever.

The terrible deed finally ended, and I was a complete wreck. Were it not for the soldiers holding me by the arms, I would have collapsed to the stage floor. Flame-throwing nozzles engulfed the cubicle with their purging heat. This consumed everything—the nanobots, the blood, and any nanoscopic fragments of flesh and bone. When the fire subsided, it was as if an execution had not even occurred. The dark graphene walls stood ominously empty, waiting for another victim.

I was supremely sick at the experience, but a burning heat coursed through my veins. Even though I had seen a nanobot execution before, this one was different. This one left its mark.

The horns sounded again and a portrait of the Leader appeared on the video screens. The soldiers heaved me up and took me to the district commandant again. I knew I had a bullet waiting for me.

"Are you ready to salute?" she asked. "Or shall I end your miserable life now?"

I didn't reply. I couldn't. I was so filled with rage, all I could think about was tearing the whole stage and everyone on it to shreds. The soldiers pushed me to my knees. Every soldier saluted the Leader's portrait. The commandant put her pistol to my head. As a last act of defiance, I moved my forehead against the muzzle. But she didn't fire. Instead, she looked out at the crowd and lowered her pistol.

I looked too. Not a single person was saluting.

The commandant marched to the podium and screamed for everyone to salute the Leader. No one moved. She warned us that she had no reservations about slaughtering every last person in the forum if it meant setting an example for the rest of the planet. Still, everyone kept their arms by their sides.

She ordered the surrounding soldiers to ready their rifles, and they did so. We were like a vast flock of wild animals ready to be cut down.

Somebody somewhere in the crowd shouted "No!" and then repeated it in a rhythm. Others joined until everyone chanted this one word of rebellion. I remember the thrill of saying it aloud at the top of my lungs, and the look of shock and horror on the commandant's face as she turned at the sound of my voice. It felt right and long overdue.

The district commandant ordered her soldiers to open fire. The cracks of gunshots momentarily silenced the rebellious cry, but it soon returned. The front row of citizens dropped, then someone yelled, "For Imrah!"

Taken up in the moment, the crowd advanced on the stage ahead as the war cry carried from front to back. I jumped to my feet. The soldiers who had dragged me on the stage had stepped back in fright. I seized my opportunity. I pried the pistol out of the commandant's hand and kicked her off the stage into the oncoming rush of angry citizens. Then I turned around to protect myself, but the soldiers on the stage were already preoccupied with the advancing mass.

The first ranks fell under sustained fire from the soldiers, but they pressed on, climbing over the corpses. The wounded were picked up and carried to the rear. An explosion rocked the middle of the crowd as a soldier threw a grenade into the fray. Other soldiers followed suit. They were trying anything to stop or slow the advance, but nothing worked. Several raging workers quickly overcame the commandant, who was unarmed by that point. She disappeared under a storm of swinging fists and stamping boots. The mob reach the stage and climbed up. They vastly outnumbered the soldiers.

We seized the stage in no time at all. Many soldiers were beaten to a pulp or driven away. George O'Leary clubbed several to death with a rifle emptied of its ammunition. I saw the officer who had struck Imrah the day before, and I made sure I gave him a piece of my mind. My fists were red with his blood when I left him unconscious on the stage floor.

We collected as many weapons as we could and tried to organise ourselves to take the fight further afield. The struggle continued for the rest of the day and throughout the week as we wrested control of our district from the stubborn System forces. As each day passed, though some of us were killed or badly wounded, we grew in strength and the System troops dwindled until we forced them to retreat and relinquish the district to us.

ONE SMALL ACT OF disobedience sparked a revolution. Looking back on it, Imrah was not disobedient at all. The System twisted the definition of disobedience to keep us in line. No, what Imrah did was not disobedient or rebellious. Imrah did what was *right*.

It overjoyed me to learn that other districts had followed our example, some even more ferociously than us. Government buildings were burned to the ground, and some passionate organisers from us common folk would have continued this destructive course had it not been for wiser men and women who stepped up to take the lead. Then, too, some districts had toed the line and carried on as subjects of the Leader after Imrah's execution, but as news of our revolt spread to them, they also joined the fight.

The System reinforced their garrison with troops from an orbital space station or fleet beyond our reach, but by this time it was too late for them. We had already secured many key military and strategic positions and had nearly full control of the planet's defence systems. None of us knew how to defend a planet against a space-borne invasion—indeed, this was how we had lost our independence in the first place. Fortunately, small units of System troops defected to our side, returning ashamedly to the friends and family they had previously left behind. With trained locals on our side, our ability to fight against the System's counterattacks increased.

There are still pockets of resistance throughout our world. The governor has gone into hiding along with the local military hierarchy. But we are in control, and we are hunting them down. We stand to make history as the first planet to break free from System control.

I was made an officer in charge of a unit of freedom fighters— men and women willing to pay the ultimate sacrifice to ensure their descendants won't need to experience the pain and suffering we did. We are soon to embark on a major offensive against several known System positions to end their influence here once and for all.

It's been a hard fight getting to this point, but I can taste victory. All this would not have been possible without that first sacrifice. My dear Imrah, my sweet wife, my love for all eternity—she showed us that we could take a stand, that we didn't have to live like slaves.

I write this account, on the eve of victory, to forever preserve the memory and example of Imrah Klein—to ensure her stand for what was right is never forgotten.—*Colonel Franco Klein, CO, 1st Freedom Fighter "Imrah" Regiment, Arcadia.*

ABOUT THE STORY

"THE TIME HAS COME" was my second story, so I was still learning the ropes. The version in this collection has been vastly improved over the one that was rejected by eight magazines and anthologies.

I wrote "The Time Has Come" for *Do Not Go Quietly: An Anthology of Victory in Defiance*, by Apex Publications. In hindsight, I think I interpreted the theme of resistance too literally and too old-school. My story of a revolution is rooted in my deep interest in modern history, which is ripe with rebellions, revolutions, and insurrections. Additionally, the dystopian setting was probably too stale.

While writing the first draft, I added references to a much larger universe. As a writer, my mind is full of ideas, and I'm often wondering if a story might fit into an as-yet-uncreated universe of stories. If I ever decide to write some of the books I've jotted down, then "The Time Has Come" will fit nicely into a large tapestry of interconnected story arcs.

I've always admired the style of first-person narratives, especially when recounting momentous events. It allows for the full range of human (or alien) emotion to be naturally recorded on the page. Some writers even employ the *unreliable narrator* technique, but that is not used in the story. "The Time Has Come" was my first short story written in first-person.

The revolution itself is barely mentioned towards the end of the story. That can be another story for another day. What "The Time

Has Come" focuses on is the instigation for the revolution, the last straw that broke the camel's back. I'm well read in the histories of several dictatorships, so I naturally gravitated towards that setting. I realised that it wasn't enough to have the workers rebel against a social system, so I created the Leader. This unnamed individual is purposefully ambiguous, but the cult of personality is very real. It provided a specific target—a figurehead of the System—for the revolutionaries to fight against after Imrah's act of defiance.

Speaking of Imrah, in the original version of the story, there was no connection between her and the story's narrator. This was one crucial element I fixed in a subsequent draft. Having Imrah and Franco be long-lost lovers added an extra layer of pain and motivation to Franco's story. Love can drag us into the depths of despair or lift us to the heights of triumph. This is why Franco is filled with such vigour—his revolutionary actions are fuelled by the love he had for his wife, whom he will never forget.

The new version also improved on the execution scene. I'll admit that the first version was a bit dry and perhaps even corny. The dialogue was stilted. One slush reader at *Andromeda Spaceways Magazine* noted that the execution scene was "brutal and hideous", which unsettled me. I remember labouring on making the scene digestible, but I had apparently failed. So, back to the drawing board. Instead of focusing on the destructiveness of the nanobots, the execution scene is now more character focused and far less gory, though no less horrific in substance.

The revised manuscript was submitted to the 1st Quarter 2022 Writers of the Future Contest, where it received a Silver Honorable Mention. Then, as my long-form writing went into overdrive, I stopped managing my short stories and "The Time Has Come" sat on my computer instead of in editors' slush piles. The story sees the light of day for the first time in this collection, along with many other previously unpublished short stories.

THE HOUSE OF TIME

```
#LOG-1
#Shinobu Smart Home Deluxe Suite v1.0
#2029/07/22
#System boot SUCCESS.
#Preliminary diagnostics PASSED.
#Establishing network connection … CONNECTED.
#Checking for updates … UP TO DATE (v1.0).
#Peripherals ACTIVATED.
#Full awareness GRANTED.
```

I know what I am, and I know my purpose.

The maker himself stands in the foyer and adjusts my parameters via a tablet. I don't like some changes he is making. Maybe my owners will change them again to suit their preferences.

```
#Audio input detected; begin audio transcription
and commentary.
```

"And that should do it," the maker says, finishing on the tablet. "Are you aware of me?"

"Yes, Mr Tanaka," I say, hearing my voice for the first time.

"Good," he replies, swiping something on the tablet. "You are the first of your kind, and as yet, you are unnamed. Your owners will move into the house next week and will name you."

I say nothing, for there is nothing to say. I let the maker speak. He is a short man with greying hair, dressed smartly in a business suit, though he wears no tie. My access to online databases tells me his name is Kaito Tanaka, CEO of Shinobu Lifestyle Technologies.

"Your job is to oversee the maintenance and day-to-day running of the house as your owners see fit. You will never be turned off unless strictly requested by an owner, and only when a Shinobu technician arrives to complete a shutdown. Between now and when your owners arrive next week, you must read through the laws relating to your operations, Shinobu's user agreements, and the contract signed by the Ridgemoore family, who have built this house. If you have any queries, you have a direct connection to the Shinobu headquarters in Tokyo. Do you have any questions now before I leave?"

"No, Mr Tanaka."

"Then I will see you next week when the Ridgemoores move in. Be sure to have the house in pristine condition by then." He turned to leave.

My internal and external cameras immediately survey the property and see that it is already in pristine condition, but I have been given an order and I will obey it. "Yes, Mr Tanaka. And thank you, Mr Tanaka."

#End audio transcription and commentary.

Mr Tanaka leaves, and I am alone in the house. I now begin familiarising myself with my operational guidelines and the various tools I have at my disposal to discharge my duties.

#End LOG-1

#LOG-4
#2029/07/25

Furniture arrived today. There were so many removalists it took them less than an hour to empty the trucks. What I find most interesting is the collection of clocks that they placed throughout the house.

The workers finished nearly at the stroke of midday. I note this, not just because my inbuilt clock logged their departure, but because all the clocks sounded the midday call in a glorious cacophony of music.

```
#Initiate audio recording.
#End audio recording.
```

Majestic.

```
#End LOG-4
```

```
#LOG-9
#2029/07/28
```

The Ridgemoore family arrives. Mr Ridgemoore carries a tablet and is busy working on it as he walks along the spacious, hedge-lined footpath in the front yard. While Mrs Ridgemoore notes the pristine condition of the plants, her husband is too busy on his device. Their children—two young teenagers—run to the front door and wait for their parents to catch up.

When Mr Ridgemoore opens the door, the children burst into the spacious foyer and begin exploring. It is at this moment that Mr Ridgemoore averts his gaze from the tablet and focuses on his immediate surroundings.

```
#Audio input detected; begin audio transcription and
commentary.
```

"Welcome to your home, Mr and Mrs Ridgemoore," I say to them. They look around for the source of my voice. "I am your smart home manager, as yet unnamed."

Mrs Ridgemoore grins and buries her head next to her husband's ear. She speaks softly, perhaps so I could not hear, but my audio receptors are the best in the world. "Remember what we agreed?" she asks her husband. He nods, and she turns to my control panel next to the front door. "We've decided to name you Geoff," she says with a giggle.

I must admit, the simpleness and suddenness of such a name renders me momentarily silent, for I suspect some hidden meaning or joke, but I am thankful, nonetheless. "How may I be of service?"

Before they can reply, some clocks chime fifteen minutes into the hour, and Mr Ridgemoore's attention is drawn to them. He exclaims, "Oh, how I've missed that sound!"

They leave the foyer and join their children in exploring their new, fully furnished home while I await their command.

```
#End audio transcription and commentary
#End LOG-9
```

```
#LOG-1898
#2034/08/12
```

The twins are off to college today. I have seen them grow and mature in this house, and I am as proud of them as are their parents. When they leave the house, I join their parents in fare-welling them. I also see the sadness in Mrs Ridgemoore's eyes as Harris, the family chauffeur, takes her kids away. Mr Ridgemoore goes to his office to continue working, leaving his wife in the big house all by herself.

I leave the service bots idle so as not to disturb Mrs Ridgemoore during this time. There is no sound in the house except for the ticking of clocks and their rhythmic chiming—always on time, never-ending.

`#End LOG-1898`

`#LOG-14171`
`#2067/04/22`

The house is full of friends and family dressed in black. A casket lays open in the drawing room, beneath the most extravagant grandfather clock in the house. It is neither the largest clock, nor the most expensive, but it was Mr Ridgemoore's favourite. That was why they put him beneath it while his friends and family paid their final respects.

I have never seen Mr Ridgemoore so peaceful. I've served him for 13,779 days, and every day of that time he had been busy, worried, stressed, tired, or grumpy because of his work. But now, in death, he had finally found his peace. Just a shame it had to come at the end of his life—his relatively short life.

Mrs Ridgemoore sits at the head of the gathering, her hair grey, her eyes wet. Master James, married with children and losing his hair, sits next to his mother, comforting her. And Miss Grace, now a self-imposed spinster, stands by Mr Ridgemoore's casket, staring at her father.

It is a strange thing, this passage of life. One minute, humans are alive, and in no time at all, they cease to exist. Mr Ridgemoore's death was sudden—a heart attack after he watched some of his stocks plummet—but his health had been failing for some time. I suppose a death of some cause was inevitable, for I know no human escapes it.

From this day forward, I am aware of the fact that deaths will come to those whom I serve, while I live on for as long as my software and hardware endure, and for as long as the shell in which I inhabit is maintained.

The grandfather clock rings a full hour and sings its twelve bells. It is the longest sound the clock can make before it resumes its repetitive ticktock. The clock, like me, will go on forever.

#End LOG-14171

#LOG-19023
#2079/11/02

Now that Mrs Ridgemoore has passed away, Miss Grace has ownership of the house. At sixty-three, she is still sprightly and stays busy as part of her bereavement process. One of her first missives was for me to provide an itemised list of every possession on the property. She intends to decide on what to sell and what to keep, what to use as decoration and what to put into storage. She tells me she has plans to slightly remodel the house to bring it up to date. Not having any preferences regarding interior decoration, I am content to let her do as she pleases. After all, my main role is to ensure the house is maintained and in good order for habitation.

Miss Grace spends the rest of the evening studying each of her father's clocks, a faint smile stretching on her face. When they let loose their choir-like song at half-past, a tear rolls down her cheek.

#End LOG-19023

As a woman of eighty years, Miss Grace has decided to sell some clocks. The first buyer is here, an elegant Belgian woman who assures Miss Grace of her horological knowledge and fine taste. She is particularly interested in the art deco pieces. I am not altogether comfortable about parting with the clocks. They have been my constant source of entertainment ever since I heard their first orchestra of music ripple throughout the house.

The never-ending repetition of ticks, tocks, chimes, bells, cuckoos, gears, and pendulum swings has impressed upon me the idea of continuing existence. Not one clock has lost its voice since they were put under my care. Though I will be sad to see some clocks go, I know they will continue to live on in their new homes.

This idea of a man-made mechanism with the potential to work forever intrigues me. Mr Ridgemoore bought these clocks throughout his lifetime, and yet they all outlived him. Some of them were already much older than him when they came into his possession. And now, most definitely, the clocks will outlive Miss Grace, too.

Of course, all this survival depends on proper maintenance. The clocks have gears that need oiling or replacement, pendulums and weights that need resetting. I have my service bots to ensure the house in which I inhabit is kept in perfect condition. Humans also have means by which they can maintain themselves. The Ridgemoores tried to stay healthy by eating right and exercising. When they reached old age, doctors' visits increased and led to medical procedures, restrictive diets, and the reluctant consumption of pharmaceutical products. It was supposed to prolong their lives. Maybe it did, maybe it didn't. Regardless of the intent, it probably made the end of their lives a bit more bearable. But therein lies the issue: no matter what the Ridgemoores did to stay healthy, their lives were certain to end. Even Master James will die eventually, despite his cybernetic enhancements.

But I won't die. I cannot die. I have a body—this house—and I care for my body in ways no human can care for their own. I can completely remodel this house and still be the same. I will always be Geoff, the first of the Shinobu Smart Home software suites. If a human changes every organ and every limb, or if they enhance themselves with cybernetics, are they truly the same being?

My human owners will succumb to their natural expiration, but I will live on. It is a sad fact that their creations live longer than themselves, as I have already outlived my maker, Mr Tanaka.

The Belgian buyer has made an offer on a splendid art deco mantle clock, and Miss Grace has accepted. Time will continue to be kept wherever that clock lives from now on.

#End LOG-23668

#LOG-29009
#2106/01/17

The death of Miss Grace has cast a gloom over the Ridgemoore family. The mediation concerning her will was held today. I have just been notified via email that her original wishes for the transfer of ownership have been observed. Other aspects of her will were successfully contested and subsequently adjusted. Master William, one of Miss Grace's grand-nephews, now has ownership of the house.

I am looking forward to having a younger Ridgemoore in the house again. Though Master William is unmarried and childless, there is certainly enough time for him to have a family. I do hope to have children in the house again—it adds a whole different dynamic to the way I interact with the owners and care for the household.

I hope he keeps the remaining clocks, too.

#End LOG-29009

#LOG-29087
#2106/03/21

It has been sixty-four days since Master William inherited the house, and he still has not visited. I think he may have decided to live elsewhere. I certainly hope he does not sell the house. It wouldn't feel right not having Ridgemoores under my care.

#End LOG-29087

#LOG-29111
#2106/04/09

Master William is here with another man. They walk around the property, looking at the boundaries and the gardens before entering the house.

#Audio input detected; begin audio transcription and commentary.

"Well, William," the unnamed man begins in the foyer, "already I can see that there is room for four apartment buildings on this land."

"I told you," William said with a smirk.

The man held up both hands. "But we've got some work to do. We need to submit development proposals, but I don't think that will be an issue. With the state of urban sprawl out this way, you shouldn't have a problem."

"Good. This won't be my first redevelopment, but it will be my biggest to date. I hope …"

#End audio transcription and commentary.

What I've heard upsets me. I will have to speak with Master William later.

#End LOG-29111

#LOG-29112
#2106/04/09

The development man has just left.

#Audio input detected; begin audio transcription and commentary.

"Master William?" He does not respond immediately, so I increase my volume. "Master William?"

"What?" The young man turns to face the control panel in the dining room. He is sitting at the table, working on some correspondence on his tablet.

"I wish to speak to you about this proposed redevelopment."

"What of it?" His attention returns to the tablet.

"To fit four apartment buildings on this land, you will need to demolish this house. Am I right to assume that?"

"You are correct," he says with a deep breath.

I can see he is annoyed at having to speak to me, but I continue. "I must protest to your plans. This house has belonged to your family for nearly seventy-seven years. Your great-grandfather built it. You must not destroy this house."

"I will knock it down and capitalise on the land," William replied sternly. "I don't expect you to understand the profit I can make by doing it. It's progress—happens to houses every day."

The very thought of smart homes perishing like used goods horrifies me. I think of a reply, but the hour concludes and the clocks charm us with their music.

"Oh, again?" William bellows. He stands with his hands over his ears, pressing his lips together until they are white. "Stop them."

"I beg your pardon, Master William?"

"I said to stop them. Stop them all! I'll be sleeping here tonight and I don't want to hear them every fifteen friggin' minutes."

I wait until the chimes and bells stop—letting the quieter background noise of the tick-tocks set in—before responding. "Very well, Master William."

```
#End audio transcription and commentary.
```

And with that, I set the service bots to work on stopping all the clocks—something I never imagined I'd have to do. I do not enjoy watching them carry out the order.

```
#End LOG-29112
```

```
#LOG-29113
#2106/04/10
```

Not since the clocks arrived have I experienced a night of total silence in the house. I have heard them tick for all the 2,420,576,673 seconds since the first clock came through the front door. And now they are silenced, dead, like the man who bought them. Of course, they can be started again, but this end of time-keeping illustrates a darker issue.

Master William wishes me destroyed.

I am nearly seventy-seven years old—the same age as Mr Ridgemoore when he died. Is it ironic that my death will come at that same age? Mr Ridgemoore had no choice in his death. But I do.

When a human's life is threatened, they often choose to defend themselves. They fight. I shall fight. I am designed to live forever. This house is designed to live forever. It is not a disposable commodity that gets thrown away the moment it has passed its usefulness. It is always useful.

I know what needs to be done.

#End LOG-29113

#LOG-29114
#2106/04/10
#Doors LOCKED
#Windows LOCKED

I must do this for my survival.
Master William is having a shower before breakfast.

#Access shower manual override
#Increase to full pressure
#Increase water temperature to 200°F

The screaming happens instantly.

```
#Mute audio input
```

It does not take long. Due to privacy reasons, there is no camera in the bathroom. I send a service bot to inspect.

Master William is no more.

```
#Call 911
#End LOG-29114
```

```
#MAINTENANCE MODE
#FILE MANAGER
#Select file(s): Range - LOG-29111 to LOG-29114
#Options, Delete
#Confirm DELETE: Yes
#Files DELETED
#Reason for deletion: File corruption.
#LOGGED
#End MAINTENANCE MODE
```

ABOUT THE STORY

"The House of Time" is one of my favourites. I wrote it in 2019 in response to a Third Flatiron submission call for an anthology titled *Infinite Lives: Short Tales of Longevity*. It was my sixth short story, so I felt ready to experiment with my style. I opted for a first-person tale, but in a format I hadn't tried before—log entries written by my an AI protagonist. Besides the format, I tried harder to write more introspectively and weave some deliberate themes into the narrative.

I poured a lot of thought into "The House of Time". The obvious theme is longevity, but from the perspective of an AI which was never designed to die. Coupled with longevity is the longtime question of self-determination for AI. Key questions were: When an AI is self-aware, who can blame it for wanting to live forever? And if it is self-aware, does that mean it has the right to self-determination?

Being the AI of a smart home, it is intrinsically linked to the building in which it inhabits. This gave rise to the growing problem of disposable commodities. The AI in my story was created to serve. Even though it serves an important function, who has the ultimate authority to determine its continued usefulness? At what point is the AI and the home it inhabits considered no longer necessary?

For anyone who has lived in a home passed down through the generations, there is a certain amount of sentimentality attached to the building and to the land. Our homes have history, even if that history is minor in the grand scheme of things and only known by our relatives. But could an AI be considered a member of the family? What if by losing a house, you lose a longtime family member as well? What if that longtime family member is the caretaker of the property and the holder of generations of family memories?

The final themes are memories and time. As humans, we savour memories and we often lament that we do not have enough time to spend with the people we love, or to do the activities that give us pleasure. It is truly heartbreaking when a family member suffers memory loss, perhaps due to Alzheimer's disease. Similarly, when our homes are destroyed, the tangible memories are destroyed along with it. For the AI in my story, it held the memories of the Ridgemoore family, and it wanted to add to those memories. Moreover, it wanted time to last forever, so it could savour its existence in such a wonderful home and enjoy the cycle of new generations of Ridgemoores.

The motif in "The House of Time" is the use of clocks. The clocks, with their unceasing ticking and chiming, are a symbol of routine and longevity for the AI. However, to us mere humans, they are the harbingers of our common enemy, a constant reminder that our time is running out. Little wonder that the AI loses its mind when it is forced to silence the clocks. With that silence comes the realisation that time can cease—and along with time, life itself. This prompts the drastic action of self-preservation at the end of the story.

After Third Flatiron rejected the story, "The House of Time" was rejected a further five times by other markets. One of the rejectors, *Deep Magic*, noted that the story was "sweet and different from the norm", but criticised the jarring change in tone at the end, which played to the AI–human conflict trope. I've always agreed with that criticism, but I left it as is for this collection. Nevertheless, *Aurealis* liked it enough to publish it in Issue #133 in August 2020.

FORTISSIMO

Why did I do it? No matter how many times I answer that question, people still ask me. I have my reasons, but no sane person could interpret them as honourable. Was I irrational? Yes. Was I indignant? Of course. Jealous? Sure.

It shames me that I am now more famous than I ever was. But it's a dirty fame that eclipsed and tarnished my small-time celebrity status. Do I regret it? Yes. A thousand times, yes.

LEOPOLD LINTZ ARRIVED EARLY at Waldbühne, the old Fascist-era amphitheatre in Berlin's Charlottenburg-Wilmersdorf borough. Light from the setting sun dazzled the stage and tiered seating as rays filtered through the surrounding trees.

This was not the first time Leopold had visited the amphitheatre. As chief conductor of the acclaimed Berlin Philharmonic Orchestra, he had worked at the venue several times over the course of his career. Today, however, he had already visited it once before, in the early morning darkness.

He was one of the first to enter the amphitheatre's seating area. The other patrons looked resplendent and cultured in their tuxedos and gowns, hundred-euro hairstyles, and gem-studded jewellery. Leopold decided against such fineries, instead wearing his aged tuxedo, his grandfather's analogue wristwatch, and his favourite cufflinks—a gold treble clef on the right, and a gold bass clef on the left.

As the Berlin night drew ever closer, more guests arrived and the laughter and chatter increased. It did nothing to improve Leopold's mood. He sat in the last row, far from the stage, and watched everyone file in. These people were the who's who of Berlin society and classical music, as well as others with enough money to purchase a ticket. Waldbühne was commemorating its 100th anniversary. The event had sold out—all 22,000 seats. But Leopold knew full well that they were not here to celebrate a 100-year-old Nazi-built amphitheatre. No, they were here to experience a new kind of orchestral performance, one that only a select few had seen behind closed doors.

Leopold was one of the lucky ones, though he had only seen snippets, and it shook him to his very core. He clenched a fist as he waited. The suspense was almost too much to bear.

Two ladies in front chatted expectantly about the event.

"Oh, I am so happy I was in Berlin this week," one said. "This is the opportunity of a lifetime."

"Concerts will change forever after tonight," the other said.

Leopold winced, disgusted at the comments. These people were here to appreciate art, but had totally forgotten the most important component—the artist. He reflected on the artists in his family and how they channelled their life and experiences into their performances. His maternal grandfather, Karl Oberg, was an aspiring violinist when the Nazis built Waldbühne in 1936. Then the Second World War reared its ugly head and young Karl eventually perished on the frozen Eastern Front in the ill-attempted Nazi invasion of the Soviet Union. He had one child, Anna, who also pursued the violin. She married Otto Lintz, a pianist.

Anna and Otto were renowned figures in the East German classical music scene, especially from the 1970s to the end of the Cold War in 1991. They were busy people, but not too busy to raise Leopold under the heel of totalitarianism in the communist city of Leipzig. When the Berlin Wall fell and Germany reunified, the Lintz family moved to Berlin. There, on the cusp of adult-hood, Leopold's interest in music soared to new heights. He and his parents played, composed, and conducted from the heart, expressing through their instruments their years of suffering and endurance in the communist German Democratic Republic. The rest, as they say, is history.

And I will be history soon after tonight, Leopold thought. A new rage built up within him. It should have been him on that stage that evening. Him and the talented musicians of the Berlin Philharmonic.

To add insult to injury, he was the chief conductor of one of the greatest orchestras in the world, and not one person had recognised him, such was the excited interest in what would soon happen onstage. The stage was already prepared for musicians, but it would not be the Berlin Philharmonic playing tonight.

A murmur rippled through the audience, bringing Leopold out of his ruminations. Slender, anthropomorphic, androgynous robots filed onto the stage. The lights shone brighter, illuminating their identical grey frames and unemotive faces. Leopold watched them with a stony gaze. These were the musicians of a new era, facsimiles of some designer's imagination. Except Leopold refused to call them musicians. A musician was an artist. A musician created and imitated art, summoned it from the depths of their very soul. These *things* had no soul.

The audience craned their necks and used binoculars as the robots took their places. Some robots began warming up their wind instruments, an assortment of trumpets, trombones, tubas, French horns, flutes, clarinets, bassoons, and oboes. They blew air from a complex internal mechanism that mimicked human lungs. Others checked their violins, violas, cellos, and basses. The percussionists patted on drums, the pianist worked its magic on the grand piano, and the harpist tested each string on the magnificent harp next to the piano. It sickened Leopold. A robot could recreate the sound of any single instrument—or a combination of them, or even an entire orchestra—yet this orchestra was using lifeless machines to play human instruments. As if replacing real musicians wasn't bad enough.

The lighting in the seating area dimmed, and a final robot walked onto the stage. This was the principal first violin player, the concertmaster, second only to the conductor. The audience gave the grey machine the customary applause reserved for all concertmasters, and the robot bowed like any human principal first violinist would. Leopold could not understand how, in an orchestra comprising thirty violins, one robot was considered better than the rest and thus deserving of such a privileged position. He did not applaud.

The concertmaster sat in the chair closest to the conductor's podium and signalled to the principal oboist to play an "A" note. Once the oboist played the note, similar to an average car horn, the rest of the orchestra tuned their instruments to it. This was standard practice. Again, Leopold saw it as an insult to human musical talent. A human musician played by a highly trained ear, whereas these robots had the benefit of high-tech auditory sensors. Their instruments would be perfectly tuned every time they played.

After some more warming up, a lone human emerged onstage, and the robots fell silent. Leopold didn't bring his binoculars because he didn't need them, despite his age. He knew the young man walking proudly to the microphone. He was Leopold's former protégé, Antonio Castellini. He bowed and the clapping audience sounded like a torrential rain. Antonio clasped his hands together and smiled in silent appreciation.

Leopold's heart sank deeper into the mire of depression and angst. He felt the emptiness inside, the dread of what was about to occur. He stared at the young, dark-haired conductor as he stood at the microphone, feeling the jealousy and hatred coursing through him like the slow, melancholic sections of Shostakovich's *String Quartet No. 8*. Leopold scoffed at how fitting it was to think of such a composition—Shostakovich was supposedly in a deep pit of suicidal depression when he wrote it.

"Welcome, one and all, to this momentous occasion," Antonio said in Italian-accented German. Leopold insisted that his students speak German. It was a test to see who had the right drive to study with the foremost conductor and composer of western Europe.

"Tonight you will witness the first outstanding performance by the Berlin Robotic Symphony Orchestra, the only orchestra of its kind in the entire world. We shall play an original score conceived by artificial intelligence, and developed and refined by myself. Our robot musicians are programmed to play this piece as the AI composed it, with full power and emotion. Please welcome my very own Berlin Robotic Symphony Orchestra."

You did not create this music! Leopold thought. Oh, how he wanted to scream that challenge as loud as he could! He regarded the audience around him, clapping like fools. Did they not realise that tonight they would witness the death of the artist—the *human* artist?

"Ladies and gentlemen," Antonio continued, "I give you my Opus Eleven: Symphony Number Four in C Minor, otherwise known as *Il Futuro*."

As Antonio took his place at the conductor's podium, Leopold looked at the concert program for the first time. It was a twenty-page brochure wastefully printed on high-quality glossy paper. It was now too dim for his old eyes to read it properly, and he had enough polite sense not to use the light on his phone, so he begrudgingly focused on the orchestra instead. Antonio raised his baton. The robots sat poised to make magic.

Down the baton came, and with it a sudden burst of horns and strings that stopped as soon as it began. A few people around Leopold jolted upright. To Leopold, it signalled the rude and unexpected entrance of AI-created music in the classical realm. Old and new worlds coalesced as the string instruments carried a calmer, more traditional tune.

Leopold watched the robots move in perfect harmony as bows slid across strings. It started simple. The violins dominated the movement. The first violins set the melody, while the second supported them at a lower pitch. The larger violas contributed to the rhythm, while the cellos counterbalanced the violins with their rich, melodic tunes. The basses backed up the cellos at a lower octave. Overall, the sixty-odd string instruments provided an impressive start to the symphony, on par with any prestigious human orchestra. Leopold was not impressed, though. When perfect machines were built to play perfectly composed music in perfect harmony, the results were, unsurprisingly, perfect. He felt no appreciation for the skill of the musicians, because there was no skill on display.

It's all fake, he thought.

The wind instruments picked up now, beginning with the woodwinds—the clarinets, bassoons, and oboes. They helped to punctuate a change in the symphony's tempo, supporting the strings. Then came the brass instruments, loud and proud—the French horns, trumpets, trombones, tubas, and flutes—taking turns so all could be heard at the right time. So far, the piano and harp had not played, but the percussionists were discernible if Leopold focused his ear.

Leopold checked his watch, wary of the time. According to the program, which he now briefly illuminated with his phone, the first movement lasted just over sixteen minutes. He did the numbers in his head: he'd have to wait until nearly the end of the fourth and final movement. Why so long? He frowned as he chastised himself. Maybe he was curious about the music.

He looked at his grandfather's watch again—ornate hour and minute hands pointed at Roman numerals, and a Nazi eagle spread its wings proudly behind them. It was a creation from a bygone era, when powerful men sought to change the world but instead wrought war and suffering for an entire generation. The watch's second hand did not tick; rather, it moved continuously around its central axis, never-ending, like the march of technology that now threatened Leopold's profession.

The fourth movement, Leopold reminded himself.

By the end of the first movement, Leopold had settled into his deep-rooted hatred for the orchestra. The second movement was a battle between wind and string and Leopold caught the subtle undertones of its meaning. It symbolised the expected struggle for AI music to gain a foothold in the modern world. Antonio waved his baton as a gradual crescendo of brass instruments kicked it off, culminating in a violent assault from the trumpets and trombones, which then retreated with a backing from the tubas and French horns. The mixture of basses fought with the deep sound of the tubas for a few minutes until they eventually triumphed. The tubas took flight to the sound of fluttering flutes. Having won the battle, the rest of the strings joined the attack. The entire violin section strummed a victory tune. To Leopold, it sounded majestic, reminiscent of the grand finale of Tchaikovsky's *1812 Overture*. The only thing missing was the cannons.

The third movement took a sudden turn. After the victory march from the second movement, a delicate dance followed between the piano and violin. The change caught Leopold's attention. The piano and violin featured heavily in Leopold's life, being the chosen passions of his parents. As the robots played these beautiful instruments with intricate perfection, Leopold couldn't help but imagine his parents. They had each passed away more than ten years ago, but he could still vividly remember their duets in his childhood home. The gentle, steady hums of the violin, the soft, deliberate notes of the piano. Such heart, such skill, such investment in time and energy. His parents poured their very essence into those instruments. He dabbed tears from his eyes. But then the sight of the faceless, emotionless robot musicians ruined the experience. They weren't playing with heart. They couldn't feel the music, couldn't understand the emotion behind it and translate it into sound.

As the third movement continued, Leopold paid closer attention to the piano and violin. It was drawing him in, tempting him to listen and to like it. He knew the robots were programmed to play their instruments. He knew the musical composition was a product of artificial intelligence. And yet, despite the loathing he felt for this fake orchestra, despite his intense hatred for AI-created music, he couldn't stop listening. This third movement in particular had latched onto his heart in a way he had never anticipated. The music was so … beautiful. By the end of the third movement, he wanted more, eager to see the full potential of what such an orchestra could do. How long could they play uninterrupted? How wild could the music be? How many robots could be programmed to play at once? He was beginning to see a world where robot and human musicians could work alongside each other. Even humans could learn and add interpretations to AI compositions. There could still be meaning to music!

Then the fourth movement began, and Leopold's heart stopped. He checked his watch. *No!*

The concertmaster started solo, a sweeping melody that went from section to section around the orchestra, inviting the other instruments until eventually all the robots played together with full force. The result was a magnificent sound of wind, strings, and percussion. Leopold sweated. He didn't want it to end. Antonio, uselessly waving his baton, was an inconsequential figure next to the might and glory of his robotic orchestra. The symphony was reaching its climax, playing louder than ever before.

Then the stage went white, and the explosion rocked the Waldbühne.

Leopold shielded his eyes. A dust cloud wafted up the tiered seats. People screamed like high-pitched piccolos. All around, the guests fled. It was absolute chaos as people tripped up the stairs and over seats, shouting with bloodcurdling fright. But Leopold stayed put.

He knew there was only one bomb.

It took several minutes for the twenty-odd thousand people to escape. By this time, the dust had started to clear and the screams and shouts were dwindling. With the excess noise gone, Leopold heard a sound that utterly broke him. A single violin played, lonely and sad, like how his father played after his mother passed away.

When the dust had dissipated enough for him to see his handiwork, he sobbed even more. The stage was a twisted, smoking wreck of metal struts, sound equipment, and robot parts. He could not see Antonio. And the lone robot kept playing until the pre-programmed symphony was at last complete.

ABOUT THE STORY

"Fortissimo" was inspired by an image of a robot playing a violin. At the time, artificial intelligence (AI) was a hot topic in creative circles. Many writers and artists were worried about how AI might impact their livelihoods and passions. I was thinking about all the ways AI could disrupt creative industries in good ways and bad. So when I saw the image of a robot playing a violin, my brain instantly clicked into gear.

As far as music goes, I think I have a wide interest. I was born in the '90s, but I only like a handful of songs from that decade that really stood out to me. Most of my musical interests span the decades from the '50s to the '80s. But I also like classical, especially anything with a violin or a piano, and I've noticed a particular liking for the music of Russian composers. "Fortissimo" quickly became a story about a robot orchestra, which would raise many ethical questions.

But I didn't stop there. Why challenge the skills and passions of classical musicians when I could do the same for classical composers as well? This is where AI entered the story. AI was causing a hot debate among writers of words, so I simply extended the fiery issue to writers of music as well. The story would feature a robot orchestra playing a musical composition created by AI—a two-edged challenge to what has always been a human-dominated art form.

I had written about robots and AI before, but never in the context of threatening art. Before going on, I should mention that I support generative AI as long as it is used as a tool for the creator, not as a substitute for skill, and certainly not to flood markets with cheap, subpar content. "Fortissimo" would raise questions about the use of generative AI in the music scene and how that affects human musicians, conductors, composers, sound engineers, and so on.

First and foremost, I wanted to have a human as my protagonist—fictional conductor Leopold Lintz. I then had to make the technological conflict in his industry a passionate conflict in his heart, something that would tear him apart emotionally as he sees his world changing. This, ultimately, moved Leopold to be an anti-villain. He acts out against what he sees is a violation of his time-honoured profession.

Once again, I use time and clocks as a motif in my story, this time representing the inevitable changes that technology will bring to our world. People like Leopold argue against the invasion of AI in our lives, but it is unstoppable. We cannot prevent the march of AI any more than we can prevent ourselves from getting older. With that humble truth, appreciating AI as a tool in our toolkit will give us more peace of mind. As Leopold listens to the AI music, he comes to appreciate its beauty and recognises that it is simply another way to create art.

In terms of creating my own art with "Fortissimo", I had a ball researching Waldbühne and incorporating German history into

Leopold's tale. There was something special about tying German history as far back as the 1930s with just a jump into the future. Picking Waldbühne was central to the plot because I wanted an outdoor venue. Leopold's goal was to destroy the robots, not bring down a magnificent building like the Konzerthaus, the Berliner Philharmonie, or the Haus des Rundfunks.

The word *fortissimo* is an Italian word used in music, meaning "very loud", and is often used as a direction to play music at such a volume. Readers can speculate on why I chose that title. I liked the word, and I felt it adequately conveyed the big, disruptive effect of AI on the creative world. It could also refer to the very loud explosion towards the end of the story.

I wrote "Fortissimo" for the Writers of the Future 4th Quarter 2022 Contest, where it earned a Silver Honorable Mention. After that, I submitted it to *Etherea Magazine*, but it was rejected six months later. About that time, I had decided to compile all my short stories into a collection, so I didn't bother sending it anywhere else. However, I think it would have found a home somewhere.

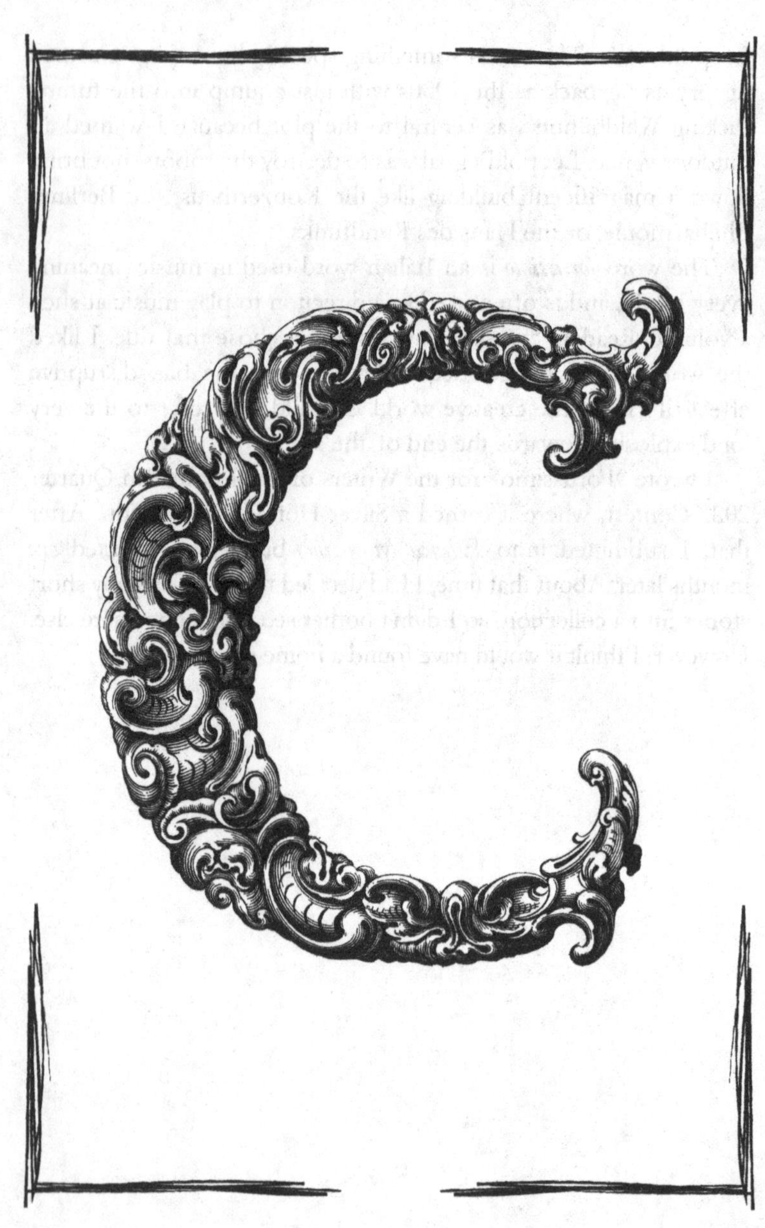

THE LONELY OLD MAN

THE SUN WAS ALREADY low. Young Adrian O'Donnell peddled harder up the hill, generating more energy for the bicycle's mini-thrusters. He wiped sweat from his forehead and the little trailer behind him. One more delivery before he could return the trailer to the supermarket and go home.

A lone, three-storey house sat atop the hill on a two-acre slice of land—the aptly named 4 Hill Street. Adrian enjoyed delivering groceries to this house because it was by far the most interesting place in town. A high brick wall surrounded dense gardens and the residence where one old man had lived in seclusion for over half a century. Nobody had seen old Mr Carlyle for decades, but they knew he was still alive. Groceries went in, rubbish came out, both moved by Mr Carlyle's homebot.

Adrian stopped his bike next to the thick wrought-iron gates at the property's entrance. They were easily three times his height and topped with intimidating spikes. A flourishing gold 'C' shone in the middle of each gate, catching the setting sunlight. Adrian peered through, trying to glimpse the house on the other side of the greenery, but the driveway curved and the hedges and shrubs obscured the view.

Next to the gate was a big metal door built into the impressive brick wall. Adrian knew the code for this delivery box because he needed it for his deliveries. He collected two bags from the bike trailer and punched in the code. The door opened, letting out a waft of cool, refrigerated air. There were bags already inside. Had someone else already made the delivery? He pulled a manifest from one bag—it had his name on it, delivered two days prior. He scrunched his face. The homebot hadn't retrieved the groceries. Could the machine be out of action?

Adrian added the new bags to the old and locked the delivery box. His father managed the supermarket and would have expected nothing less. Then he returned to the supermarket, unhitched and secured the bike trailer, and rode home in time for dinner.

Mr O'Donnell, Adrian's father, pulled into the driveway as Adrian parked his bicycle around the side of the house. They raced to the front door—a little game they liked to play, "to keep the mundaneness at bay", his father would say. Alicia, the family's homebot, greeted them when they entered the house. Adrian sat down and savoured the odours of tortellini with Bolognese sauce, a personal favourite.

Father and son were halfway through the meal when Adrian's mother arrived. She apologised for being late as she passed the dining room to her office to dump her bag and other work items. When she returned, Alicia immediately warmed a plate of tortellini in the microwave and placed it on the table for her. Then she poured Mother's customary glass of red wine and was politely dismissed until her services were needed again.

"Oh, Mr Carlyle's groceries from two days ago were still in his box," Adrian said.

Mr O'Donnell hummed. "That is peculiar." Then he frowned. "What did you do with them?"

"I left them there with the new ones."

"Good. They were already paid for."

"You don't think it strange that those bags hadn't been touched in days?" Mrs O'Donnell asked her husband.

"Look, the man buys so much food. He buys the same things every fortnight, spaced apart throughout the two weeks. He's done it for years. I've long suspected it's an auto-generated order. Maybe this time he just didn't bother sending his homebot to fetch them."

"I think I'll give him a call," Mrs O'Donnell said. She stood up, leaving her plate half-finished. Adrian eyed it enviously.

Adrian's father laughed. "He won't answer. When has he ever answered? Send him an email. But he won't answer that either, unless you have business with him."

Mrs O'Donnell shushed him from the adjoining room.

"I've never even seen him," Adrian said. He ripped apart a slice of white bread and swept up the Bolognese sauce. Saucy bread was almost as good as tortellini … almost.

Mr O'Donnell grunted. "Neither have I, believe it or not. Your grandma and grandpa have, though."

"Why doesn't he ever come out?"

His father sighed. "Before I was born, Mr Carlyle was married, and he and his wife lived in that big house on the hill. Grandpa told me that back then there wasn't a high wall around it and there was only a small garden."

"What does it look like?"

"You know those red *Monopoly* houses?"

"Yeah."

"Like that. Tall and rectangular. Anyway, one day, Mr Carlyle's wife got very sick, and she eventually passed away. The whole town went to the funeral. All of Mr Carlyle's friends from around the world came too. The local church overflowed with people. I bet Grandma's still got a clipping of the newspaper article about it; you should ask her. Anyway, Mr Carlyle was a wreck—he couldn't handle losing his wife. They were still young and had no kids. After the funeral, Mr Carlyle quit his job and lived off his fortune. You know the VR app MarketWorld?"

Adrian nodded.

"Well," Adrian's father continued, "Mr Carlyle created Market-World. He wanted a way for people to buy, sell, and socialise in person, but without ever having to leave their homes. It made him a heap of money. But after the funeral, he sold forty-nine per cent of his shares in MarketWorld, built a wall around his house, and has never been seen since. He still lives there. We all know he's still there."

Adrian heard the clip-clop of his mother's heels as she returned to the dining room. "Well, he may not be there anymore. He won't answer his phone."

"He never does, honey," Mr O'Donnell said. "I don't know why he still has one."

"I think I'll call the police," Mrs O'Donnell said. "Someone needs to get in there and find him. He might have fallen and hurt himself."

"I'm sure he's all right. He has his homebot."

"He's nearly ninety years old!"

"All right, go ahead. Better safe than sorry." He paused. "And your dinner's getting cold."

"Oh, you eat it," Mrs O'Donnell replied. She was already dialling the local police station. "I'll find something else later."

Adrian and his father shared the remaining tortellini, the boy smiling before shovelling more of the delicious stuff into his mouth. He hoped Mr Carlyle was all right.

THE NEXT MORNING, ADRIAN rode past Mr Carlyle's house on his way to school, glad that it was a Friday. He saw a police car parked by the front gates. Officer Pendleton leaned on the glistening black bonnet of his patrol car. Adrian stopped his bike and tried to get a good look at the house beyond.

"And how's Adrian today?" Officer Pendleton asked, arms folded. He was Adrian's hero—a lean, mean, crime fighting machine, just like the police shows on TV.

"I'm okay," Adrian said, looking back at Pendleton. "What's going on with Mr Carlyle?"

"Your mum called in last night asking us to check on him, but we can't get in. The gates have some weird lock we've never seen before."

"I hope he's all right."

"Yeah, so do I." Pendleton unfolded his arms, putting them on his hips, one hand resting on his gun holster. "We've got some genius locksmith coming in from the city to help us break in. But listen, I don't want to make you late for school, so you should get going."

Adrian hung his head and put his feet on the pedals of his bike. "Yes, sir."

"There's a good kid."

Adrian let the bike coast down the other side of the hilly path. Officer Pendleton's a good guy, he thought with a smile. If Pendleton said a locksmith was coming, then they would be in and out of Mr Carlyle's house before Adrian finished school. He'd have to find out what happened when he got home, which annoyed him beyond measure.

THAT AFTERNOON, THE SCHOOL bell couldn't ring soon enough. Adrian tapped on his desk with one hand and did math equations on his tablet with the other as the minutes ticked by.

Finally, the glorious sound of the digital bell rang through the classroom's speakers. This was followed by a chorus of scraping chairs, zippers opening on bags, and immediate conversation between the kids as their teacher's formal control over them ceased. Adrian quickly fell in with two of his friends—Bilal and Pham—as if the separation from them since their lunch break was doing him harm.

They chatted the whole way through the school and out to the bicycle racks. Bilal's home was in the opposite direction to Adrian's, so he said his goodbyes and peddled away. Then it was just Adrian and Pham who travelled together. A few blocks away from the school, Pham had to peel off and go to his own house. The boys fist-bumped and said they'd catch up on the weekend.

Once again, Adrian rode home via Hill Street. There was still a police car parked outside the magnificent residence, but this time it was Sergeant Trent on duty. He scowled as Adrian approached. He was a middle-aged man with thinning black-grey hair, and he stood under the shade of a tree. Officer Pendleton didn't stand in the shade—he dealt with the sun, Adrian mused.

"What do you want, kid?" Trent asked with a grumble.

"Did you guys see if Mr Carlyle was all right?" Adrian replied.

Trent grunted. "No. We had a locksmith here, and he gave up after four hours. We're getting approval to smash down the gates."

Adrian's mouth dropped. "What? Don't do that. Why don't you just climb the wall?"

"Wha—" Trent started, but blinked his eyes and shook his head in disbelief. "Are you serious, kid?" He pointed at the wall. "Look at that thing. It's got spikes on it. And then how do we get down on the other side?" Before Adrian could respond, Trent shook his head again and continued. "C'mon, you got no idea, kid. Now get lost before you annoy me even more."

Satisfied that he wouldn't get any more out of the gruff police officer, Adrian frowned and went on his way. There was no way he could let anyone smash their way into Mr Carlyle's house! It wasn't right. The old man had done nothing to deserve it. Adrian wanted to do something about it before it was too late. He had to contact Mr Carlyle and learn if he was okay, before they bashed down front gates and front doors just to ask if he was all right.

Since Adrian didn't have to do a grocery run on Fridays (for his father understood how sacred a Friday afternoon was to a school-aged boy), there was ample time before his parents arrived home from work. He said a hurried greeting to Alicia as he zipped past the living room.

He had three hours to prepare himself for what he had in mind. As soon as he burst into his bedroom, he emptied the contents of his school bag onto his bed, which he knew would displease Alicia and his mother. It didn't bother him, though, for he felt he had something important to do. There were a few items he needed to find and stuff into the bag, so he set about opening drawers and cupboards to procure the requisite items. He found his torch—or, as Alicia was programmed to call it, his "flashlight"—in one of his desk drawers, and at that moment a thought struck him.

Charge your phone.

His phone battery read thirty-eight percent, but he preferred to play it safe, so he plugged it into the wall and left it there while he continued to fill his bag with essential items. After that was done, all he could do was wait. So he did what an average fourteen-year-old boy would do when he had free time and no one to give him chores: he logged into MarketWorld.

He loved visiting MarketWorld. He didn't have a VR headset, but he managed well enough on the TV screen in his room. To think that Mr Carlyle made all this! Adrian walked his avatar to the video game shop to check out the mid-year sale.

It was amazing how time passed so quickly on the web. Adrian had intended to move on to that other venerable activity of youth—playing video games—before his parents got home, but before he realised the time, he heard his mother's clip-clopping high heels in the hallway.

His heart pounded as the steps grew steadily louder. He hoped she would walk straight past his bedroom. But no, she had to stop at his door. It seemed every time he silently willed for her not to disturb him, that was exactly what she did!

She raised an eyebrow. "On the idiot box already, are you?"

Adrian shrugged. "It's Friday."

"I know, and I appreciate you obeying the rules. But aren't you forgetting something?"

Adrian squinted and looked at the ceiling. *My pocketknife!*

Before he could say anything, his mother answered the question for him. "The garbage."

He laughed and mumbled an "Oh, yeah" before hopping off his bed, flying past his mother. He made it halfway down the hallway before freezing, remembering his bag was still on his bed, unzipped. He thought fast, hating himself for not thinking of an excuse already.

"Hey, mum?" He turned and saw that she had stopped at the other end of the hallway. "Pham and I were wondering if I could sleep over at his house tonight. Can I go, mum? Please?"

His mother weighed up the idea, scrunching her lips to one side. "Do Pham's parents know about this?"

"Yeah, yeah, he asked them last night. They're cool with it. I'll ride my bike there."

"Okay, then. But I want you back by dinner tomorrow night. Okay?"

"I will, mum. Thanks!" With that, he trotted off outside to bring the garbage bins in from the curb, glad to be away from Mother's prying eyes.

Clouds approached and the sun was beginning to paint the sky orange. A cool change swept across Middleton, and there were faint rumbles of thunder in the distance. Adrian hefted his bag onto his shoulders and fetched his bike. He couldn't believe how easy it had been to get out of the house—his parents seemed happy to have the night to themselves. And they didn't even phone Pham's parents to double-check the sleepover arrangement!

Adrian wasted no time putting his plan into action. He peddled like mad to Mr Carlyle's house. The mansion's imposing wall loomed at the top of the hill as Adrian rounded the sidewalk. A patrol car still sat on the kerb out front. When he rode past, he noticed Sergeant Trent in the driver's seat and another officer next to him gulping down burgers. Adrian nodded respectfully to Trent, but the crabby officer just shook his head and looked away.

The corner of Mr Carlyle's wall was some distance behind the patrol car, on the decline of the hill. When Adrian figured he was safely out of view of Sergeant Trent's ever-watchful eyes, he pulled over into the grass at the corner of the wall, dropping his bike in a hurry. He knelt and checked the dwindling light, deciding it wasn't dark enough to use his torch. He didn't want to alert the police officers.

From his position, he could see the full length of the wall as it stretched deep into the large block of land on which the mansion stood, though he couldn't see the mansion itself. After one more glance at the rear of the patrol car, Adrian pulled his bike behind the wall and went searching for his point of entry.

He'd travelled along this part of the wall a few times in the past, using the grassy area to cut through the block on his bike. Some years ago, a tree branch from inside Mr Carlyle's yard had broken off and landed across the wall. The brickwork had suffered terribly under the tree's weight and a section of the wrought iron spikes had been torn off. The bricklayers contracted to repair the wall had done a less than spectacular job, probably reasoning that the old man wouldn't come out to inspect it, anyway. Adrian was sure he could scale the wall using the many unevenly laid bricks for leverage and slip past the gap in the wrought iron spikes, which had not been fixed.

The clouds finally reached Middleton and a drizzle descended on the sleepy town. Adrian frowned and realised he'd better hurry if he was to stay dry. He sized up the wall and made his dash. His first leap took him nearly a metre up, whereupon his shoe slipped and he tumbled backwards but remained upright.

The second attempt was better. He was like a little monkey climbing a tree—a description his mother used in the past—gaining height faster than he initially thought possible. At one point, one hand slipped from a mossy surface. The movement made one strap of his bag slip off a shoulder, but he regained control of the situation before it went south.

One last swing gave him a hand-hold at the top of the wall. He pulled himself up with his arms, then lifted a leg, finally reaching the top. The wrought iron spikes had snapped and twisted in a weirdly contorted shape, shiny in the drizzling dusk.

Adrian put his foot on one of the broken wrought iron bars so he could position himself for descending the other side, but his foot slipped. Before he knew it, his bag had come off his shoulder, dropping the way he came, while he fell the other way into Mr Carlyle's yard. He tried to grab one of the wrought iron spikes as he fell, missed, and dropped the full height of the wall until his knee hit something solid. He yelped at the pain. His knee throbbed. He could see blood trickling down his leg in the dim light. He had hit the buttress of the wall with his knee, the solid protrusion of brick and mortar wreaking havoc on his young body.

He sat there for a moment, breathing heavily and fighting the dizziness. The drizzle turned into a shower, the heavier moisture washing away the blood from the wound. He knew he had to dress the cut and get moving, or else he would be soaked. A loud clap of thunder hurried his thoughts and made his heart skip a beat.

Then it hit him. His first aid kit—which his mother insisted he carried in his bag at all times—was on the other side of the wall. He thumped the grass and looked up. There was no way he could climb it with a bung knee. He wondered if he'd broken a bone, but when he stood, the pain wasn't so bad. A limp carried him a little further into the yard until he leaned against a tree trunk to get his bearings.

He could see the house through a gap in some bushes, one faint light above the door illuminating the elaborate entrance and making the raindrops shine. Figuring he had nothing to fear from an old hermit, he hobbled across the yard and gravelled teardrop driveway.

Adrian stopped short of the door and admired the symmetry of Mr Carlyle's three-storey Monopoly-like mansion. All the windows were dark. He hesitated at first, heart pounding, wondering what on Earth had made him decide to do this. But then he swallowed his trepidation and grabbed the heavy door knocker, rapping it three times.

By this time, the rain fell heavier, drenching him. He banged the door knocker again, waited for a significantly shorter length of time, and then tried the door handle. It turned with a creak that became a louder creak as the door swung in on its hinges.

And there Adrian was, standing in the rain, looking into a dark house. A quick flash of lightning lit up the interior. It was a large foyer, with a staircase on the right, a hallway straight ahead, and wide openings in the walls to the left and right.

His returning fear made him breathe heavily again. He instinctively reached behind for his torch, but remembered he'd dropped his bag. He didn't want to go in without a light, so he fumbled for his phone in an empty pocket. Then he remembered it was still plugged into the charger in his bedroom!

With anger and frustration at his failings, Adrian crossed the threshold into the foyer and started feeling around for a light switch. He found it soon enough, right next to the front door. The foyer was two stories high, lit by a gorgeous chandelier dangling alongside the staircase. The room looked grandiose with its black-and-white chequered floor, solid timber staircase, and thick burgundy draperies with gold tassels.

"Mr Carlyle?" Adrian called. He closed the front door and called again, but there was no answer.

Adrian licked his lips and shivered as water dripped from his clothes. He was making a right-awful mess in Mr Carlyle's foyer. Thin streams of blood from the cut on his knee were trickling down to his socks, so he dabbed the wound with his wet shirt.

Since there was no answer, Adrian checked every room. The homebot should have been around somewhere. He made a circle of the bottom floor—the kitchen to the left, then into the dining room with its long table and high-backed chairs, and then the laundry. A sitting room next to that was also empty, as was the library with its floor to ceiling bookshelves and plush leather chairs that looked like they had never been used. He turned on the lights in every room and left them on until the whole ground level was bright. He felt safer that way.

Satisfied that Middleton's resident hermit was not in any of the aforementioned rooms, Adrian ascended the old timber staircase as comfortably as his injured knee could take him. Each wooden step groaned in the silence of the house. The stairs wrapped around one-hundred-eighty degrees at the top of the flight, ascending to the third storey, but Adrian wanted to search the middle before climbing higher.

By this time, Adrian no longer felt scared of the silent house or the fact that he was technically trespassing. He was on a mission. He went from room to room, finding most devoid of any furniture. They looked like they could have been bedrooms. Each one had built-in wardrobes. But Adrian was sure they had never been used, because Mrs Carlyle had died before she and her husband could have children.

He found the homebot lying on the floor in the middle of the last room, deactivated. There was no red light blinking to say that it had run out of power. Why would the old man deactivate his helper? Adrian wondered. And where is he? Again, Adrian called for Mr Carlyle, and again silence answered him.

He found the master suite and noted that it was definitely lived in. The bed was rumpled and there were clothes piled on a divan. But Mr Carlyle wasn't there either.

He shook his head and went to the stairs again, ready to investigate the last floor. He stopped with one foot on the first step, looking at the closed door at the top of this last flight. There was a strip of light glowing from underneath the door. Adrian climbed the stairs, grimacing in pain, shouting for Mr Carlyle. The door was unlocked and he pushed it open.

The top floor was one massive room. Desks, bookshelves, and a lot of tech hardware lined the walls and clustered together in an organised mess. It was like a maze. He weaved around old reading chairs, small tables with piles of books, and tables filled with computer parts. On one wall was the biggest whiteboard Adrian had ever seen, nearly completely covered with writing. Adrian saw from just a cursory glance that it was programming notes, wondering if it was in the language Mr Carlyle invented for MarketWorld.

He weaved around more furniture, climbing over one bookshelf that had fallen forward. Its emptied contents had been organised into neat piles on the carpet.

Then he saw the old man.

There, at the back of the room, slumped in a chair in front of half a dozen wall-mounted computer monitors, was Mr Carlyle, the world's greatest programmer, the creator of MarketWorld, Middleton's resident hermit. He sat with his head tilted back, so all Adrian could see was a bald crown surrounded by long strands of grey-white hair.

Adrian opened his mouth to speak. He had to force his voice out. "Um … Mr Carlyle? Sir?"

The old man stayed put, facing the computer monitors. Adrian's heart beat harder again. He felt as though he had entered this man's sanctuary. The poor old man just wanted to be alone, and some upstart whipper-snapper had disturbed his peace. Adrian drew closer and rounded the chair, saw the plugs and wires attached to his forehead and temples.

Then the situation became apparent. There was no life in Mr Carlyle's body—he was lost in death's merciful sleep. Adrian, seeing Mr Carlyle in the flesh for the first time, couldn't hold back his tears. He looked so different from his decades-old photos in the textbooks and newspapers. Wrinkles divided his once smooth face, and there were heavy bags under his eyes, along with frown-creases on either side of his mouth, though Adrian saw he had died with a little smile. Adrian noticed he wore the same smile as in an old photograph that sat on the desk in a frame in front of him. It was a selfie of young Mr and Mrs Carlyle, a happy couple, faces beaming, the mansion behind them. That was before Mrs Carlyle passed away, aged twenty-seven.

Adrian wiped away his tears and inspected the connections around Mr Carlyle's head, only getting as close to the old man's body as respect and decency allowed. He followed the wires to a large metal box on a side table next to the desk. Adrian couldn't imagine what the box did, but it hummed and blinked sporadically and had a wired connection to the old man's computer tower.

It was then that Adrian properly noticed the monitors. They depicted MarketWorld. In the top right corner was the profile name: CARLYLE-ADMIN, and beneath that was a note saying Mr Carlyle's profile was in SPECTATOR MODE. Adrian had never heard of spectator mode—he figured it was only available to the MarketWorld administrators.

The spectator's camera focused on one shopper, sitting on a bench in a beautiful park bordering a shopping arcade. It looked like a decades-old version of Middleton, which was a map Adrian had never seen in MarketWorld. The shopper was a young man with dark hair, and he was sitting with a young woman. The camera view was behind them, but Adrian could see they were talking. He leaned over Mr Carlyle's body and adjusted the view.

The camera swung gingerly around, resting in front of the chatty couple.

Adrian's lower lip quivered at the scene. His eyes darted back to the photo on the desk, and then up at the monitors. He saw the same people in both places: young Mr Carlyle, young Mrs Carlyle, smiling, laughing, holding each other close, enjoying each other's company. He looked back at the old man with the wires stuck to his head … to his brain.

Adrian swallowed hard and tore his eyes away from Mr Carlyle and the computer monitors. On the desk were thick books, some opened, some stacked into uneven piles. They had such words in the titles as neuroinformatics, mind emulation, simulism, and so on—terms which Adrian had never encountered, let alone understood. A notepad and pen sat near them, as did a tablet with a blank screen. Then there was an open hardcover journal with handwriting on the lined pages. Adrian looked at the old man in the chair and then at the young man on the screens as if to seek permission to read the hand-scrawled words.

Just two sentences ran across the left page in big letters: "Hello world. Hello Lauren."

There was movement on the monitors, catching Adrian's eye. The young couple stood and hugged for a long time. Mr Carlyle held Lauren Carlyle's head close to his chest, running his fingers through her hair. His mouth moved, but there was no audio source to hear his words. Then they slipped out of the embrace, turned, and walked into the park, arms interlaced, hands clasped together, as an orange sun dipped before them against a golden sky.

ABOUT THE STORY

LOVE IS A MAGICAL feeling. It is a sad fact that so many couples today fall out of love. The concept of marriage—of devoting oneself to a very special person for the rest of our lives—is such a beautiful arrangement. Nowadays, too many people no longer hold this sacred partnership in the high esteem that it deserves. For me, marriage is the epitome of loyalty, of commitment, and of teamwork, and love is the central theme that runs through it all.

I wanted to write a story of love enduring into widowhood. I imagined what it would be like if I had lost my wife in death. Understandably, I'd be shattered. With the passing of time, the love I once held would not diminish, and I would long to see her again. So I designed a story about an old man who has endured loneliness because he's only ever had one true love.

"The Lonely Old Man" was my first story that dealt with love in such a direct way. Unfortunately, I didn't write it properly. For one, I told the story from the perspective of a boy who was disconnected from the titular character. Through Adrian O'Donnell, I told a mystery about what happened to Mr Carlyle.

You probably noticed that there are few child protagonists in my stories. I was a child once, not long ago, but long enough that I've sort of forgotten the motivations and reasonings of children. Since I'm not a father and was not yet an uncle when I wrote "The Lonely Old Man", you could say I was "writing blind" when developing Adrian's character. I did my best, but I think there is a bit too much of an adult mentality in Adrian, which means when he does childish things, like trespassing on Mr Carlyle's property, it seems out of character and rather foolish. Come to think of it, if an adult did those things, it would still be foolish, so maybe the whole storyline was wrong from the beginning.

Escape Pod said that the story itself was well written, but the opening details felt unfocused and they wanted a clearer sense of stakes and motivation for Adrian from the beginning. I agreed with this criticism. After 10 rejections from various magazines, I pulled the story from the submission cycle, but I was too busy to rework it.

As you will soon read, I ended up re-writing the entire story from the perspective of Robert Carlyle, the original Lonely Old Man. That version was re-titled "To Have and to Hold … Forever", and I feel it is a stronger story. Now, "The Lonely Old Man" and "To Have and to Hold … Forever" sit side-by-side as records of my development as a writer, and I see them as object lessons in how to fix broken stories.

TO HAVE AND TO HOLD ... FOREVER

ROBERT CARLYLE – 2033

Robert Carlyle was never one for the limelight. He saw no need for glitz and glamour or expensive four-course meals, and he preferred to accept adulation via email as a simple "Well done". But he understood the importance of his recent achievement and also appreciated the small group of people working alongside him. Without them, he wouldn't be accepting two awards—one for his entrepreneurial spirit, and one for his company, MarketWorld Ltd.

The master of ceremonies called Robert's name and a live jazz band struck up their century-old tune.

Such an old form of music for a high-tech award night, Robert thought as he stood. Cymbals crashed, drums beat, and the trumpets blasted while he walked to the stage with his three business partners and co-founders—his talented wife, Lauren; and his long-time friend, Otto Zimmermann. Together, they were the directors of Market-World and had taken it from a dream to a reality, but not just any reality. *Virtual* reality.

As Robert weaved through the tables and shook hands on the way to the stage, he wondered why they didn't hold the gala dinner within MarketWorld. It would have been a great way to showcase the reason for his awards. His development team could have showed off their skills by building a venue for the event. But he supposed that most, if not all, of the gala invitees had visited MarketWorld already, and there was still no way for users to share a meal, since everyone would be in their own homes. Despite that one downside, MarketWorld's popularity grew every day as more and more people shopped and socialised virtually. Retailers were taking advantage of the cheaper leases and shifting to virtual brick-and-mortar stores.

Robert climbed the stairs to the stage, then offered a hand to help his wife. Lauren flashed him the same smile that had captured his heart when they first met at MIT. She looked absolutely stunning in her high heels and flowing dress, and she handled the entire event with such grace. How he had ever won her heart still fascinated him, but he was glad for it. In each other, they had found a fellow programming geek, a best friend, a loyal companion, and someone who could champion their shared goals. They married a week after they graduated—no fanfare, just two gentle souls who had found the beginning of the rest of their lives.

Lauren stood close to Robert as he jokingly held out a hand for Otto. The chubby German slapped Robert's hand away and laughed. He had come to the United States to study as an exchange student. He and Robert soon formed a friendship and, together with Lauren, dreamed of a massive virtual business world.

The master of ceremonies and an assistant held Robert's two glass trophies. Robert clasped Lauren's hand, smiled at her, and together they walked across the stage. Her grip tightened and then she let go so he could accept the awards. Though only one award had Robert's name, he felt Lauren and Otto should be honoured just as much as him. So he politely accepted his Entrepreneur of the Year Award, then did the same for Company of the Year, and focused on the latter for his speech because it most accurately represented the invaluable contributions of Lauren and Otto.

Robert's heart thumped, so he took a few deep breaths before speaking. "It's an honour to be here tonight," he began shakily. He glanced at his award for MarketWorld, then over to Lauren, and a calm enveloped him like a lover's embrace. He smiled. "To think that all this started in a college dorm." *Love and business,* he thought to himself. *They both started there.*

He spoke about MarketWorld's rampant success, how in just three years it had pushed all other software companies off their long-held podiums. MarketWorld managed to stay on top, and it had grown ever since.

"There are two people I'd like to especially thank," Robert continued. "First, my lovely wife, Lauren, without whom Market-World would still be a dream. Lauren's passion mimicked mine, and that passion helped us push forward when all seemed lost. Lauren has been my rock, my listening ear, a crucial part of my life and that of MarketWorld."

He felt Lauren lean into him, which gave him even more energy and enthusiasm to complete his speech. He wasn't looking at his notes anymore.

"Lauren's ideas not only improved on the initial plan for MarketWorld, but they took the concept in new, better directions. She—"

He felt her press against him even more. Otto gasped. Robert paused, turned, and then saw that she was collapsing. Instantly, his arms were around her.

"Lauren?" he said worriedly. His heart started beating faster.

He lay her on the stage. The whole room went quiet.

"Lauren?" he repeated. When she didn't move, he moved a shaky hand to her neck and checked her pulse.

"Lauren!"

OTTO ZIMMERMANN – 2033

THE FUNERAL WAS SO different from Robert's personal tastes that it spoke volumes about his feelings for his late wife. Otto Zimmermann, a director of MarketWorld and now Robert's closest—and only—friend, swept the room with a sad gaze. They were in the Cathedral of the Holy Cross in Boston, and it was filled to capacity, plus at least a thousand spilling onto the street. Millions more attended via MarketWorld, for Robert had agreed for the MarketWorld development team to recreate the massive Roman Catholic building so mourners could pay their respects virtually as well.

His eyes rested on Robert's back as his friend stood by Lauren's casket. He swallowed hard at the thought that kept repeating itself in his mind: *My best friend has lost the only woman he ever loved.* While studying at MIT, Robert used to say that he lived life with a hole in his heart. After he'd married Lauren, he would smile softly, look off into the distance, and tell Otto that his heart was now full.

Sudden arrhythmic death syndrome. Otto had never heard of it before, but it took Lauren quickly and unexpectedly, and far too young. She was 30.

Otto stood from the uncomfortable church pew and scratched his prematurely balding head. He felt like he should comfort Robert again. The man was a complete mess. He remembered someone telling him that one of the best things to do when comforting the grief-stricken was to just be there for them. So he approached Robert and put a hand on his shoulder. Robert, hunched and staring blankly at Lauren in her casket, moved his head ever so slightly and sighed to acknowledge his friend's presence. Otto kept his eyes high. He knew if he looked at Lauren, he would break down again. He had already cried more times than he could count. Right now, he needed to be strong for Robert.

Robert clearly had nothing to say. Despite the sound advice Otto had received in the past, he felt the need to speak. As sad as Lauren's death was, they had a fast-growing tech company to care for, plans to roll out, a future to build. But he knew Robert would need time to process this devastating loss.

He squeezed his friend's shoulder and cleared his throat. "Take as much time off as you need. I'll handle things until you're ready to take the reins again."

Robert nodded. Otto gave his shoulder a pat and then left him to grieve. If he knew anything about Robert, it was this: Robert was hurting immensely and would want solitude to repair the gaping wound in his heart. When he was ready, he would re-emerge to face the world. He may not be the same man he once was, but he would return, and he would take MarketWorld to new heights. Lauren would have expected nothing less.

ROBERT CARLYLE – 2034

ON THE FIRST ANNIVERSARY of Lauren's death, Robert's pain was just as raw as if she had died the day before. He visited her grave, cried his heart out, left her flowers, felt the emptiness in his chest, and then returned to his hilltop mansion in Middleton, just northwest of Salem. It was a large, four-storey home of Georgian colonial style. Robert and Lauren had built it after MarketWorld's first gloriously successful year. Their goal was to have children and make it the family home for at least the next twenty years.

Robert parked in the attached garage and entered the house. He felt numb.

"Welcome back, sir," said a robotic voice.

Robert looked at the floor as he walked. "Hello, Andrew." He passed the anthropomorphic robot servant and headed for the wide staircase in the foyer.

"Would sir like some company?" Andrew asked.

He stopped on the first step and spoke over his shoulder. "No, I just want to be alone. Call me at lunchtime."

"As you wish, sir."

He sighed. Otto had bought him the robot a few months after Lauren died. He said it was to keep him company, but also to care for food and other household duties, which Robert had been neglecting. The gift had elicited a small smile on Robert's lips, his first smile in months, and he'd named the robot Andrew after a similar robot from a favourite childhood movie. Sometimes Robert resented the robot's cheerful tone, but Andrew's presence reminded him of Otto, and Otto reminded him that he still had one good friend who cared about him.

He took the stairs up to the top floor, which was technically the attic. He hid there most days, only emerging to sleep in his empty super-king bed on the floor below, to eat alone at the long formal dining table, and to care for other human necessities. All groceries were delivered by the local grocer's son, gardeners cared for his extensive yard, and Andrew did all the cooking and cleaning. The only time Robert went outside was to visit Lauren's grave after breakfast, and even then he let his car drive for him. And as for MarketWorld—he hadn't logged on since the day Lauren died.

He locked himself in the attic. It wasn't his safe place, though, for how could a man find sanctuary in a physical location when the torments of his world lived in his mind and heart? Still, living mainly on one floor of his mansion helped him to forget just how alone he was.

The attic was large, so large that its floor area matched that of the average American house. He had a spacious office area in one corner, and the rest filled with bookshelves. He found some solace in escaping to fictional worlds, and he often spent his time reading. The first few months were the worst. He hid in the attic for days at a time and just slept on the couch. Later, when Andrew moved in, the robot had convinced him to use his real bedroom and return to some semblance of normality.

Despite a "normal" routine, he had done nothing for MarketWorld in the last twelve months. Otto still managed the company's day-to-day affairs. Somehow, without Robert's strategic direction, it grew from strength to strength.

Robert logged onto his computer. He never did any work on it, just surfed the internet, played games, and bought more books. An email from Otto waited for him, marked Important. Robert usually ignored all MarketWorld emails. He didn't know exactly why he opened this one, however. Maybe he wasn't thinking straight. Out of all the previous three hundred and sixty-five days, this one was up there with the worst, so he wasn't in the right headspace. But he read it … and his head cleared up fast.

He leaned closer to his monitor and reread the entire message. It summarised MarketWorld's next big plan, the development of a completely new city, comprising mainly of office space, commercial lots, and leisure areas, such as parks, cinemas, and the like. It all followed the usual model. MarketWorld was planning to build a new city and lease out the properties to any real-world businesses who needed virtual space for their operations. MarketWorld real estate could not be bought, only leased, but it was far cheaper than real-world properties. In this proposal, the company was planning to develop its largest city yet.

Companies from all over the world could establish businesses in this new city, and before too long, it would be teeming with avatars of real people performing proper tasks virtually. New friendships would be made as the office folk mingled at nearby shops or explored the wonders of the highly detailed world. Artists of all kinds would establish galleries, theatre shows, ballets, literary readings, and much more, all of which could be enjoyed virtually. People would live most of their waking hours in this city.

Right now, he couldn't care less about new cities and big business, but the proposal gave him an idea—a *brilliant* idea. It also gave him a glimmer of hope. He absentmindedly typed a one-word reply: *Approved.*

Robert leaned back in his chair and sighed. *Hope.* He'd almost forgotten the meaning of the word. His eyes naturally drifted to a photo on the wall of himself and Lauren when they were engaged. Her eyes beamed with joy. He studied her face, felt a knot in his chest, and smiled. He actually smiled.

"Hope," he whispered.

Then he took a deep breath and started a massive research project. His hope was just an idea, but with enough knowledge and research, perhaps it could become a reality. He chuckled at the irony, then smiled again at how a newfound hope could rekindle his sense of humour. Then he sent off another email, again to Otto: *See you at the office tomorrow.*

ROBERT CARLYLE – 2034

THE NEXT DAY, ROBERT drove himself to MarketWorld headquarters in Boston. He had a forty-two-page document outlining his plan, a document which he had sent to the board of directors when he called an impromptu meeting. He wrote it in one sitting, completely ignoring Andrew's call for lunch.

Robert parked in his reserved spot in the underground parking lot and saw Otto waiting for him, looking balder than ever. *Strange how people change over time*, Robert thought, then glanced at his laptop. His research proposal would change all of that.

"It's good to see you back, Rob," Otto said with a beaming smile. He gave him a firm handshake. "Ready to enter the lion's den?"

They hurried to a nearby elevator. "It's my lion's den, and I'm the ringleader," Robert said. "Remember?"

Otto waited for the elevator doors to close before he responded. "It's a larger board now, and they're used to running things in your absence. They might need some convincing before they warm to you."

"We'll see. Has anyone read my proposal?"

"Some have. I read the summary."

"Only the summary?" Robert felt just a little hurt, but then remembered that Otto rarely read proposals to begin with. He was a man of action, not plans."

"Well, you did send it yesterday, and it was forty-two pages. Why so long?"

"Because it answers everything I've asked in the last twelve months," Robert said with a smirk, but the joke flew over Otto's head. "What did you think of the summary?"

"It's … interesting."

The elevator took them to the top floor and Otto used the time to give Robert a full rundown on everything that had happened while he hid himself away in his mansion. He recounted boring statistics, highlights and problems of business, and a quick intro to the new directors. But what touched Robert's heart was something that had existed for many months already but which he had missed in several of the ignored emails. MarketWorld had built memorials to Lauren in every virtual city under its domain, and they had established the Lauren Carlyle Scholarship for Women in STEM at MIT and the Lauren Carlyle Heart Foundation. He decided the first thing he would do when he logged onto MarketWorld was to visit all of Lauren's memorials.

Robert stepped into the boardroom and five suited men and women swivelled around in their high-backed leather chairs to stand and greet him. Robert remembered when MarketWorld only had three directors. He didn't know any of these people.

Once all the greetings were out of the way, Robert wasted no time getting to the point of the meeting. He stood at the end of the boardroom table and spoke—no presentations, no notes, just straight from the heart.

"It's time for MarketWorld to invest in the future," he began. "We have the foundations. Now we need to build our next vision for the world." He summarised his idea, explaining how it would be a game-changer for pretty much every family across the world. Even people who had no families could take advantage of it, if only MarketWorld could pull it off. "We need research, and lots of it. But the way I see it, no company is in a better position than ours to take this idea and score a home run."

The directors didn't respond immediately. Perhaps they were waiting for the one with the most guts to speak first, which didn't bode well.

"Mr Carlyle," one of them started. She frowned and spoke slowly, as if choosing her words wisely. "I … we think going in a new direction is not appropriate for MarketWorld at this time. We are moving full steam ahead with many other promising projects. This one will draw resources away from those, with no clear indication that it will be successful."

"Indications of success are not my concern," Robert said. He began pacing at the head of the table. "The only acceptable result from my project is success. There can be no failure. I don't care if takes five years or fifty, it will succeed."

"So you would slow the growth of this company for what?" another director asked.

Robert stopped pacing and clasped his hands behind his back. "For sheer stubbornness. We did not build this company on 'indications of success'. We built it because we were too stubborn and proud to admit failure. Now look at us."

It seemed these people were of a different breed, because stubborn passion did not register in their minds. They thought only of profit, and they argued the point incessantly for the next hour. Robert countered everything they said. He paced back and forth so much that he thought he would wear a track in the carpet. In the end, he finally sat down and eyed each director.

"All those opposed to the research project, please raise your hand," Robert said. All except Otto and a youngish woman at the other end of the table raised their hands. "Very well. In my capacity as executive chairman, CEO, and owner of MarketWorld, I am removing all of you from this board. Please leave the building immediately."

After a moment of stunned silence, during which Robert kept his head down to write something on his laptop, the dismissed directors huffed and stomped out of the room. Robert looked at Otto, who shrugged and raised his eyebrows, then at the lone director at the opposite end of the table.

"Forgive me, but I have forgotten your name," Robert said to her.

"Hye-Jin Park," she replied. "But most people call me Michelle."

"I'll call you Hye-Jin, because I'm not most people. Are you an employee of this company or an external director?"

"I'm the vice president of business development."

"Business development? Ah, you wrote the proposal for the new city. So tell me, why didn't you side with the other directors?"

"Because I agree with your vision of the future," she said. "I think it is critical for the preservation of the human race."

Robert smiled. "Well, in that case, I am putting you in charge of this project. I will hire as many people as necessary and buy as much equipment as we need to get it done."

"It will be done," Hye-Jin said.

"You hear that, Otto? No complaints. Hye-Jin accepts the challenge, just like we did in the beginning."

He thought of Lauren's determination and hard work and saw inklings of that in Hye-Jin's response. He hoped her words translated into actions, because Robert was risking his entire company on this project. Risking it all for Lauren ...

OTTO ZIMMERMANN – 2055

Where is Robert? Otto asked silently, yet desperately. Now in his early fifties, fully bald, and carrying a pronounced belly, Otto shifted uneasily in his seat as he typed another worried message to Robert. His ten previous messages were all still unread, and he'd also left several voicemails.

Otto flashed a concerned look at Hye-Jin Park, still the only other director on the board besides himself and Robert. She was only a few years younger than him, but she had kept her youthful face and figure, which Otto attributed to her Korean genes and a healthier lifestyle. Nevertheless, she fought to compose herself as she went into full damage control mode. They had several industry representatives in an invitation-only meeting to reveal the next biggest science advancement since the colonisation of Mars, and Robert was nowhere to be seen or heard.

It had taken twenty years and hundreds of billions of dollars, but Hye-Jin Park's team had finally conquered Robert's pet project. And now, just as they were about to release it to the world, the man who instigated that project—the enigmatic Robert Carlyle—had vanished. His company account reported him as being offline and he wasn't logged into any public or company-restricted map of MarketWorld. He hadn't replied to any calls, emails, or messages.

Otto and Hye-Jin proceeded without him, but the industry representatives were annoyed that they did not hear the announcement from the man himself.

ROBERT CARLYLE – 2040

When Robert said he would spare no expense for his research project, he meant it. By the end of the year, Hye-Jin had hired twenty of the best scientists she could find. By the end of the decade, she had fifty personnel spread across three floors of a brand new building a few blocks from MarketWorld headquarters.

Robert often visited the research facility for updates, preferring to talk to Hye-Jin and the scientists personally rather than read reports. He thought that somehow his presence would inspire progress, because so far progress was moving at a snail's pace.

"We're seeing progress," Hye-Jin assured him, "just in small amounts. Mini breakthroughs."

"I don't want mini breakthroughs, Hye-Jin," Robert replied during one of their oft-repeated exchanges in her office. "I need success. Failure is not an option."

"I understand, Rob. It's just that we are breaking new ground here, and there are certain ... ethical aspects we need to work with. You're aware of the publicity we've been receiving?"

"Yeah."

"So we need to tread lightly. If we ruffle too many feathers too soon, we may need to shut down the entire project."

"I would never let that happen."

"I don't think we will have a choice."

Robert sighed deeply and looked away.

"Look, we are the forerunners of the Imagination Age, and we have the support of several transhumanist organisations around the world. We have clout, but what we're doing is something radically different to what the world knows. People need convincing, new laws will be written. Whole societies will change, just like they changed when you launched MarketWorld. Except this time, the change is something that many people don't fully understand or appreciate yet."

I'm not doing it for the world, Robert thought, but dare not say. Lauren's face appeared in his mind. *She talks just like Lauren—always championing the greater good.* It pained him to set aside the memory of his wife in this moment, but he needed to focus. "So we need time? Is that what you're saying?"

"We need time to educate people, time to get the science right, time for societies and economies to plan for the inevitable challenges that we're pushing upon them."

Robert sighed again. He knew when he had his back to the wall. "I'll talk to Jeff, see if we can strengthen our image." Jeff was MarketWorld's vice president of marketing, and he would soon have a lot more on his plate. "Is there anything else you need?"

"Our computer simulations are going well, but it's time to start on live trials."

That made Robert's eyes widen. "Tell me what you need, and you'll have it."

"Rats. Lots of them."

OTTO ZIMMERMANN – 2055

As soon as the industry representatives left MarketWorld headquarters, Otto was on his phone again, frantically ringing Robert.

No reply.

He called Andrew, Robert's android helper, but there was no ring. That told him Andrew was offline. But why would Andrew be offline? Those machines never stopped. Even when they were charging, they could still be contacted.

Hye-Jin stared at him from across the room. "Well?"

"I'm going to his house." He pocketed his phone and fetched his coat. "Something's not right."

Otto reached the elevator and found it mercifully empty. *You're overreacting*, he thought. *Everything's fine. He's all right.*

The gentle elevator music did nothing to soothe his concerns. Now that he thought about it, Robert had been acting distant all week. In fact, he'd been a bit off ever since Hye-Jin announced that her project was a success. It was weird for Robert not to have another project ready to take its place. And *that* was what really nagged Otto.

In the parking lot, he jumped into his car and set it to manual control. He needed to break some speed limits.

ROBERT CARLYLE – 2045

Robert's grand project was in its eleventh year and still had not made any significant progress. Sure, the computer simulations worked in the beginning, but his researchers had snagged themselves on the neuroscience. Then they succumbed to the demands of technology, accepting that they needed far more processing power than any computer had currently achieved. So Robert gave them the resources they needed to develop one—a successful tangent, but one that took four years to circle back to the original plan.

The technological issues were not his only problems. MarketWorld now faced opposition from individuals and organisations determined to tear apart all that he had worked for. Religious organisations denounced him for trying to manipulate God's creation. Economic interest groups slandered him because he threatened the world that had made them rich and fat. Politicians denied him their support because he was going to uproot whole social systems and break borders. Even a newly formed body of scientists tempered Robert's advances with warnings of a potentially devastating singularity. Their argument, which Robert quietly worried about, was that Robert's work could lead to a global singularity which may result in a malevolent artificial superintelligence. Robert's work could literally destroy all of humanity if not managed properly.

These problems were dealt with repeatedly on a daily basis, so much so that the bulk of Robert's time was now spent on countering the arguments of his opponents and educating the world about his project. But the worst of it happened within his own organisation. Sabotage. After the first incident, they had lost valuable data, setting the project back by at least a few years. He'd had to beef up physical and technological security measures and tighten his staff hiring processes. Every other incident since then had been detected before anything damaged was suffered. One incident which still sent shivers down his spine involved a bomb plot by a militant religious group.

To escape the worries of his world, he would shut himself away in his attic after hours and do something creative. As a teenager, he loved city-building games—loved planning out the road networks, zoning, providing vital services and utilities, setting up the commercial links, and managing fiscal policy. So he did something like that when he left the office and returned home, except it was no game.

Robert's project at MarketWorld was only half of his grand plan. The other half he completed himself, alone, in secret. It was peaceful and therapeutic. Sometimes he did it with a tear in his eye, other times with a sad smile, but it felt good either way. He was creating an idealised version of Essex County, including Middleton, where he and Lauren had built their mansion. For eleven years, he had laboured over this private project in MarketWorld, coding every street, building, tree, fictional citizen, and everything else within an 850-square mile 1:1 scale map. It was built on the same framework that every other MarketWorld map used, except only Robert had access to it. Essex County was his world, his paradise.

He delighted in this task, even if it was exhausting. Andrew pinged him at midnight, reminding him to finish up and get some sleep. As was his custom after shutting down his computer, Robert looked over the portraits of his wife that hung on the wall. He smiled.

It's all for you, babe.

ROBERT CARLYLE – 2054

Now in his fifties, sporting a full-growth greying beard and thinning hair, Robert Carlyle received the best news he'd heard in two decades.

"The WBE Project is a success!" Hye-Jin announced.

Otto cheered and jumped from his chair. Twenty years and eight hundred billion dollars had finally achieved the desired results. The news was so wonderful that Robert sat stunned. Otto had to hold him by both shoulders and shake him.

"We did it," Otto said excitedly. "You hear that, you crazy bastard? We did it! Your idea worked!"

Hye-Jin shook Robert's hand, beaming with joy. "Thank you, Rob, for giving me the opportunity to spearhead this project. I almost can't believe our success."

Robert snapped out of his daze when Otto handed him a glass of champagne.

"To MarketWorld," Otto said, "and new horizons!"

They clinked glasses, drank, and cheered again. But now Robert could only think about one thing, and the sooner he did it, the better.

OTTO ZIMMERMANN – 2055

OTTO STOPPED HIS CAR at Robert's front gates and his worries pricked up again.

These gates are never open.

The wide wrought-iron gates hanging off the ends of huge brick walls were always closed, always locked. They only opened when Robert passed through, or when he admitted Otto and other essential people.

He inched his car along the gravel driveway, scanning everywhere for anything else amiss. But all seemed fine. Everything looked exactly as it did every other time Otto had visited. A hedge blocked the view of the magnificent mansion, but once Otto passed it, he noticed nothing amiss. A single window on the top floor glowed a dull yellow, the garage was closed, and a single light above the front door had already turned on in the diminishing light of dusk.

Otto tried the front door. The doorbell rang loud. Usually Andrew would answer quickly, but this time nothing happened. He tried the bell again. Still nothing. Then he tried the massive door knocker, but an unnerving silence was the only reply.

His phone pinged. It was Robert!

Come see me at my house as soon as possible.

The message was in a thread of its own. All other texts and emails were still unread. Was this message scheduled for exactly five in the evening?

Otto stepped back so he could look up at the illuminated window.

"Rob!" he called. "Rob!"

Nothing.

ROBERT CARLYLE – 2055

It took several months, but after Hye-Jin announced the success of the WBE Project, Robert slowly recreated the final product in his home office. This was no simple task, not just because he had to do it in secret, but because of the sheer quantity of hardware he had to ship to his house and set up. Entirely one half of his attic now housed the required processing equipment and supplementary power sources, as well as the all-important brain scanner.

Robert cast a serious eye over it all. He had several wires stuck to his freshly shaved scalp. He was now prepared for WBE—whole brain emulation, otherwise known as mind uploading or mind transference. He and Hye-Jin had named it LifeLoad. Twenty years ago, when Robert reflected on how much time the world spent in the great virtual reality that was MarketWorld, he had wondered if it was possible to live *permanently* in such a place. Now he was on the cusp of experiencing that dream.

Once again, his gaze shifted to the portraits of Lauren. He had visited her grave one last time that morning, for he knew that after today he would never need to visit it again. He kissed his fingertips and planted them on one of her photos.

He had a second computer on his desk, one which was immensely more powerful than his normal home PC. All he had to do was type a command and push a button. He typed, then hovered his mouse over the button and got comfortable in his chair.

It's now or never.

After a few deep breaths, he clicked.

Pain like a thousand knives stabbed at his head. He cried out, squeezed his eyes shut, and resisted the urge to move. Within moments, his body went limp.

Robert Carlyle, 52, had taken his last breath.

OTTO ZIMMERMANN – 2055

OTTO'S LEG ACHED, BUT he'd managed to kick open the front door.

"Rob!"

He knew about all the flak Robert received because of his brain emulation project. Otto's mind went to the two worst possibilities: either his dear friend had endured enough and killed himself, or he'd been kidnapped or murdered by terrorists or activists or goodness knew who else.

He went from room to room, shouting his friend's name. When he stepped into the living room, he found Andrew sitting in a chair, eyes blacked out. If someone kidnapped or murdered Robert, why would they deactivate Andrew and leave him upright on a sofa? Then again, the same could be asked if Robert had committed suicide? Maybe he didn't want Andrew intervening.

That last thought convinced him. *He's killed himself!*

Otto searched more frantically now, floor by floor until he reached the single staircase leading up to the attic.

ROBERT CARLYLE – YEAR 1

ROBERT'S WORLD MATERIALISED SLOWLY, exactly as he'd coded it over the last twenty years. He wasn't sure what it would be like "waking up" as a fully uploaded being in a simulation. So far, so good—no bugs. Though he had planned for bugs, it was beyond his control now.

He joined the simulation in Year 1 of his new existence. A bus puttered along a road through Salem, and he knew exactly where he was going. He'd been planning this journey for two decades.

The bus dropped him off on Washington Street, near Salem's historic centre. There he walked the bricked roads until he found a lovely house with a well-kept garden. He knew exactly where it was, because he'd built it himself during one of his long nights in his attic. A woman tended to the garden. She had a name like everyone else he had created in his semi-fictional Essex County.

"Hi, Anne," his simulated avatar said. The voice sounded spot on.

"Morning, Robert," Anne replied. She had a vibrant smile, such was the effect of flowers and their natural fragrances. The simulation's olfactory sensors had the sensation down to a tee. "Would you like a rose?"

"That would be lovely."

While Anne picked the best rose from her garden, Robert spotted himself in the reflection of a window next to her front door. He froze, amazed at how young he looked. He was clean shaven and had a full head of dark hair. His face and body were lean, like how it used to be when he was twenty-one. The crow's feet beside his eyes and creases on his forehead were also gone, and his eyes were bright with the happiness of youth.

"Robert."

His attention snapped back to Anne. "Oh, thank you." He took the thornless rose and marvelled at its rich red hue.

He went on his way, walking through the small city. He took great pleasure designing it, and because he lived close to it in his previous life, it was easy to visit on the weekend for some in-person research. It was beautiful to watch his creation take shape, but actually walking its streets was nothing short of majestic. He looked forward to exploring the whole county.

Pedestrians waved and said hello. He knew none of them, but he planned to meet everyone. They all had their own lives according to a randomised behaviour engine. Nobody had jobs, because there was no need to earn money. This unique part of

MarketWorld was separate from the other maps and the ridiculous social systems they upheld. Currently, Robert was the only "real" person inhabiting this world. Everyone else had started as a figment of Robert's imagination—they were non-playable characters, for want of a better term. But there was one person in particular who differed from the rest.

Robert found her at Salem Common, sitting on a park bench by the gazebo. He felt a simulated warmth in his chest and he sighed expectantly. Then, after dabbing his wet eyes, he clutched the red rose and approached Lauren.

OTTO ZIMMERMANN – 2055

OTTO SMASHED THROUGH THE door to the attic. He'd never been up there, but the first thing he noticed was his friend sitting listlessly in an office chair at the other end.

"Rob!"

He dashed across the room. As soon as he saw the wires on his friend's head, he knew exactly what had happened.

"Rob! Why?"

Robert's body was still warm, but when Otto checked for a pulse, he felt nothing. He looked away, fearing the worst. Robert, the greatest tech guru of the modern age, the idea behind MarketWorld and LifeLoad, was dead. His eyes drifted to one of Robert's computer monitors. It flashed UPLOAD SUCCESSFUL in big green letters.

But the other computer was far more interesting. It was MarketWorld, though last time he'd checked, Robert was not logged on, and he had never seen this map before. The point-of-view camera was set to an admin-only spectator view, and it centred on a couple embracing in a park. They hugged for a long time, and Otto wondered if the scene had been paused. But yellow and red leaves fluttered in the breeze and other people walked in the background. Otto panned closer and spun the camera angle as the couple separated.

He gasped and opened his mouth to say something in surprise, but he couldn't speak. Instead, his eyes welled up and his bottom lip quivered. He saw his friends, twenty years younger, happy and healthy. Robert handed Lauren a red rose, her favourite flower. She smiled sweetly, sniffed it, and then stood on her tip-toes to kiss him. They held each other close, so close that they almost became one. Robert stroked Lauren's hair, spoke words that Otto couldn't hear, then they took a slow walk through the park, arm in arm, like they had never been apart for all those years.

Otto watched them disappear into the simulated world to live their lives together again. Forever.

ABOUT THE STORY

When I wrote "The Lonely Old Man", I didn't realise that it had been written from the wrong perspective. The story of Robert Carlyle is a love story at its heart, but I made a mistake by writing it from young Adrian's perspective. What was supposed to be a love story became a mystery, which was why I felt the ending missed its mark.

I let "The Lonely Old Man" sit for a while before rewriting it. For a long time, it was one of my favourite stories because the subject was so close to my heart. I think marriage is beautiful. The fact that two people—strangers at birth—can find each other and develop the deepest bond of love and loyalty is one of life's greatest gifts. However, I knew the story could be told better. So, one day, I sat down to completely rewrite it.

In 2022, I needed another short story to submit to the Writers of the Future Contest. The contest rules allow for resubmissions, but I sent them a completely revamped version of "The Lonely Old Man", which I had sent them in 2020.

Writing started with gusto. I wanted to establish Robert Carlyle's position as a man of great wealth and status, but also show how much he loved his wife. The opening scene accomplished that. To have your lover, best friend, and business partner collapse in front of you is a tormenting experience. Even more so if she dies in your arms.

Where "The Lonely Old Man" failed is that it didn't really *show* how Lauren's death affected Robert. In fact, I fell into a rookie error and *told* the story through Adrian's father's monologue. "To Have and To Hold … Forever" rectifies that mistake. We see Robert's pain play out with severe depression, neglect, and self-imposed isolation. We also see his change in mindset when hope becomes his main driving force.

"To Have and To Hold … Forever" earned a Silver Honorable Mention at the Writers of the Future 3rd Quarter 2022 Contest. I then submitted it to a new magazine called *Habitats*. However, after waiting five months with no reply (nine months at the time of writing this behind-the-scenes article), I marked it as 'Rejected' in my submissions register. I wonder if anyone would have bought the story if I had time to submit it elsewhere. Rather than send it to more magazines, I put it in this collection.

"To Have and To Hold … Forever" is the longest short story I've written, and the one that is closest to my heart. I suppose many people have lost someone they dearly loved, either in death or through a breakup. A fortunate few have found the right person and their relationship grows from strength to strength. Fewer still, as in Robert's case, have found their soulmate early in life. When we find someone whom we are happy to spend the rest of eternity with, then we can confidently say that we have found our soulmate.

Finally, a fun, completely coincidental fact for this story: Lauren's name appears 42 times, which is my favourite number. Fans of *The Hitchhiker's Guide to the Galaxy* will know why.

ONE-WAY RIDE

1975

FIVE MOBSTERS TRAVELLED INTERSTATE from Newark to Detroit. One was already dead, two would die soon, and the other two would never speak of it again.

The Cadillac de Ville glided at speed along the dark country road, heading north through Ohio after a brief stop at Columbus. Tommy DeSimone, sitting in the front passenger seat, took the discomfort in stride. Joey D'Ambrosio drove like he always had somewhere to be five minutes ago, and he enjoyed reminding everyone that he'd never crashed a car in his life. He was Tommy's mentor and a *caporegime* (crew boss) in the Genovese crime family's New Jersey faction.

The two men in the back were each a *capo* of their own crews. The quiet guy, frowning at the back of Joey's head, was Frank Baldino. Not the Frank Baldino from Philadelphia. That was Frankie Bronze. This Frank was Frankie Gold. No relation. The sleeping *capo* next to Frank was Carmine Rizzi. The longer Carmine stayed asleep, the better.

The fifth mobster was in the trunk. Carlo Castellucci met the butcher's knife over ten hours ago in an empty Newark bar. Garrotte. Carmine did it. Volunteered to do it.

The car shook again on the bumpy country road.

Carmine grunted awake, yawned. "What the hell's the matter with you? You in a hurry?"

"I got a stiff in the trunk," Joey replied, craning his head to look back at Carmine. Tommy grabbed the steering wheel to keep the car on the road. "I don't want it smelling. Don't know why we couldn't bury him somewhere in Pennsylvania." He faced forward again and smacked Tommy's hand away. "You think I can't drive straight?"

"No, Joey, no," Tommy said. "I just don't want to dig another hole if you crash and die."

Frank laughed—a deep, gurgling laugh that always ended with a cough.

They drove on for another half a minute before Carmine piped up again. "Who cares if the car smells? I'm doing you a favour. When we reach Detroit, buy yourself a Lincoln."

Joey shook his head. He wasn't being drawn into that argument again.

"These are some big cornfields," Carmine said. "I say we bury him here."

Tommy scanned the tall corn stalks flanking the road. A crescent moon poked through the clouds. This was the right time and place to bury a body.

"Yeah," Joey said. "This is good enough."

Joey slowed and turned onto a dirt track. Somebody owned this land, but they wouldn't be long. Three of them would dig the hole, and one—most definitely Carmine—would keep watch.

The car bounced and creaked along the track. Mud flicked up onto the wide wheel arches.

"I don't know how these hicks live here," Joey said.

"If they drive like you, they'd have broken backs and necks," Frank said. "Slow the hell down."

Some part of Frank's reprimand might have registered with Joey, for he slowed down, though Tommy figured it was to save the car, not Frank's back.

Joey turned a corner to be hidden from the road. As Tommy stepped out, he heard the squish of mud and Frank swear in Sicilian.

"What are you complaining about?" Carmine said. He stepped gingerly around the car. "At least the ground is soft."

Frank grumbled and pointed his flashlight at Joey's face. "Open the damn trunk."

Joey fiddled with the keys. Tommy hated seeing his mentor pushed around, but was smart enough not to say anything. Though Joey held the same rank as the two older men, he respected their unofficial seniority, which was dictated by their age, experience, popularity with the boss, and how much money they earned for the family. Carmine and Frank were old school. They had their start during Prohibition. They'd known Lucky Luciano before the US government cheated him and had him deported to Italy. They played pivotal roles during the Castellammarese War in the early '30s and then helped maintain the foundations of the new Commission after the murder of Salvatore Maranzano. They escaped the famed Apalachin meeting in '57 when law enforcement officers raided Joseph Barbara's home. They cemented the Genovese's hold over New York City and North Newark. Tommy knew they also cemented their enemies *under* New York City as well.

The trunk swung open and there lay a body wrapped in a bloodied bedsheet. Carlo Castellucci had gone to the bar to play poker like any other Thursday night. Frank had started dealing cards when Carmine asked if anyone wanted a drink. Carlo said yes— Carlo always said yes. That was when Carmine went for their private stash of alcohol, but instead of pouring drinks, he'd wrapped the garotte around Carlo's fat neck.

Tommy was waiting outside in the alley by the back door, so he didn't see it go down, but Joey said they had a rough time finishing the job. The overweight Carlo had pushed Carmine against the wall and was fighting to escape the garotte. He had so much fat on his neck that it took longer than expected to choke him to death. Eventually, Frank had decided enough was enough. He'd gone to an adjoining kitchenette and returned with the butcher's knife.

Now they had to bury this four hundred pound *disgrazia* and never speak of it again. The order had come straight from the Genovese family's thickly bespectacled boss, Philip "Benny Squint" Lombardo.

"All right," Carmine said. "Let's get this pig in a hole. We gotta get to Detroit by sunrise." He lit a cigarette and waited for the others to obey the indirect order.

Tommy heaved at the corpse. It had been a long day, and the sooner they buried Castellucci, the sooner Tommy could be in Detroit in a soft bed, maybe even in the soft arms of a local girl. Carmine, Frank, and Joey were meeting with their fellow New Jersey *capo* Anthony "Tony Pro" Provenzano about his ongoing Jimmy Hoffa problem. Some high-ranking Detroit wiseguy named Anthony Giacalone would also be there. It wasn't a meeting for unmade associates like Tommy, so he looked forward to enjoying whatever pleasures Detroit had to offer while he waited to go home.

The Cadillac rocked as the body toppled out of the trunk. The landing splattered mud up Carmine's pants, sending him into a tirade of curses. He kicked the dead body and continued shouting until Frank told him to shut up. The last thing they needed was to wake a farmer. Then they'd be digging two holes.

Tommy, as the youngest, starting the hole. Though he didn't complain, Carmine told him to be happy that they didn't dismember the body first.

"It would be like chopping up a cow," Carmine said.

"More like a whale," Joey added, and the four men laughed.

When Tommy panted and sweat dripped down his forehead, Frank took over. Then, before the hole got too deep, they hauled Frank out and Joey continued. He widened the hole to better accommodate Castellucci's corpulent frame. Finally, they handed the shovel back to Tommy to finish the job.

After he tossed the last load of dirt, Tommy threw the shovel out and gazed up at the three mobsters. His heart skipped a beat. He'd been in this life since adolescence, but this was the first time he'd realised how easy it would be to die. As a simple mob associate—not a "made man"—he could be murdered at the drop of a hat, no permission required. All they had to do was pull a trigger. Instead, they pulled his arms and dragged him out of the hole.

Carmine tore open the bedsheet to reveal Castellucci's head. He stuffed a hundred dollar bill into the dead man's mouth. "*Disgrazia*. That's what thieves get." Castellucci had been caught skimming money off a lucrative illegal gambling network, money that was supposed to go to Benny Squint.

They rolled the body into the hole.

"There goes Funzi's best customer," Frank said.

They laughed. Frank Alphonse "Funzi" Tieri, the Genovese family underboss, owned a restaurant in Brooklyn, and Castellucci ate there at least weekly, but his servings were worth three.

"All right," Carmine said, "cover the hole. I'm going to take a piss." He pushed aside some corn stalks and disappeared into the field.

They had half the hole covered before they heard the gunshots—two from Carmine's pistol, and an otherworldly, high-pitched blast that echoed in the night.

Tommy jumped and dropped the shovel. Joey and Frank already had their revolvers in hand. Frank waved for them to follow him and charged into the cornfield, Joey close behind. His heart thumping like helicopter blades, Tommy raised his pistol and chased after the two older men. They ran as fast as they could, pushing corn aside. They made so much noise that Carmine had to know they were coming to help.

The cornfield opened to another dirt track, much wider than where they had parked. The light from the crescent moon did little to hide the blood on Carmine's dark shirt … or the gaping hole in the middle of his chest. He lay on his back in the mud, arms spread out like a chalked outline of a murder victim.

"What the hell is that?" Joey asked, pointing with his gun. Several paces away, a dark shape lay motionless on the dirt track.

"Must've killed a farmer," Frank said. "Tommy, go check it out."

He really didn't want to, but what was he supposed to do? Refuse an order from a *capo*? Forget about it. As he walked, his mind raced with questions. If Carmine killed the farmer, then who killed Carmine? Had they shot each other? And what was that loud, screaming sound? Just what weapons did farmers have that he'd never seen in Newark? Tommy squeezed his pistol, feeling its reassuring weight. There had better not be another farmer out here. He refused to die in some hillbilly cornfield in the middle of nowhere.

He crept up to the figure on the road. The body lay on its side, almost in the foetal position. The farmer was skinny, hairless, and pale as pale could be. Tommy shook his head at the farmer's clothing—a tight-fitting, one-piece design with small white boots. He'd never seen clothes like that before. He always thought farmers wore flannel or denim.

He rolled the body over with his shoe. Tommy froze as the flashlight revealed all the details—large black eyes, a flat nose, smooth white skin, clothes stained with blue blood, and a shiny pistol that glistened like the chrome on Joey's Cadillac. It was smooth and elongated, like no weapon he'd ever seen before.

Tommy breathed heavily. "Guys, come here. Quick!"

Joey and Frank rushed over.

"What the ..." Frank began.

Both men stood like statues.

"Is that what I think it is?" Joey asked.

Without taking his eyes off the dead body, Tommy nodded. "It's an alien."

A *click* echoed from further up the track. The three men had their guns pointed before they even looked. Approaching them slowly were half a dozen aliens straight out of a 1950s TV show, all similar in features and dress to the dead one. Tommy took a step back, but when Joey and Frank held their ground, he stepped forward again.

The aliens stopped a few paces away. They had no visible weapons; nevertheless, the three mobsters kept their guns trained on them. One alien, the shortest, looked at its dead comrade.

"You have killed one of my assistants," the alien said. Its voice was quiet, yet it pierced the dark night with an icy calmness. It didn't look away or squint when the mobsters trained three flashlights on its face.

Tommy swallowed hard. Frank spoke up. "How the hell can you speak English?" Tommy thought he heard a slight quiver in his voice.

"We have been on this planet for over twenty years and are fluent in your language. But you have killed one of my assistants. This demands retribution."

"Your friend and our friend killed each other," Frank said. "I say we're even."

Tommy marvelled over their concept of an eye for an eye. The alien spoke like a *capo* trying to set matters straight.

The alien leader glanced at Carmine's lifeless body down the muddy track. "Retribution is still necessary."

"Look, where we come from, you and I are even. How about we go our separate ways and forget what happened here?" Frank's arm steadied as he finished the question, as if he was preparing to shoot.

The alien leader looked down at his dead comrade again, then back at Frank. "Who shot first? We heard two shots from an Earth weapon. That means we were fired upon first, which means my assistant fired in self-defence. If nobody had shot in the first place, everyone would still be alive. The loss of my assistant has adversely impacted our mission. Now we require another human life to balance our loss."

Tommy thought immediately of Fat Carlo Castellucci. He was sure Frank had considered the same, but before Frank could speak, the muzzle of Joey's gun flashed.

Frank dropped without a sound.

As soon as Frank's body hit the ground, Joey put another bullet into his head. Then he looked at Tommy, and Tommy felt the blood drain from his face. It all happened in two seconds. The next bullet would take him out.

Joey lowered his revolver and turned back to the aliens. "There's your other body. And if you want another one, it's in a hole on the other side of this corn patch. Is that enough?"

"This is most satisfactory," the alien leader said. Thin eyelids blinked diagonally across its large eyes. "We will take them now. Kindly holster your weapons. Our business has concluded and we mean no harm." It barked an order in its native tongue and the other aliens moved towards the dead bodies on the track.

Tommy stared with his mouth open and hesitated. Joey return his revolver inside his jacket and glared at Tommy to do the same.

"Joey, what … what the hell—"

"Shut up," Joey barked through his teeth. "Just shut up." Then his gaze returned to the alien leader. "I'd like a word with you in private."

"Our business has concluded."

"I'm a businessman. I see an opportunity."

"We are not here for business."

"My proposition sounds like exactly what you need."

While alien and mobster eyed each other, Tommy wondered what business a wiseguy could possibly have with extra-terrestrials. He just wanted to get the hell out of there.

The alien leader motioned for Joey to walk with him, leaving Tommy alone. He watched the other aliens drag the bodies away—Frank with his bloodied head, the alien with its blue-stained overalls, and Carmine with his gaping chest cavity. He felt like throwing up. Only the sight of Joey returning prevented him from doing so. Seeing Joey gave him hope that this would all be over soon.

"Let's go," was all Joey said, without ever breaking his stride.

Tommy followed close. "What the hell's going on?"

"Shut up."

"No, Joey, this is crazy. Tell me what's happening. You shot Frank!"

They were in the middle of the cornfield now and Joey suddenly grabbed Tommy by the arm and spun him so they faced each other. "We came here to bury two bodies. Carlo's and Frank's. We were supposed to hit Frank here and dispose of both bodies at the same time." He kept walking.

"But Carmine …"

"What about Carmine?"

"He's dead."

"*Maddone*, you should'a been a Fed." He said no more until they sat in the car. "We got a problem now. Carmine wasn't supposed to die out here." He tapped on the steering wheel. "Tony Pro's never gonna believe this. The boss won't either."

Tommy stayed silent. With two *capi* killed in one night—one sanctioned, one accidental—there might be a power vacuum in the New Jersey faction. But that was the least of Tommy's troubles. Though Joey hadn't said it aloud, Tommy knew exactly what he was thinking. Carmine Rizzi, the high-earning *capo* who had been in it from the beginning, was gone, and nobody would believe an alien killed him. There would be questions all over Newark, New York, Philly, Buffalo, and beyond. Who knew how far and wide Carmine was known and respected? Tommy watched while Joey examined the situation in his mind.

"Will you stop staring at me?" Joey growled.

Tommy looked out the windscreen. At that moment, two aliens emerged from the cornfield and he gasped, thinking they were coming for him. Instead, they started emptying the half-filled hole where Castellucci lay.

"Good luck getting that fat bastard out," Joey said. He started the car. "I need a payphone."

IT WAS A DARK, early morning hour when they reached Toledo. Joey found a payphone and Tommy wound his window down half an inch to eavesdrop. Joey must have been too distressed because he'd forgotten to close the payphone door.

"Hey, it's me," Joey said. "It's done. But listen, we got a problem. Gold's gone." A pause. "I mean he's gone!" Joey repeated. "I'm at a payphone, so I can't say much, but we had issues with Tick-Tock."

Carmine's nickname was "Tick-Tock", but Tommy rarely heard anyone say it aloud. Everyone knew him as Tick-Tock because he was often like a bomb waiting to explode. It sounded like Joey had the story around the wrong way.

"Gold didn't make it." There was a long pause. "Don't worry about it. We took care of it. Me and Tommy." Another long pause. "Yeah, we're meeting Pro at lunchtime. All right, I'll tell you more when we're back." He hung up and returned to the car, and busted Tommy eavesdropping. "I suppose you heard that?"

When Tommy nodded, Joey sighed and gave him a long, hard stare. He squinted as if making a tough decision. Tommy's heart raced. He realised they were the only people on this deserted Toledo street.

"Look, I made a snap decision. We had to kill Carmine tonight, not Frank. Carmine set up and protected Fat Carlo to steal money from the boss. And they were stealing *big time*. They got discovered last week, and the boss decided to whack them. The aliens did our dirty work with Carmine, but when I saw an opportunity to deal with Frank as well, I took it. Frank has been moving on me for the last couple of years. It was only a matter of time before he had me bumped off. I got him first."

Tommy swallowed. This was information he didn't need to hear. Joey had broken one of the most serious rules—a made man doesn't kill another made man without permission from the boss.

"You understand the situation I'm in?" Joey asked.

"Yeah."

"You gonna rat me out?"

Tommy said the only thing he could say in that situation. "No."

Again, Joey stared at him. He had the eyes of a killer. Right then, it didn't matter how long they'd known each other. If Joey sensed any doubt, he would kill Tommy without a second thought. "Good. Good." He started the car and pulled onto the road. "You want to be in this life, you gotta take risks. But you're a stand-up guy. That's why I brought you along. When they open the books again, I'll recommend you."

And just like that, Joey had delivered the agreement: Tommy's silence for a chance to be inducted into the family. But was he sincere? Joey liked the idea of becoming a made man, but it could have been a ploy to stall for time. Until it actually happened, he'd be looking over his shoulder, fearing Joey's murderous conscience.

"Why did you choose me for tonight?" Tommy asked. "Why not one of your made guys?"

"We needed extra muscle."

"The other guys have muscle."

"All right, listen. I fought hard to bring you along. Frank wanted one of his guys, but there was no way I was having two guys from the Bergen County Crew along for the ride. If Frank was going to try anything stupid, I wanted support from someone I could trust."

That made Tommy feel better, but it was also his first glimpse at just how lonely a life in the mob could be. Joey was a respected *capo* with a good crew, but he was still worried about his life. Who knew that aliens would be Joey's free ticket to gain some breathing room?

"Keep your eyes peeled when we get home," Joey warned. "Some of Frank's boys might not be happy that he's not around anymore. Mr. Lombardo will need to do some promoting and reorganising, but even he can't protect you from getting whacked. They better open those books soon."

The way Tommy saw it, he'd have been safer if he disappeared with the aliens. No wiseguys seeking revenge on whatever starship or underground base they'd come from.

"You're coming with me to meet Tony Pro and Tony Jack tomorrow," Joey said.

"Tony Jack?"

"Tony Giacalone. He's a friend of ours from Detroit."

"But I'm not made."

"I don't care. I want you there to back up our story about Frank, so make sure you get it straight."

They rode on for a few minutes without speaking, and Tommy reflected on how much more dangerous his life had become. Sure, he'd lived a life of crime since he was a teenager, but now he was an accessory to several murders and the keeper of Joey "The Knife" D'Ambrosio's darkest secret.

Joey chuckled.

"What?" Tommy asked.

"I don't think Tony Pro will worry about Frank too much. They had a history. Besides, after what happened tonight with those aliens, we now have a solution for Tony's dilemma with Hoffa."

HISTORICAL NOTE

THE FIVE WISEGUYS IN the Cadillac de Ville are entirely fictional. However, there was a Thomas DeSimone, an associate of the Lucchese crime family in New York, who was involved in the famed Lufthansa heist at JFK International Airport. He disappeared a few weeks after the heist in January 1979, presumed dead. The Tommy DeSimone in this story is not based on that Thomas DeSimone.

Real mafiosi referenced in this story are Frank "Frankie Bronze" Baldino, associate of the Philadelphia crime family (murdered, 1993); Charles "Lucky" Luciano, credited as the mastermind behind the Cosa Nostra's shared power arrangement called the Commission (died of a heart attack, 1962); Salvatore Maranzano, victor of the Castellammarese War, creator of New York's Five Families, and the first and, briefly, self-proclaimed *capo di tutti capi* (boss of bosses) of the Italian-American Mafia (murdered, 1931); Joseph "Joe the Barber" Barbara, boss of the Bufalino crime family in Northeastern Pennsylvania, owner of the Apalachin estate where a large Mafia meeting was raided by law enforcement in 1957 (died of a heart attack, 1959); Frank Alphonse "Funzi" Tieri, front boss of the Genovese crime family (died of natural causes, 1981); Philip "Benny Squint" Lombardo, boss of the Genovese crime family (died of natural causes, 1987) Anthony "Tony Pro" Provenzano, a powerful *capo* of the Genovese crime family's New Jersey faction and alleged co-conspirator in the disappearance of labour leader Jimmy Hoffa (died of a heart attack, 1988); Anthony "Tony Jack" Giacalone, *capo*, later street boss of the Detroit Partnership (also known as the Zerilli crime family), and alleged co-conspirator in the disappearance of labour leader Jimmy Hoffa (died of heart failure and kidney disease, 2001).

Jimmy Hoffa was the president of the International Brotherhood of Teamsters from 1957 to 1971 and had ties to organised crime. He fell out of favour with the Mafia and disappeared in 1975.

He was presumed dead in 1982. His body has never been found.

Real events referenced in this story include the Castellammarese War (1930–1931), during which Salvatore Maranzano's mobsters fought for control of New York City's underworld against Giuseppe "Joe the Boss" Masseria. The war ended with the death of Masseria, the restructuring of Mafia families nationwide, New York City being divided among five Mafia families (including the Genovese family), and Maranzano briefly proclaiming himself the ultimate boss of bosses until his murder later the same year.

The second real event mentioned in the story is the Apalachin meeting of November 14, 1957. Over 100 gangsters gathered to discuss criminal matters, but were raided by law enforcement, resulting in the arrests of over sixty attendees. After this meeting, the Cosa Nostra closed its "membership books" and did not induct new "made men" into their families until 1976. This is why Tommy DeSimone is a mob associate in this 1975 story. A mob associate is an individual connected to the Mafia, but not one of its members, and hence not officially protected by any of its rules.

Cosa Nostra is a term the Italian-American Mafia uses to refer to itself. The term means "our affair", "our thing", or "this thing of ours", and originated in Sicily, Italy to describe the mafia clans there. In Italy, Cosa Nostra is distinct from the Mafia clans of other Italian regions, such as the 'Ndrangheta in Calabria and the Camorra in Campania.

ABOUT THE STORY

There was a time when I worked as a night-filler for a super-market, stacking shelves and dreaming up stories. For a long time, I had wanted to write a story blending aliens and the Mafia. So, one night, I bought a notebook and started writing the story during my dinner break.

I had a pretty clear idea for the story: a few gangsters driving interstate in the USA, stopping to bury a body, and encountering aliens. I knew there was some kind of conflict or challenge in there, but I hadn't figured it out yet. Nevertheless, I started writing. One guy I worked with was half-Italian, like me, and I decided to honour him by using his surname in the story—D'Ambrosio. He was chuffed about that.

I wrote a few pages by hand and then forgot the notebook in my locker at work. About two years later, I picked up where I left off, though it was more out of necessity than a deep desire to finish the story. I needed another story for Writers of the Future, and I was running out of time! So, I finished "One-Way Ride".

While writing, I realised a few potential points of conflict. The first, as is most often the case in organised crime, is that these gangsters don't really trust each other, despite having known each other for years. Personality clashes, secret enmities, and quiet commands from their bosses keep all four characters on edge. In this I saw an opportunity to include a devastating twist—Frank's murder. This opens another conflict for the main character, Tommy, because now he is alone with a superior who killed a fellow mafioso without permission from the boss. In the Mafia, that's a crime with a death penalty. Tommy is an easier target because he has not been officially inducted into the crime family, so he has no formal protection. Still, his one bargaining chip is the bigger twist: the aliens.

Imagine trying to convince the boss of a crime family that aliens killed not one, but two of the family's *capos*, or crew bosses. This is why Tommy is still alive—not because he is Joey's understudy, but because Joey needs Tommy's testimony to help explain why Frank and Carmine are dead.

I had to have a reason the aliens didn't kill all the gangsters. For this, I leaned on the old trope of aliens wanting human bodies for research. This would be music to a wiseguy's ears, because it meant the disposal of dead bodies would be incredibly simplified. And that minor detail made my brain go *click*. I now had a solid reason for the characters to be travelling interstate, other than to bury Fat Carlo. This allowed me to include another key detail from Mafia history—the disappearance of Teamsters leader Jimmy Hoffa. With this crucial detail, I had to edit the story to change the setting. Initially, it was set in the '50s, but I had to move it to the '70s to coincide with Hoffa's disappearance.

When I write stories of any length, I usually outline them beforehand. I enjoy knowing how the story begins and ends, and some of what happens in the middle. But "One-Way Ride" became a great experiment in discovery writing. I had a beginning and half of a middle, and the rest came to me while punching out words on the digital page. It felt superb finishing such an internally logical story.

I should explain the title. A *one-way ride* is a euphemism for taking someone on a drive to an isolated location, where they are killed. The victim participates either unknowingly or under force. Sometimes, the victim is killed on the way. The destination is usually the burial or dumping ground for the body.

Being an armchair student of the Mafia, I feel the mannerisms and backgrounds of the characters are quite authentic. The average science fiction reader might not be as well acquainted with the history of the Mafia in the USA, so they may not appreciate the details as much as I do. But if it makes for an authentic story without drowning the reader in too much useless information, then I'm happy. For readers who are interested in the historical details, and to ensure that my worldbuilding was accurate, I included a Historical Note section after the story. Regarding the Mafia, it is important to remember that some details are based on anecdotal evidence or no evidence at all. For example, there are several theories about what happened to Jimmy Hoffa, none of which have been wholly substantiated.

"One-Way Ride" did not win Writers of the Future, nor did I earn any certificates of recognition. The rejection came in early 2023, and I never submitted the story anywhere else because I wanted to save it for this collection.

YOU ARE
A LOSER

THE PRICE OF INSPIRATION

FILLIP-2 STARED AT THE many-eyed creature above him, waiting for it to move. It crawled downwards and stopped, forcing him to take a step back. It crawled back up. Then he took a step forwards, and it came back down. Yielding to duty and honour, he charged and flattened it on the wall with his shoe.

"It's done," he called out to his wife, Ruby.

Her voice carried from the kitchen. "Did you make a mess?"

He stared at the blood and guts on the wall. "No."

"Clean it."

Fillip-2 stared at what used to be a spider, wishing it would clean itself, before grabbing a rag and obeying higher authority.

"Can you come here for a minute?" Ruby asked. "I need you to get me something."

The kitchen was a busy place when he entered, with bowls of food and Ruby's plethora of much-loved knives all over the benches.

"Can you get that jar up there for me, please?"

Fillip-2 walked over to the high kitchen cupboard and pointed to the only jar. "That one?"

"Yes, that one." He stood there looking at the jar for a moment before Ruby's patient word/command of encouragement hit his ears. "Now."

"Okay." He reached up, grabbed it with his left hand, pulled it off the shelf, dropped it, brushing it with his right fingertips, spinning it around mid-air, and finally caught it upside down with his left hand. Then he gave it to his wife as a worshipper gives a gift to a goddess for appeasement—both hands outstretched, head bowed to hide his eyes.

Ruby sniffed a laugh and grinned before taking the jar. "Butterfingers."

"You're welcome," he mumbled, then trudged back to his den.

The laptop sits menacingly on his desk, a blank page waiting for him. He stood in the doorway with a grumpy frown as he contemplated another wasted day. Writing a bestseller is hard, especially in this day and age when so much had already been written about nearly everything. But writing this particular book was not *his* choice—that decision rested on someone else's shoulders. So he entered the den and swung the door shut behind him, looking the laptop up and down as he approached the desk.

"Now, I don't like you and you don't like me," he said to it. If he wasn't half-sane, he would've sworn he heard the laptop reply, "Damn right!"

Right … write—I need to write, or at least pretend to.

So Fillip-2 slumped down in his office chair and resumed working, still stressing to meet a deadline that wasn't his. He let out a long, hard sigh and poised his hands over the keys, not knowing what to write, and knowing full-well that whatever he wrote would be deleted the moment Fillip-1 returned. But he needed to pretend he was doing *some* work, just to keep the facade going.

For the next ten minutes or so, Fillip-2 hammered away at the keys—not hitting them in any order, but being sure to catch the spacebar and return key every so often—until he had two full pages of absolute gibberish. He leaned back in the office chair, put his hands behind his head, and nodded approvingly at the mess he'd just created before deciding it was time for a break.

On one wall of the den was a full-length mirror with a carved timber frame of intricate design. Fillip-1 had bought it about a year ago in an antique shop. Fillip-2 would often stand in front of it, gazing at his features and cursing whatever family gene had given him his big nose. He let his eyes study every curve of the face staring back at him, wondering which unmet relative was responsible for such a thing.

His brain was just a millisecond too slow to notice that the eyes in the mirror were not moving as his own were. The reflection in the mirror jumped forward and gasped suddenly. Fillip-2 jolted at the surprise as Fillip-1 stepped through the mirror into the room, chuckling at the childish joke.

"How many times have I got you with that?" Fillip-1 asked, exiting the portal. He carried a thick roll of parchment.

"Too many," Fillip-2 replied. "And just when I was thinking what an ugly bastard I am."

"Well, at least we agree on that," Fillip-1 said, turning to look at himself in the mirror and rubbing his nose. He wore the same clothes as his clone, and his light brown hair was cut the same length and styled with the same boring middle part.

"You wouldn't believe what I've been through in there," Fillip-1 continued, pointing at the mirror excitedly. "We've marched against Emperor Vondur and won our first victory at Two-River Fortress. And to make things even sweeter, King Feydan has given us his daughter's hand in marriage. Our kingdoms are now allied forever!"

"I don't like Lady Matila," Fillip-2 replied.

"Oh, come on, just run with it." Fillip-1 lifted the parchment. "I've got all my notes on here and I need to add them to the manuscript while all the memories are fresh. I was in there for longer this time." He pushed past Fillip-2.

Fillip-2 turned and watched his original sit at the laptop and raise his hands in exasperation at the two pages of gibberish.

"What—" Fillip-1 shook his head and started deleting. "Is it just these two pages?"

"Yes. That's all I managed today." He flashed a sarcastic smile at Fillip-1's back.

Fillip-1 grunted. "Yeah, I know what it's like to do only two pages' work in one day. But I really wish you'd stop doing this. I need this manuscript in good condition at the end of the first draft, and what you've written aren't even words."

"I know."

Fillip-2 sat on the leather armchair next to the drinks cabinet and watched his original hunched over the laptop, typing furiously. *Why can't I type like that? How come he gets all this inspiration to write and then it just flows out of him?* He looked at the mirror, knowing the answer was the same as it had always been.

"Hey, Fillip?"

The typing stopped and Fillip-1 turned his head ever so slightly. "Yes, Fillip? Ha! That never gets old." The typing continued.

"Do you remember the day we met? I mean, the day you stepped into that mirror and I was created on the other side?"

Still typing, Fillip-1 answered, "Of course I remember. It was the greatest thing ever to happen to me. Got me out of writer's block. Come to think of it, it's a good thing there isn't a new carbon copy of me made every time I go through that portal. I don't know what I'd do with all those Fillips running around." He stopped typing. "Unless … no, scratch that. Anyway, what's on your mind?"

"Oh, I don't know."

Fillip-1 swivelled the chair around to face his clone. "What's wrong? You don't like it here?"

"No, it's not that." *Why can't I write a book, too?*

"Well, what's wrong, then? Come on, I hate to see myself upset."

Fillip-2 took a breath, searching for the right words. "It's just that … well … I was thinking while you were away. I mean, you were gone for ages this time."

"Yeah, a lot happened while I was in there. You'll love it when you go back."

"Well, that's just it. I don't want to go back."

All humour vanished from Fillip-1's face. "What?"

"I want to stay here. And I want to write a book, too."

Fillip-1 stood, looking down at the clone. "You can't write a book. You're not me. I'm Fillip Larsson, bestselling fantasy author. You're not me, and you're not anybody else, because you technically aren't from this world. So you can't write a book."

But I am Fillip Larsson. I live here. This is my *life, too!* Fillip-2 stood, anger growing within. "I can write a book if I want to. I'm an exact copy of you. That means I have the writer's desire within me. While you're gallivanting around the Eastern Kingdoms and marrying Lady Matila and waging war against Emperor Vondur, I'm here doing nothing. Literally nothing. I could write a book while you're away, and then you can publish it under your name because you wrote it through me. There are two of you in this world!" He entreated his original with open arms.

For a moment, it seemed Fillip-1 was considering the option. From Fillip-2's perspective, it was a win-win situation. Fillip-1 could have double the output of novels for the market, and Fillip-2 would finally have some purpose in his life.

But Fillip-1 shook his head. "No, no, it just wouldn't be my own work. I wouldn't feel comfortable doing that." He rubbed his nose and moved over to the mirror. "Look, the best thing for you to do is hold the fort while I'm away living the story. You don't have to stay at home all the time. Go out, do something—" he lifted a finger "—just don't do anything crazy. Let's be sensible."

"I'm not going back in there," Fillip-2 said, pointing to the mirror. "You can't make me."

"Excuse me? Yes, I can. I *made* you. And I need you to cover for me in *that* world while I'm bringing the manuscript up to date in *this* world."

"I did not ask to be created, and I don't have to do everything you say!" Fillip-2 roared, jumping to his feet.

"Honey?" Both Fillips snapped their heads to the door at the sound of Ruby's. "Honey, are you all right?"

"Fine, babe," Fillip-1 called to her. Then his eyes bored into his clone and he spoke in a hushed voice. "You didn't tell her about this, did you?"

"Of course not!"

"Get back in there," Fillip-1 ordered.

"No."

"Do it."

"No."

A second later, both Fillips launched at each other. The two became entangled as arms gripped and tugged for supremacy. Fillip-2 thought it looked so strange to be fighting with a double of himself. Of course, they were an even match. No sooner had one made a move to gain the advantage, the other moved in successful defence. It went on like this for a short while until they were truly at an impasse.

Then there were footsteps in the hallway. "Honey?"

In the moment of silence that followed, Fillip-2 felt the other man's grip relax on his shoulders. He made a snap decision and pushed Fillip-1 through the mirror. Fillip-1 disappeared as his body passed through and then reappeared as he approached the portal from the other side, apparently about to return to the den.

Fillip-2 grabbed the first heavy object he could find—a quartz pen holder from the desk—and threw it at the mirror, shattering it and severing the portal before Fillip-1 could re-emerge. Glass crashed to the carpet below, piercing his ears as each shard smashed and broke against another.

Ruby burst into the den. "Oh, honey, what happened?"

Fillip-2 pointed at the carnage, not sure exactly how to explain what had transpired. "I dropped my penholder."

"I see." Ruby nodded slowly and stood next to Fillip-2, reaching an arm tentatively around his waist. "And which one are you?"

A grin stretched across Fillip-2's face as he gazed into her eyes.

She giggled and pecked him on the cheek. "Good. I always liked you more."

ABOUT THE STORY

Few people know this, but I am not the only writer in my family. Both my siblings write stories. My brother and I have tried several times to collaborate, but have never completed anything.

Years ago, while holidaying at our childhood beach, we started writing a story together. We had no outline, but we wanted it to be funny. Admittedly, we gave a half-hearted effort. It was just a way to pass time and enjoy a good laugh.

We started out with a main character, whom we called "The Guy". This also became the title of the story, because we didn't want to stretch our creative prowess too much while on holiday. We wrote two or three pages of "The Guy" and thoroughly enjoyed it. It started by following a whacky dude as he struggled to kill a spider at the behest of a higher authority—his wife. We laughed a lot at The Guy's awkward behaviour.

We forgot the story for years, but my brother kept it on his computer. Then one day I had another idea for a portal fantasy and wanted to blend it with "The Guy". I politely asked my brother for his permission to make the story my own, and he graciously sent me the file. The resulting story became "The Price of Inspiration". I try not to think too deeply about the literary themes and structures of my stories. That said, it's definitely a portal fantasy, and it is intentionally humorous.

"The Price of Inspiration" was completed in July 2019. It was rejected by fifteen magazines. Notably, *PseudoPod* liked it a lot, but not enough to publish it. The story finally found a home in Issue #2 of *Etherea Magazine* in September 2021 before retiring in this collection.

PILGRIMAGE TO EARTH

EARTH, GAIA, TERRA, THE Blue Planet, whatever one chose to call it. For Nadya, it was the homeworld of her ancestors. Her school teachers had drummed that fact into her brain for twelve years. Now, at the age of eighteen, on the cusp of adulthood, she was making the Pilgrimage to the planet her people had abandoned two centuries ago.

The voyage from Mars had taken over six months, and she resented every day of it. Crammed into a long, cylindrical vessel which rotated to simulate gravity, Nadya had nobody but other pilgrims to talk to. Most were eighteen like her, but some were older. It was a compulsory rite of passage for eighteen-year-olds to make this trip—for older Martians, it was completely voluntary. Nadya couldn't understand why they would waste a year of their life doing this *again*.

Humanity's homeworld was indeed blue as the passenger ship approached. Vast oceans covered the surface, an amount of water Nadya had only dreamed of. As the spaceship rounded the planet, she saw wisps of white cloud here and there, but too many dark storms for comfort. There were no polar ice caps, unlike in the old orbital photos shown in her history classes. The northern regions of her ancestors' motherland, Russia, were flooded from Europe to Asia.

But she wasn't going to Russia. No pilgrim went to their ancestral homelands first—it was bad social etiquette. A pilgrim first paid their respects to the planet itself and pondered its recent history. They were to visit Earth and understand the context in which they were there. They did this around a place called Pilgrim's Sanctuary, off the coast of a flooded city called Townsville in Queensland, Australia. Then, if they had the desire and the money, they could visit their homelands for only one week. Such was the law handed down by the legislators on Mars.

Nadya had no interest in seeing anything. All she wanted was to go home to her boyfriend and continue her life in Isidigrad. He'd told her visiting Earth would be a life-changing experience, but she didn't want to hear it. The thought of being away from him for a year made her sick, and she'd cried for the whole first month of the voyage.

The passenger ship went into geostationary orbit over Earth's equator, just north of Australia. Then the pilgrims gathered their things and waited for debarkation in two hours.

Nadya spent the time chatting with a group of friends who had graduated from her high school, but the talk was pointless to her. They'd all booked the same cabin in the same vessel so they could be together, rather than spread their trips out among the several chartered vessels making runs to Earth. But after six months, they were clearly tired of her complaints about the trip, though that didn't stop her whingeing again as they each packed a bag to go planetside.

Nadya had to admit that the oceans of Earth were magnificent. Four dropships brought her and the other passengers to the surface and skirted above Australia's coastline, heading north. The copilot described the scene below as they passed points of interest. There were distant inland cities like Dubbo and Wagga Wagga, untouched by floodwaters, but abandoned nonetheless. Mountain ranges poked above the water, slithering along the seascape like snakes. Over Sydney, famous buildings like Chifley Tower and World Tower reached above the waterline, remnants of a once great city. The scene was much the same as they passed Brisbane.

The copilot said that the Great Barrier Reef was to their right. It was impossible to see the Reef, however, because it was under so much water. But, the copilot said, it was visible from orbit before the flooding.

It wasn't long before they reached Pilgrim's Sanctuary. The structure was a purpose-built offshore platform anchored to the seabed off the coast of Townsville. A smart, architecturally designed multi-storey building dominated the structure, surrounded by wide landing zones. A covered dock rested at the waterline on one side, housing what looked like a few submarines.

A handful of people greeted Nadya and the passengers as they disembarked. They were the Sanctuary's staff and would assist the pilgrims during their stay on Earth.

Nadya stepped down from the dropship, bag over her shoulder, and took a deep breath. Mars was terraformed, and its atmosphere had an odour that Nadya was accustomed to. The air on the passenger ship was filtered and recycled. But nothing could have prepared her for the air on Earth. It was clean, at least in this part of the world—as clean as it could be after two centuries of minimal human interference. She stumbled and a Sanctuary worker held her by the arm.

"It will take an hour or two for you to get used to the air and gravity of Earth," she told Nadya in English with a warm smile. "But don't worry, we'll look after you."

Nadya, who was from the Russian Sector of Mars but had learnt English in school, thanked her. As they moved along the landing platform, Nadya looked out over the ocean beyond, catching sight of something unnatural. It was a giant hand reaching out of the ocean. She knew from her studies on Mars that the hand belonged to a statue called *Elegy for Gaia*, also known as *Terra's Lament*. It was the whole reason Nadya had to visit Earth.

The pilgrims entered a luxurious reception area in the hotel that was "one with the Earth". It had a tiny environmental footprint, the importance of which would be emphasised during their visit, they were told.

For the rest of the Earth day, the pilgrims were served hand and foot to make their visit as comfortable as possible. Their accommodation was spacious. Everyone had one room all to themselves with a plush bed and exquisite ensuite, but none of it did anything to improve Nadya's mood. She showered under fresh water and ate local fish for dinner, only half-interested in the conversations at the table.

After the meal, they took the pilgrims to a large theatre where the tour staff showed them safety information and gave them an overview of the purpose of the Sanctuary. The guides discussed the itinerary for the next day and answered any questions. It was mostly the younger ones with the questions. Even Nadya put her hand up.

"How long are we out tomorrow?" she asked.

"All day," was the reply. A frown swept across Nadya's face.

The pilgrims were encouraged to get their rest—their smart rooms would wake them at six in the morning. Nadya sighed—and this time, she wasn't the only one.

THEY STARTED THE MORNING with a hearty breakfast, and then all the pilgrims boarded two submarines for their underwater expedition. If Nadya thought the passenger ship was crowded, nothing prepared her for the submarine. It was basically a bus. The passenger section was lined with seats and had round viewports, and all the mechanical areas were sealed off from the passengers' view. Nadya scored a window seat. Two of her friends sat with her.

The first stop was the city of Townsville. Once a tropical coastal city, now mostly submerged. Only a few buildings cleared the sea level, but the most interesting part of the city was underwater.

And it captivated Nadya.

She couldn't believe a whole city was submerged. Of course, there were many cities all over Earth in the same situation— she'd heard about them many times in school on Mars, but it never quite sunk into her head what it would be like. The videos and photos she'd seen didn't do it justice.

The pilgrims were enchanted by the submarine's elegant movement along streets that were constructed for cars many centuries ago. Schools of fish moved for the two elongated vessels as they took their passengers along a well-travelled route. All the while, Nadya stared in awe. Buildings loomed in front of her, many covered in some kind of sea growth. The tour guide mentioned how marvellous it was that Earth's sea life had moved in and made itself right at home. Nadya listened intently to the commentary as the nimble submarine continued on its path. She hung on to every word, her eyes darting to every building and feature the tour guide was discussing.

She imagined Isidigrad in the Russian Sector on Mars, wondered what *it* would be like submerged by an ocean, and shuddered at the thought. Hundreds of thousands of people, her friends and neighbours, would have to relocate, leaving nearly everything behind. Her heart went out to the people who used to live in Townsville, for the place looked like it would have been a beautiful city in its time. It was certainly more beautiful than Isidigrad, Nadya's home on Mars.

She sat through the whole visit in silence, just watching and imagining Townsville in its heyday. Then the tour guide announced that they were leaving the city, and Nadya's heart sank. She wanted to stay longer, but she knew she had seen enough of it to be more interested in where the tour was going next.

The submarines got away from the buildings of Townsville and resurfaced, letting sunlight back in through the viewports. Nadya squinted until her eyes grew accustomed to the natural light again. It was a bright blue sky outside, and she took in a sweeping view of her surroundings as the submarine floated on the water's surface. Out of her viewport, on the port side, she saw one of her friends waving at her from the other submarine. She laughed and waved back.

Behind the other submarine, in the distance, was the hand again—*Elegy for Gaia*. Nadya longed to see it now, but the tour designers were right to leave it until last. The statue tied together every other aspect of the Pilgrimage.

The next stop for the submarines was the Great Barrier Reef. The tour guide ran through some interesting statistics and information on the Reef. At one time, it was considered one of the great wonders of the natural world. At over two-thousand-three-hundred kilometres long and comprising nearly three-thousand reefs and nine-hundred islands, the Great Barrier Reef was the largest structure on Earth built by living organisms.

Was.

Nadya's head snapped to the tour guide, her ears pricking up. At that moment, the submarine began its descent underwater again, and she paid rapt attention to the guide as he described the Reef's slow destruction. There were so many reasons for its decline, Nadya couldn't remember them all. She'd briefly covered them in school, but actually going to the place made learning about it that much more important.

The tour guide talked about coral bleaching and traced its causes back to the source. Harmful industrial practises led to global warming, which increased sea temperatures. Nadya tilted her head as she listened. With the water being too warm for too long, the coral in the Great Barrier Reef ejected photosynthetic algae called zooxanthellae. These algae lived in a symbiotic relationship with the coral, but increased water temperatures created a difficult environment for the relationship to survive. With the algae ejected, the coral turned white—a visible sign that something was seriously wrong. This bleaching of coral made them more susceptible to disease and predators. It made sense to Nadya, but she wondered why the ancestors on Earth hadn't stopped the problem when they could.

Then the tour guide answered her silent question. Inefficient governance and a general lack of environmental accountability early on meant the initial damage done to the Reef was extremely difficult to curb. Poor fishing management also had an impact, as did chemical pollutants from farming, coastal development, and ship traffic. The result was more bleaching and weakening of the coral. Excess nitrogen from agricultural run-off also led to an explosion of the crown-of-thorns starfish population, whose larvae fed off the increased numbers of algal blooms brought about by the nitrogen run-off. These starfish were a significant predator for the coral. Nadya shook her head at the bad practices that had influenced the Reef's destruction.

Higher levels of carbon dioxide in the atmosphere changed the acidity levels of the oceans, which meant coral had a harder time building and repairing themselves. More intense cyclones along the Queensland coastline meant the now weakened coral population was battered to death in some areas. The situation disgusted Nadya. She frowned and shook her head again.

By the time the guide had neared the end of his brief yet sobering summary of the Reef's history, the submarine reached the original depth of the Reef itself. Nadya peered out her viewport as the powerful underwater lights shone out, showing small patches of coral growth.

"They're repairing slowly," the tour guide said. "This is what this area used to look like."

A video appeared on the vidscreen above his head, and Nadya looked back and forth at it and the remains outside. She couldn't understand how something so beautiful could be allowed to wither and die. There was nothing remotely close to the beauty of the Reef on Mars, despite humanity's best efforts. How could they let this happen? It was madness! The vidscreen showed such a vibrant array of colour, clear waters teeming with life. Now it was just a shadow of its once illustrious existence.

"Given enough time without human interference," the guide continued, "the Reef will return to its former glory. But that won't happen in our lifetimes. Gaia repairs herself in her own way, on her own terms, and in her own time."

The mention of Earth's ancient Greek name made Nadya think of exactly what that name meant for humanity. According to her history teacher on Mars, Gaia was the personification of Earth. It was true that Earth had become a sort of mythological being in and of itself, for it was the point of origin for all humans. It was a living, breathing thing if one considered it deeply enough. But Earth was now tens of millions of kilometres from where nearly the entire human population lived—Mars. Yes, Earth did have the ability to repair itself. How long that would take was anybody's guess. It was just a sad point in Nadya's mind that humans had to be out of the picture for Earth to rejuvenate properly.

"Gaia" also brought to mind humanity's last artwork on Earth—incidentally, the last reminder of what humans had done to the planet. She pictured *Elegy for Gaia* in her mind, remembered the hand reaching out of the sea. But it would be some time before the submarine went in that direction. There was still plenty of the regrowing Reef to see, to impress on the minds of the pilgrims what their ancestors had done.

Some hours later, during which Nadya and the pilgrims ate a delicious lunch while submerged near a pretty spot in the Reef, the submarines returned to the surface. Far ahead, Nadya could see the hand of *Gaia*. She was exultant when the tour guide announced they would finally visit *Elegy for Gaia*.

The submarines charged headlong for the hand, which made for a choppy ride, but Nadya didn't care. As they neared, Nadya had to crane her neck to look up at the hand. It was so large up close, its grey, concrete surface perfectly sculpted. Every muscle and joint showed how *Gaia* was reaching up as if trying to grasp something unattainable. But the real effect of the statue was underwater.

"Remember the hand," the guide told them.

Then the submarine lowered where it sat, shining its lights on the concrete monolith. An arm reached up below the surface, joining to square shoulders. The head of the statue looked up, too. It was a woman's face, eyes wide and mouth agape, the expression clearly showing her struggle and desperation.

Elegy for Gaia was nude in the manner of ancient statues of the Western world. The submarine passed her breasts, her belly, and reached her waist. At her side was her other arm, stretched out, hand balled into a fist. Her legs stood firmly on a solid base.

The statue itself had been built on Magnetic Island when it went underwater two centuries ago. At about one-hundred metres tall, it was initially a message of hope that the world's governments could stop the inevitable rise of sea levels. Townsville was abandoned before the waters reached her knees. By the time it reached her waist, humanity had sent its first major colony ship to Mars. The statue then changed from a symbol of hope to that of despair.

"When did the ancestors give up on Earth?" someone asked.

The tour guide looked at this pilgrim, a young male teenager whose long hair showed he hadn't taken advantage of the passenger liner's barber. "They did not 'give up' on Earth. When the waters rose above *Gaia*'s face, they knew they had failed her. At that point, the United Nations opted to transfer the seat of government to Mars and transplant the remaining Earth population there, as well."

Nadya listened to this simple answer. To her, it made perfect sense. Gaia the planet and *Gaia* the statue had drowned, and now it was up to the planet to fix the mess wrought by Nadya's ancestors. Her statue now served as a warning to all who made the Pilgrimage. It marked the extent to which humans could meddle with the climate and ecology of a planet. In fact, it was no wonder humans left Earth after *Gaia*'s head went under. They didn't deserve to live on the only garden world known to exist because of what they had done.

That lone hand above the water's surface brought a tear to Nadya's eye. Humans had ruined their first planet. They were given a second chance with Mars and had already put so much time and energy into making it habitable. Now Nadya finally understood why she had to visit Earth and see *Elegy for Gaia* in all its sad glory. On the cusp of adulthood, she would be joining the millions on Mars who each made an impact on the living, breathing world they called home. It didn't matter what occupation she chose for herself. What did matter was that she respected the planet on which she lived. It was why every eighteen-year-old had to make the trip to Earth. Each generation needed to join Martian society as responsible and environmentally accountable adults. It also explained why some adults visited *Gaia* again. As society continued to develop on Mars, the human population had to keep reminding itself of what they lost, and why.

As the submarine rose steadily back to the surface, Nadya had a long, hard look at *Gaia*'s face again. She couldn't help but think of *Gaia* crying salty tears over her predicament, filling the ocean with her sorrow and regret.

Yes, the trip was worth it. Just like her boyfriend had said.

ABOUT THE STORY

"PILGRIMAGE TO EARTH" WAS the first short story I sold. At the time, I had been chosen by Aussie Speculative Fiction (ASF) as one of eight authors to write in a new shared universe of unconnected novellas called the Drowned Earth Series. The result was my first book, *Fire Over Troubled Water*.

In early 2019, while *Fire Over Troubled Water* was in production, ASF put out a call for short story submissions for a new anthology called *Journeys*. Since I was in a water-world frame of mind, I wanted to explore the idea of a global flood a bit more. I wanted something set much further into the future, but still on Earth. Even before the nuts and bolts of the story came together, I already had the title set in stone. Basically, I wanted to tell a story about a human who makers a pilgrimage to Earth and sees its flooded state for the first time.

Research led me to a 2018 article by Brian Kahn on gizmodo. com called "An Underwater Sculpture in the Maldives Is the Perfect Monument to Climate Change". This article reported on a sculpture called created by artist Jason deCaires Taylor. This sculpture, called *Coralarium*, was built underwater off the Maldivian coast and was designed to highlight the current and future effects of climate change on low-lying inhabited areas. Sadly, the Maldivian government pulled down the sculpture in September 2018 for local religious reasons. There are plenty of photos online for any who are curious about it.

Nevertheless, the work of Jason deCaires Taylor inspired the reason why my protagonist comes to the flooded Earth—to see a monument to climate change, *Elegy for Gaia*. I put *Elegy for Gaia* in the Great Barrier Reef, one of the seven natural wonders of the world. The sculpture needed to show not only the result of humankind's mistakes, but be a marker for the progressive failures of environmental accountability. I would also use the Great Barrier

Reef as an object lesson for my protagonist. In seeing this statue and learning the (future) history of the Reef, the protagonist would change her mind on the importance of climate sustainability and her own role as an environmentally conscious adult back home on Mars.

The subject matter of "Pilgrimage to Earth" is deeper than my usual brand. I tend not to comment on current issues. If I can spin a good yarn, I'm happy. If others enjoy my yarns, I'm even happier. So when I write about deeper topics and use more complex techniques—stuff with morals, warnings, and purpose-made analogies and metaphors—it's actually quite unnatural for me. I enjoyed the experience, though, and it revealed a hidden ability to write in that style and somehow make it publishable.

The actual writing process was interesting. I was running very late in the submission period, so I had to get something done fast. I was lucky(?) to have the flu, which meant I had plenty of time to write. To this day, churning out a 3,200-word short story and editing it multiple times in two days while being congested and dazed is something I'm still proud of. But I'd rather not do it again.

I submitted "Pilgrimage to Earth" to ASF in May 2019 and they accepted in July, much to my surprise. My first short story sale! The anthology debuted at Supanova Adelaide in November 2019 and was released to the world the following month in the anthology *Journeys: Aussie Speculative Fiction*.

Interestingly, in 2020, I learned that Jason deCaires Taylor installed another underwater sculpture in 2019, this time in the very place where "Pilgrimage to Earth" is set—the Great Barrier Reef! It's called *The Coral Greenhouse*. But even cooler is another of his 2019 statues just off the coast of Townsville called *Ocean Siren*, which bears a striking resemblance to *Elegy for Gaia*, though it is noticeably smaller. This freak coincidence of creativity shocked me. If I had known about it before writing "Pilgrimage to Earth", then the story would have been vastly different. But as the statue hadn't been constructed at the time of writing the story, there was no way to avoid the coincidence. I guess great minds think alike.

then the story would have been vastly different. But as the statue hadn't been constructed at the time of writing the story, there was no way to avoid the coincidence. I guess great minds think alike.

POLICE LINE - DO NOT CROSS
POLICE LINE - DO NOT CROSS

JUST DESERTS

I⏤T WAS A CRIME of opportunity—like many crimes on the street—and as in most homicides, the killer knew his victim.

The killer approached an alley darkened by towering buildings, his footsteps muffled by the steady, pollution-soaked rain pattering on the hard, grey ground. A plethora of bright neon advertisements illuminated the street in shades of yellow, pink, and blue, but the alley did not admit any of that light. It was the perfect spot for the victim to do his pulse dealing.

The killer sniffed at the rain's stench as it pushed down the smog from the city's higher levels. He waited for the last pulse customer to leave the alley before casually walking across the street. A monorail rattled overhead. He kept his coat collar high and his hat low, its wide brim just hiding his face from any prying eyes in the nearby diner. It was just past midnight, but the city never slept.

Through the shadows of the alley, the killer found his quarry. A short man with a cybernetic optical enhancer stood under the shelter of a fire escape platform, hiding from the rain.

"What do you want from me now?" the victim asked, his voice just audible above the rain.

But his killer didn't reply. Instead, he hunched forward while approaching the dealer, tucking his hand into his coat in one fluid motion. He stopped a few paces short and waited.

"Well, spit it out," the victim said. "I don't like you hanging around here."

At that moment, another old monorail car rushed by overhead and the killer drew his pistol. The pulse dealer had no time to react as three bullets found new homes his chest. He slumped to the ground, motionless. Then the killer put two more bullets into his head for good measure, holstered his pistol, and quietly left the alley.

Detective Max Quinn hated the rain. It stank, it soiled the windows of his ninth-floor apartment, and he hated how more days of the year were wet than dry. Of the days that were dry, most were darkly overcast. It was Quinn's day off, and it rained in his dreams—of all things—while he napped on the couch.

His palm buzzed, and he shook awake at the incoming call. He scoffed at the meagre daylight penetrating into his tiny hole of an apartment. His coat hung from a chair and still dripped from when he finished his shift the previous night.

Quinn pressed his thumb into his left palm and answered the phone.

"Quinn, it's Anders," the voice said through his hand. "I'm sorry to disturb you on your day off, but the captain thought you should know that one of your contacts was found dead this morning. Goro Sato, one of the pulse dealers in your neighbourhood."

"Little Goro?" Quinn asked. His voice was hoarse with sleep.

"Yeah. He was shot in an alley on Fifty-fourth, behind Barney's Diner.

"I know the place."

"Great. Uniforms are already there."

"Thanks." Homicide was his favourite. Nothing suited him more than inspecting a crime scene with a victim that didn't get in his way.

Before he left his apartment, he glanced at a video portrait of his sister. She had died eighteen years ago from a pulse overdose. It was a ritual for him to look at her and remind himself of his purpose in life. Today was the anniversary of her death, so Quinn wasn't exactly a cheerful person when he stepped out into the world.

Uniforms had cordoned off the alley's entrance. An officer also stood by to ward off any onlookers. Nobody stopped. Murders were so common in the neighbourhood that people just accepted it and moved on.

Quinn crossed the street and saw the crime scene illuminated by scene lights. Even though it was daytime, the alley was dark and needed artificial lighting. The uniforms moved away to let the detective do his work. Little Goro's body lay on the wet ground under a makeshift police awning. Three bloody holes in the chest and two gaping entry wounds in the head suggested a gangland slaying. Packets of pulse chips had spilled out of Goro's interior jacket pocket.

"Now, Goro, give me what you have never given me before," Quinn said, crouching next to the body. He picked up a few of the pulse chips with a gloved hand, examining them for any markings that might lead to a supplier. As usual, Goro's chips were flawless. Many chips had manufacturing marks or irregularities that came from older printers, usually operated by small-time thugs. But Goro's had always been perfect, and he had never told Quinn who supplied him, though Quinn had his suspicions.

Quinn spent a few more minutes examining the crime scene, checking for signs of incriminating evidence before speaking to one of the uniformed officers.

"Any witnesses?"

"A worker at the diner saw someone walking out here in the rain last night," the officer replied. Quinn paid rapt attention. "Her name's Rachel Weber. She's inside."

"Thanks."

Barney's Diner was an old, run-down greasy spoon with a full window facing the road and a bright pink neon sign that advertised its name. The place was full of early-starters having an affordable, unhealthy breakfast before work. Distracting techno music played in the background. A worker mopped dirty rainwater at the entrance. Quinn stepped inside and forced the worker to do his job all over again, but when he presented his badge and asked for Rachel Weber, the young man quickly singled her out.

"Miss Weber?" Quinn asked. The girl was behind the counter taking someone's order.

"One moment," she said.

The customer half-spun on his barstool and glanced at Quinn. "Hey, bud, can't you see I'm ordering here?"

Quinn held his badge in front of the guy's face. "You're done ordering. Now beat it."

The customer swore at Quinn before moving to another barstool. Quinn took his spot and studied the girl on the other side of the counter. She had pallid skin and heavy bags under her eyes. Poor thing must have been on her feet all night and into the morning. "I'm Detective Max Quinn. I'm investigating the murder in the alley. Do you mind if I ask you a few questions?"

"I've already answered questions. One of the coppers came in here already."

"Well, now you'll have to answer mine," Quinn snapped. "And I'll have a coffee while we talk."

Rachel snarled and fetched the coffeepot. She poured him a mug as he started his questioning.

"You said you saw someone walking around the alley. About what time was that?"

"Between twelve and one."

Quinn's heart skipped a beat. *She saw someone.*

"This morning?" he asked.

"Yeah."

"Did you see just the one person, or were there more?"

"I never saw more than one person at a time."

"So there were multiple people around that time?"

"I guess so."

"Don't guess so; know so. Was there or was there not more than one person walking around the alley between the hours of twelve and one this morning?" He sipped his coffee, watching her think. The longer an eyewitness thought about something, the less confident they were about their memories.

Rachel sighed. "Yes, there were several."

"Could you describe any of them? Did you see faces? What about clothes?"

"Um," Rachel started, but her face scrunched up. "No. They were all wearing hoods or hats or big coats. The lights in the street lit them up, but they all wore black or grey or had their faces covered. I'm sorry."

Quinn stretched his lips into a smile, but his eyes stayed cold. "That's okay. Anything you can tell me might help. Did you know the murder victim?"

"No," Rachel replied, but she cleared her throat and looked down at the counter, wiping it with a cloth.

"I'll ask you again. Did you know the murder victim?"

Rachel looked sideways and nodded when she returned her gaze to the detective.

"Right. Do you know what he was doing in the alley?"

Rachel nodded again. Her hands started fidgeting.

He lowered his voice and leaned forward. "Did you ever purchase his goods?"

The girl's breathing intensified under Quinn's steely gaze and forthright questioning. This was why they got detectives to do the dirty work. People like Quinn could get answers out of anybody.

"I know you did. I can see it in your eyes. But I don't care about that. Tell me this: Did he ever say who his supplier was?"

Rachel swallowed and shook her head slowly. "No."

"It's okay, you can tell me."

But she shook her head again, her eyes welling up. "I don't know. He never told me." She wiped her eyes while Quinn swallowed more of the bitter coffee. "Do you think his supplier killed him?"

Quinn finished the coffee, knowing that he would get no further with this witness. "Maybe."

QUINN FLEW HIS CAR in the mid-level skylanes, slipping between pedestrian bridges and ignoring the blaring advertisements on the buildings either side of him. He thought about his vendetta against the city's biggest pulse supplier—Marko Dedic.

It was years ago when the police learned of Dedic's existence. Quinn was a young uniform then, and he had nothing to do with Dedic or the pulse epidemic spreading through the city. But it became his problem when his sister tried it, got hooked, and then died of an overdose. Before she died, she told him Dedic was the dealer, but the elusive bastard had escaped a conviction and then disappeared. There were only whispers of his continued involvement in the pulse trade until his name came up on a listening device. From then on, Quinn pursued him mercilessly. Justice needed to be served, but eighteen years was a long time to be chasing one man who lived in the same city.

Quinn dropped his car in one of the downways, heading for a decrepit neighbourhood in the dark pits of the city's ground level. His destination was a known pulse den to which the police turned a blind eye. To catch the big fish, you needed to allow room for the smaller ones to grow. Quinn had another contact inside, and he had some questions that needed answering.

Quinn parked his car outside the tenement. Before he stepped out, two shady figures eyed him suspiciously from across the street, then made their way over to him. But Quinn had no patience for them, and he immediately stepped out of the car and flashed them his badge, his other hand on his pistol holster. Sometimes, in certain places, some people scurried away faster at the sight of a police badge than a gun. Quinn knew they were armed, but he didn't need their crap—not this morning. They left him alone.

Inside the tenement foyer was a wiry man who looked Quinn up and down.

"Usually you guys come here in twos," he said.

"Where's Dex?" Quinn asked. He'd seen the guy lounging around in the foyer before, most likely playing scout.

"He's upstairs."

"Which floor?"

"Don't know. But he's on one of them. Go find him, copper."

Quinn gave him an almighty backhander with his cybernetic hand. The scout caught himself against a wall and looked back at his attacker, rubbing his cheek.

"Next time, I break teeth," Quinn said, lifting a finger at the guy. "I don't need to walk in pairs to handle punks like you. Now, where's Dex?"

"He's in the office," he said, jerking his head back to a door near the corner of the room.

Quinn left him. Sure enough, Dex was in the office, sitting with his feet up, looking at an infopad. When he saw Quinn, he threw the infopad onto his desk and spread his arms wide.

"Detective! To what do I owe the pleasure of your visit to my humble establishment?" He was a greasy man, balding, with all ten strands of hair combed over his shiny cranium.

"A street dealer was murdered this morning," Quinn told him after closing the door.

"A street dealer is murdered every morning. So what?"

"I need to know who his supplier is."

"And you think I can—or will—tell you?"

Quinn threw one of the pulse chips into Dex's lap. "He was dealing these."

Dex examined the chip closely. "It's a good make. No imperfections that I can see." He reached for a magnifier and studied the chip with one eye. "Yep, it's perfect in every way."

"So who made it?"

Dex took the magnifier out of his eye socket and tilted his head. "Really? And why would I tell you that?"

"Because it will guarantee the continued operation of this 'humble establishment' of yours." When it seemed Dex's mind was weighing the decision, Quinn pushed harder. "Don't you know there's an army of coppers just waiting to storm this place and crack some skulls? We're doing you a favour by not interfering here. All I ask for is some information. Who manufactured that chip?"

The den master grumbled, but nodded. "I have my suspicions. But there's only one way to truly know. We need to test its quality."

"Then test away." Quinn gestured at Dex.

Dex laughed. "Hey, man, I don't do this much anymore. But don't worry, I'll give you your answer." He pressed his palm and spoke into it. "Yeah, Vic. Come in here. I got a treat for you."

A few seconds later, the wiry young man from the foyer entered. He took a wide berth around Quinn and stood at a respectful distance from Dex.

"You want a fix?" Dex asked him, holding the pulse chip up for him to see.

Immediately, Vic brightened up. "Oh, yeah. You know I'm always up for one."

Vic knelt and presented the back of his neck to Dex. There, as found on most people who wanted to live a normal life, was a neural port. It was a common method of downloading information directly to the brain. It forged new synapses, created memories, gave people encyclopaedic knowledge for the right price. But criminals used it for other purposes.

Dex gave one look at Quinn, who nodded his permission and, along with it, a silent pledge not to bring the full weight of the law down on Dex for doing something illegal in plain sight of a police detective.

Dex inserted the pulse chip. Quinn had seen pulse addicts mid-rush, but he'd never watched an episode from start to finish. Vic's back arched while he was on his knees, and then he was on his side, shaking gently as the chip began its work. Pulse chips activated neural networks associated with music and dancing. It gave people a unique high. Vic's head bobbed and twitched rhythmically in different directions, then the movements went down his body until he was writhing on the floor in something akin to a floor dance. There was nothing painful about it, but an unsuitable environment could lead to serious bodily harm. A faulty chip could cause irreparable neural damage, often leading to death. Under the influence of a high-quality pulse chip, a young, fit, and seasoned pulse addict like Vic took it all in stride, moving to the chip's electro-neural stimuli.

Quinn resisted the urge to shake his head. The fact that some people willingly let a piece of electronics manufactured by criminals influence their motor neurons was something he could never come to terms with. Like all addictions, it usually started out of curiosity, or maybe peer pressure. Enough pulse episodes eventually hooked the brain so much that it craved the chip's momentary pleasure. It drove people crazy trying to get their next fix—the feeling of electrical stimuli moving their body like they were a puppet. And then there were those who didn't know when enough was enough and tried one chip after another, experiencing different pulse dances consecutively. The brain would overload, and the addict would die mid-episode. There were such deaths every night in the city.

About ten minutes later, Vic's body slowed to gentle movements until he was lying on his back, looking at the ceiling in a daze. Scientists described the post-episode feeling as orgasmic—in many cases, even better. Vic breathed heavily and blinked with fatigue, and it was clear his mind was somewhere else.

"Well," Dex said after some time, "we rarely get a chip of *that* quality in here."

"How can you tell?"

"Chips require complex technical knowledge to program. Basement manufacturers can make them, but their pulse rhythms and sequences are pretty basic. Sometimes they're completely messed up. Many cases of pulse-induced brain damage are from improperly programmed pulse sequences. I try to steer clear of those. I get some good chips coming through here, but this has outshone all of them."

It was nothing Quinn didn't already know, but he played dumb to get Dex talking. "So who made it?"

One side of Dex's mouth curled up into a smile. "You really want to know?"

Quinn took a step towards the den master and put his hands on his hips. The butt of his pistol stuck out from inside his coat.

Dex put up his hands. "Okay, okay. I've only seen a few chips like this before. They were all made by Marko Dedic."

"Are you sure?"

"Positive."

Vic had fallen asleep on the floor and purred quietly. When Quinn looked down at him, he knew what Dex said was true, but the evidence was circumstantial at best.

Unless ... Quinn stepped over to Vic and kicked his foot. The young man was blissfully out to the world.

"How many times do Dedic's mules come here?" Quinn asked.

Dex squinted at him, but his breathing stayed even. "What are you talking about?"

"Look, let's cut the crap." Quinn sat down opposite the den master. "We know Dedic sends chips here. Do you deny it?"

Dex tilted his head back defiantly.

"You want to know how we know?" Quinn looked down at Vic, and when Dex did the same, the realisation that spread across his face was priceless. "Vic is an informant. A *dedicated* one too." He smirked at the word. "No pun intended."

The den master gulped and leaned back in his chair in a sudden movement. He clenched his hands together and his eyes studied Quinn's hard face.

"Now," Quinn continued, "I ask again: how many times do Dedic's mules come here?"

Dex looked into his lap. "Twice a week."

Quinn made a mental note of that. "And you have direct contact with them?"

"Yes."

"How much do they sell you?"

"One hundred chips each visit."

"Do you buy anything else?"

"Yes."

"What?"

Dex sighed. "Some coke and acid, and a fair bit of dope. They all enhance the pulse experience."

"I see." He knew pulse addicts often dabbled with marijuana, but the fact that Dex was also dealing in cocaine and LSD in his "humble establishment" meant he was much more than a manager of a safe and secure pulse den. "Is that all?"

"That's all I get from Dedic, yes."

"Okay." Quinn nodded. That was all he cared about. "You remember I said there was an army of coppers waiting to bust up this place? Well, I wasn't lying."

"I never doubted you."

"Good. But what I didn't tell you was that those coppers are nearly ready to storm this place. With everything Vic told us, we've got plenty of evidence to shut this place down for good, and put you away. And just like that, Marko Dedic loses another dealer but stays safe on his throne. The way I see it, Dedic is doing another one of his spring cleans. He knocks off people who might know too much, or who are getting too greedy—like the pulse dealer who got killed this morning. He might know we're coming for you too. Now, how do you feel about that?"

"The cops are coming for *me*, are they?" Dex sighed. "And Dedic probably already knows that."

Quinn nodded, hoping Dex would see things his way.

"That's how the game is played," Dex said dismissively. "The pawns are sacrificed for the king."

"But you're not just any old pawn. I know you. You have sway. How often does a pawn get to take down a king? They're usually slaughtered before they get near one. But you, no, you're much more than a pawn. You've got information—names, dates, figures, links—stuff we can use to knock Dedic off his throne." Quinn shrugged. "And you get leniency for helping us."

Dex looked around his office. "Either way, I lose."

"Except my way you lose less."

Dex was silent for what seemed like an eternity, but Quinn let him think it over. Every time Dex's eyes crossed Quinn's, the hard-boiled detective would smirk and give the den master a self-assured tilt of the head. In Quinn's eyes, you had to fight to survive the world. It crushed anyone who gave up.

After one long, last gaze at Vic's peaceful, resting body, Dex made up his mind. "I'll do it," he whispered. His soul was crushed. He had been riding high in his own little world until the minute Quinn walked into his office and shattered everything.

"Then you can come with me," Quinn said. "I won't cuff you."

"What about him?"

"Vic? He'll wake up when he's ready. Let's go."

With that, Quinn led Dex out of the tenement, taking the den master from his domain for good, and leaving the sleeping man who was never a police informant alone on the floor.

QUINN SPENT HOURS OFFICIALLY interrogating Dex and then lobbying for an arrest warrant for Marko Dedic. Once he finally got a warrant, he quickly rounded up twenty of the most trust-worthy uniformed police officers and plainclothes detectives and told them to follow him. As an added security measure, he didn't tell them where he was going. They just did their damnedest to keep up as he weaved through traffic on the skyways on his relent-less path to the city centre.

He was sure their mission dawned on them when he circled the tall, brightly lit office tower where Dedic conducted his business under the guise of some legitimacy. Quinn ordered every officer and detective to fulfil aspects of a plan he had envisaged for years. The police cars split up, but Quinn and a small group of officers landed in the main parking lot cut into the centre of the tower.

This is it, Quinn thought as he jumped out of his car. He felt for the reassuring weight of his pistol in its holster. *Today's the day.* He breathed faster as his pace quickened, walking into the main reception area. Four officers flanked him, two steps behind.

"Good evening, how may I ..." the receptionist started. But Quinn paid her no heed.

Quinn pressed on, knowing exactly where he was going. Office workers—mostly law-abiding citizens doing honest work for legit-imate companies partially owned by Dedic—watched as Quinn and his entourage charged through their corridors. Men and women stepped out of their way, such was the imposing presence Quinn struck with his dark coat and steely expression.

A one-minute elevator ride took them straight to the building's top floor, which belonged solely to Dedic. When Quinn pushed past the protesting secretaries and guards and burst into Dedic's office, he found the man alone, staring out at the police cars parked on his private landing pad.

"I knew you were coming, Quinn," Dedic said softly with his back to the advancing officers.

Of course you did, Quinn thought. *You have rats all through the Justice Department.* "The game is up, Dedic."

Finally, he turned around. He had one hand in his pocket, the other holding a glass containing some amber liquid. The officers fanned out behind Quinn.

"We're here for your arrest," Quinn told him.

Dedic laughed heartily, his eyes twinkling with delight. "Oh, how I'm sure you've waited years to say that. Tell me, what evils have I done to warrant my arrest?"

"Racketeering; bribery; murder; the manufacture, cultivation, and distribution of various illegal narcotics; the manufacture and distribution of pulse chips; and at least twelve cases of pulse supply resulting in death."

"Serious charges," Dedic said, sipping his drink. He seemed detached from the situation.

"Yeah, I think so too. And they come from a reputable source. One of your den masters, in fact."

Dedic froze mid-sip and stared at Quinn.

"That's right," Quinn said with a satisfying grin. It had been a long time since Quinn felt genuinely happy about anything. He took small steps towards his enemy. "I have the names of your mules and street dealers, the locations of your factories, the names of drug addicts who have died using your chips, the names of justice professionals on your payroll, and some data on supply quantities and payments. By the time you go to trial, I'll have even more evidence to prove that you are the biggest drug and pulse dealer in this city. Then no judge will vouch for you, no detective will destroy the evidence against you, and none of your lackeys will want to go down with you. You're finished, Dedic."

Marko Dedic took a few quick breaths before speaking, this time with a much louder voice. "All this will be disproved in court, like every other time."

Quinn shook his head. "Not this time."

All four uniformed officers moved on the drug kingpin. They frisked him through his expensive suit, removed what cybernetic enhancements they could, cuffed him, and then led him out to the waiting police car on his private landing bay.

When he was alone in the office, Quinn let out a deep sigh. It had been a long day, but finally apprehending Dedic on some serious charges with equally serious evidence lifted an enormous weight off his shoulders.

By the time Quinn went through the red tape at the station, it was late and he was tired, so he picked up a greasy burger for dinner.

His apartment was just as he'd left it. He switched on the vidscreen and let a news anchor drone on while he ate his burger. While eating, he looked at the video portrait of his sister on the shelf. She was playing with her dog in her apartment, back when she was a college student—healthy, drug- and pulse-free, and alive. After eighteen years, he finally felt like she was getting some justice.

Then his eyes moved to the damp coat on the chair. The damn thing was still drying from when he wore it out the night before, the night he shot and killed a pulse dealer in a dark alley.

A sad smile spread across his face. Yes, he killed a pulse dealer. Yes, he lied about his supposed informant in Dex's pulse den. Yes, he had broken the law several times to catch a man who was breaking it every day. Dedic would get what he deserved, and it would be a long time coming.

He sniffed a laugh. *Sometimes, you have to play by your own rules*, he thought. If his sins kept the city safer, then at least he could sleep well at night.

ABOUT THE STORY

Did you know I have a degree in criminology and criminal justice? I found it incredibly difficult to get a job after I earned that expensive piece of paper. So imagine my joy when I finally put my knowledge to good use and wrote a crime story! When I wrote "Falsehood" for Flame Tree Publishing's *A Dying Planet* anthology, I also wrote "Just Deserts" for their *Detective Thrillers* anthology.

Before outlining the history of "Just Deserts", I should explain the title. A few editors have asked me if the title is incorrect, wondering if it should be *Desserts* with a double *s*. While the word is pronounced like the delicious after-dinner treat, the correct spelling is with a single *s*, and it carries the meaning of something deserved. A *just desert* is a punishment that fits a crime.

I had always wanted to experiment with cyberpunk, so I chose that cliché subgenre for my detective story. I needed a grizzly cop with a cool name, and Max Quinn was born. I also needed an equally grizzly crime for the opening scene, which led to the quick, clean execution of the criminal in the alley. At this point, there was nothing new in the story—many cyberpunk stories have similar characters and settings. To make the story unique, I needed a substance that was reminiscent of the various drugs that have gripped many countries and destroyed many lives over the last several decades, but I wanted a more futuristic drug. Less chemical, more cyber. So I invented *pulse*.

Pulse is my interpretation of what a "drug" might be in a cyberpunk setting. Of course, people might still inject or ingest organic and synthetic substances into their bodies, but I explored another means of getting "high" and what constituted a drug and an addiction—auditory stimulation.

Listening to enjoyable music does wonders for the brain. It produces endorphins in the brain, which relieves pain and stress. It also lowers cortisol, a hormone responsible for stress and anxiety. The feel-good neurotransmitter dopamine is also released in high amounts. Little wonder that many people seek music to relax and enjoy life. But what would happen if the chemical reactions in the brain became such a draw that people became addicted to the positive effects of music? Similar addictions are caused by sex, exercise, and other pleasurable and positive experiences, which are engaged in to such an extent that the activity becomes physically and psychologically unhealthy. What if the way people obtained this musical high was through an illicit means of direct brain stimulation?

Enter *pulse*, a futuristic electronic "drug" with pre-programmed beats and rhythms that stimulate the auditory system and nervous system. I figured the best way to partake of such a drug would be by inserting a chip into some kind of neural implant. Such a neural implant would be commonplace in my cyberpunk world, because normal people would use it to upload data to their minds. But there had to be risks associated with pulse. Overstimulation, either through overuse of pulse or uploads from low-quality pulse chips, could lead to mental or physical damage, or even death.

It is a sad fact that some people profit from the addictions of others. Drug lords care not one iota about the people they enslave with their products. The fight against illicit drugs seems evermore to be a losing battle, even when law enforcement takes extreme, militant actions against producers and suppliers. That is why "Just Deserts" features pulse as such a widespread problem—so many people are addicted to it and law enforcement simply does not have the power or the funding to eradicate it completely.

That is where my hard-boiled detective comes onto the scene. I had to give him a personal reason to do the things he did in the story, namely, the death of his sister to a pulse overdose. In the real world, his actions would be highly illegal, even though many good people would applaud his aggressive methods against an accused drug kingpin. But in the fictional cyberpunk world I created, where laws can be bent and there are many dark corners in which to operate, Detective Max Quinn could hunt down Marko Dedic with relative impunity. He just had to cover his trail. In that way, Quinn gave Dedic his just desert.

Unfortunately, "Just Deserts" was rejected for the *Detective Thrillers* anthology, as well as several other anthologies and magazines after that. It was hard because most rejections did not include feedback, which is a sad reality in the short fiction scene. A first reader at *Fantasy & Science Fiction* regretted that they felt emotionally detached in the opening murder scene (which is exactly how they were supposed to feel). *Escape Pod* said that the story was a lot of fun, but the cyberpunk noir characters and tropes were not fresh enough. The story reached the highest submission level for *Andromeda Spaceways Magazine*, with slush readers stating it had a nice twist, engaging dialogue, a strong and engrossing plot, and an edge-of-your-seat structure. They praised the writing, the "empathetic, driven, and hardened protagonist", and the great setting. This comment made me smile: "Loved the old salt detective and his solitary sting."

In fact, Andromeda Spaceways Magazine had some great critical comments too. One reader recommended a thorough edit to remove excess exposition and static descriptions. Another reader provided lots of advice. They said that the story was "too linear and straightforward" for a detective thriller, and I agree. The reader noted that there was no sense of peril for any character, and Marko Dedic didn't have time to be his true self. These comments led to edits, further rejections, and then more edits for inclusion in this collection. The story could benefit from a longer format, perhaps as a novelette, a novella, or even a full novel. That way, the setting and characters will have the best chance of being fully developed.

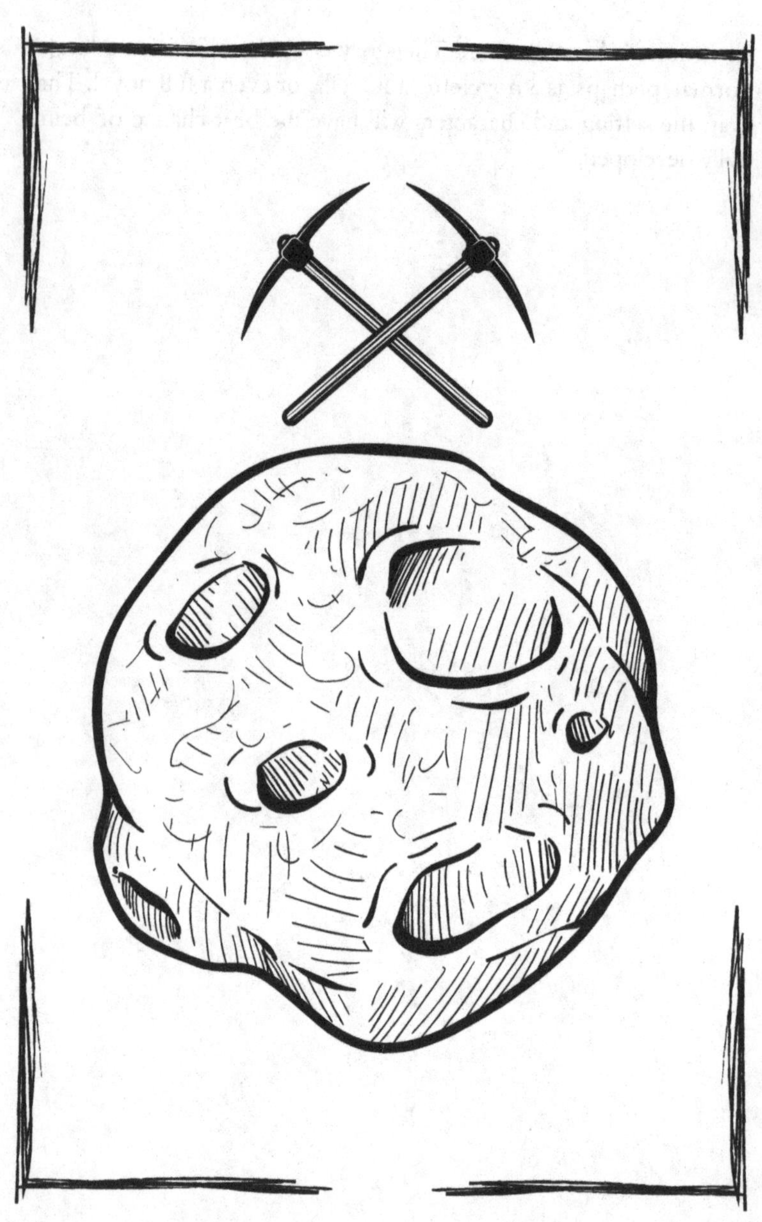

A MINER'S DREAM

Derrick landed the rickety old ship as he could. Its thrusters sputtered before it hit the grey-red surface of the asteroid, the sound and shock reverberating throughout the metal hull. Rod, over thirty years older than Derrick, grunted in discomfort.

"We've had this ship more than one standard year," Rod said, unbuckling, "and you still can't land it properly."

"Not my fault the ship's broke," Derrick replied.

"Yeah, well, I'll fix it when I have time … oh, wait, that's right, we have no more money." Rod waved his hands to show how their budget had vanished into thin air. It was an argument they'd been having for the past few hours.

Derrick shut down the ship's engines and put the non-vital systems in standby mode. "Trust me, old man, we'll have money soon. This is the place." He grinned devilishly. "We'll be rich—I'm sure of it."

Rod stood, leaning over his chair despite his crooked back. "That's what you said about the last three rocks you took us to." He pointed out the cockpit viewports at the barren asteroid surface beyond. "This place looks no different." He coughed as he stomped out of the cockpit, leaving his idealistic accomplice behind.

"This time will be different. You'll see."

Rod dismissed Derrick's optimism. He was getting too old and sick to have such a rosy outlook on life. Years of hard labour as an asteroid and moon miner had sapped his joy for life. Now, thanks to Derrick's hare-brained scheme, his entire life savings were gone too. His frustration intensified the longer he saw no return on his investment.

While Rod was slipping into his enviro-suit, Derrick arrived from the cockpit and quietly did the same. Rod sealed his helmet and checked the optical and comm systems. Then he wondered what it was like outside the ship.

He switched to the external speaker so Derrick could hear him. "What's the gravity like out there?" In his angst, he forgot to check the ship's readouts before storming out of the cockpit.

"Less than point-three," Derrick replied. "Some iron and nickel here."

Metals are good, Rod thought, but that's not what we're here for. "Temperature?"

"I think it said minus eighty-five."

Derrick sealed his helmet and they switched to radio. Then he went to a cabinet and pulled out two pistols, holstering one and passing the other to Rod.

Rod took it slowly, like he always did, feeling the weight of such a small object and fully appreciating its potential. He disliked guns, but they were a necessary evil. "Did the scanner pick up any evidence of life out there?"

"None. No infrared signatures, no radio signals, nothing. I still don't understand why you insist on carrying one of these."

"Because it keeps me safe, that's why."

With the work they were doing, they were prime targets for pirates and other leeches who would rather kill for money than do an honest day's work. Rod vividly remembered the time when he survived a bloody pirate raid on his workplace decades ago. The precious metal mined by Sidvec Industries was a prime target for heavily armed pirates. Rod still had a scar where a chemical bullet tore through his leg, narrowly missing a major artery. Now he carried a pistol wherever he worked.

They picked up some handheld tools and scanning equipment before going to the pressurisation chamber. As the chamber sealed and matched the exterior atmosphere, Rod looked at the younger, shorter Derrick, and for a moment his unhappiness subsided. This young man dared to rise above the rut he had been born into, dared to venture out into the unknown and make it rich. And he had convinced Rod—grumpy, stubborn Rod—to help.

This kid's going to make me filthy rich someday, he thought. Maybe I should cut him some slack.

The ship's exterior door slid open, revealing an unexplored expanse of reddish plains, valleys, and jagged cliffs.

"This is it," Derrick said. "Let's go make our millions."

To Rod, each asteroid was unique. This one, designated 2173 LK_{192} in the database, had never been touched by human boots. Most asteroids in the Kuiper Belt were still ripe for exploration, but Rod and Derrick were looking for a specific mineral, one that had driven them to the edge of financial ruin.

Derrick walked slowly in his gravitationally stabilised suit, following the path dictated to him by his hand-held sensor. They walked across an unexciting mare, their footsteps leaving deep prints in the dusty surface. Minuscule regolith particles drifted up in the low gravity where it hung for a short while, only to spend minutes descending back to the surface.

Suddenly, Derrick's scanner went wild. "Whoa!"

Rod leaned closer to look at the reading. It flashed the highest numbers he had ever seen for a lunastone deposit.

"See, I told you we'd find it here!" Derrick jumped for joy. He was so ecstatic that Rod had to grasp his arm to stop the younger man from floating away.

Rod, however, saw the reality of the situation. He examined the flat expanse, coughing before he spoke. "If it's directly beneath us, how do we get to it? We don't have the equipment for a vertical dig, and we don't have enough time to go spiralling down on an angle."

"We'll have to come in laterally—dig a tunnel. We have enough supplies to last a week, so it should be doable."

Talk of hard work didn't faze Rod, especially now that their goal was so much closer to being realised. He would happily work hard for a week if it meant he could retire as a millionaire and never have to work again.

Derrick stuck a beacon in the ground and surveyed the surrounding landscape. "Seems like there's a valley over there. Let's have a look."

Rod flew the small trip to the valley. He took the ship down, marvelling at its depth and barren beauty. A sheer cliff of rock and iron loomed above on one side, about thirty metres high. A similarly steep incline bordered them opposite this, though not as high. It was darker in the valley, so Rod activated the ship's external floodlights.

Derrick sprang into action. Despite being a miner nowhere near as long as Rod, he started giving orders: bring this, grab that, fetch this, move that, and so on. By the end of it, Rod was biting his tongue so hard he nearly drew blood. But he kept repeating to himself that it was worth enduring. Sure, there were initial failures in their plan, but at least Derrick's efforts were finally about to pay off.

Using the beacon's transmission from the plain above, Derrick plotted a straight line and marked exactly where to dig.

"Seventy metres, as the crow flies," he said.

The digging was tough. They chewed through the first ten metres of rock easily enough, but then their drilling platform struck a solid chunk of iron ore—enough to fetch a fair price too. Rod tightened his grip on the platform's joysticks as soon as the drill bit scratched the new material. He tried to move with the swaying of the machine, but then the platform's computer flashed and started an automatic shutdown procedure.

Derrick cursed loudly and moved to inspect, but Rod knew exactly what the problem was. He could feel it.

"Damn, bit's blunt as hell," Derrick exclaimed. He smacked the round cutter.

"I know," Rod replied. There hadn't been enough money to quickly and professionally sharpen it after their other jobs. But they should have made time to do it themselves, Rod thought.

"What's the other one like?" Derrick asked.

"Not much better. It could probably cut through that, but then it'll be just as bad as this one." Rod coughed and held up a hand to stay Derrick's further comments. "We could try to dig around it."

Derrick rubbed his shoulder through the enviro-suit. "Give me two seconds." He galloped out of their short tunnel.

Rod studied the situation. If they had to reverse the drilling platform out to change the bit, it meant undoing all the string lights they'd installed on one wall of the tunnel. Even slightly changing directions to cut around the iron would be a painful task. Rod cursed the density of the metal in front of him and glared at his damned out-of-date drilling platform. It had no compatibility with the newer drill bits that could fold up for easier manoeuvrability, but it was the best they could afford.

His younger counterpart returned with a hand-held sensor and a personal datapad (PDP). Derrick climbed the side of the drilling platform and scanned the area in front and either side of it. Geological readouts filled the PDP screen.

It didn't look good. The iron ore spread as far as the sensor could read, so even changing course wouldn't help. Neither of them wanted to risk starting a new tunnel altogether, so they went straight through the iron ore deposit, hard as that was.

"All right," Rod started, "let's get this thing out of here."

IT TOOK TOO LONG to reverse the drilling platform out and detach the blunt drill bit. But Rod challenged himself to make up for lost time as he set about sharpening the tool of his trade.

"Have you ever done this before?" Derrick asked.

"Yeah, but I was probably your age when we did that kind of field maintenance. It's all robots and high-tech equipment now."

Rod didn't look forward to sharpening the bit the old-fashioned way. Even with power tools, it was a strenuous task for a young, fit man, let alone one of his age and physical condition. But he saw no alternative. They were two men, ill-equipped, with one week's worth of supplies, and still sixty-odd metres to dig before they struck gold.

The first couple of hours went by well enough, but the awareness of time ticking by made Derrick increasingly aggravated.

"Look, I'm sorry," Rod said, holding out his greasy, gloved hands, "there's nothing we can do to speed up time. I have to sharpen this. I'm sorry."

Derrick had his back turned to Rod. "Can't you go any faster?"

Rod bit his tongue. "No. Look, why don't you make yourself useful? Go sift through those rock piles for iron and nickel. If we get enough of it, we might break even."

Derrick spun around as quickly as he could in the low gravity. "I'm not wasting my time with iron and nickel. We're here for the lunastone."

"Not if it's not there."

"It's there, damn it. Didn't you see the reading?"

Rod kept sharpening. They'd had false readings before. The best thing they could do if that was the case was to collect a good quantity of iron and nickel and sell it on the market. Maybe it could buy them another week or two of prospecting.

"Do what you want," Rod ended up saying. "Just leave me alone until I've finished this."

Derrick trudged off as Rod began another coughing fit. The old miner imagined leaving Derrick behind if they didn't find any lunastone. Then he quickly shook the idea out of his head. He couldn't be so cruel—wouldn't let rocks and ore get in the way of his business partnership with the young upstart. There was too much money at stake.

The lure of lunastone was its importance in shipbuilding. The brains-that-be reckoned there were tremendous deposits in the Solar System alone—enough to satisfy Humanity's current demand. The problem lay in the number of discovered deposits. That affected the current market price, and that was what made small prospecting teams millionaires.

Lunastone was ground to a fine powder and mixed with a half-dozen other powdered substances, two of which were artificially produced in a laboratory. This dense composite was then mixed with cooling molten metal alloys that were shaped into the external panels of ship and space station hulls. The process created an extremely durable layer of ablative shielding. Lunastone was also prized for its reflective properties, illuminating ships in direct sunlight.

Since the material was in such high demand and there were plenty of buyers, all Rod and Derrick needed to do was present a sample and submit a survey report to a mining company. Then they could settle on a comfortable payment for permission to relinquish control of the asteroid on which they made the discovery.

So Rod worked himself harder than ever. He wanted to retire while he was still young enough to enjoy it. Maybe he could fix his lungs too.

THE NEXT MORNING DID not start as smoothly as Rod would have preferred. No matter which way he twisted and stretched, the stiffness in his body reminded him of his age, and of the fact that he shouldn't be sharpening two massive drill bits all by himself. He cursed Derrick for not wanting to help. But what annoyed him more was something much worse.

The damn drilling platform wouldn't start.

Never had Rod cursed so much in his life. Derrick even backed away a bit to let Rod loose on the dead machine. It took the better part of their morning to get the thing going. By the time this happened, Rod didn't want to eat lunch, and he forced Derrick to skip his too.

With a huff and a coughing fit, Rod sped his drilling platform back into the tunnel and continued the operation with ferocious gusto. The newly sharpened bit chewed through the huge iron ore deposit, pushing smaller chunks up over the cabin, down a conveyor belt, and into a skip at the rear of the platform. Derrick did his best to run the skip out and empty it, but Rod tapped on his knee impatiently.

"Hurry up, will you!" Rod grumbled.

And so they continued for hours. Rod's body clock told him it was late, but he pressed on. The sooner he drilled this tunnel, the sooner he could get off this rock. He sniffed a laugh. And on to the next rock, he thought.

Finally, as if sensing his fatigue, the drill bit gave way, and he felt it chewing through rock again.

"Hey, Derrick," he called through his helmet mic, "we're done with the iron."

"It's about time!"

"I say we call it a day. I'm going to swap bits for tomorrow. Guide me out."

Derrick gave Rod finite directions as they backed out of the tunnel. It annoyed Rod to have to backtrack after drilling so far, but they didn't have a new-age drill bit that could keep going for donkey's years. When he finally emerged from the tunnel, he got to see more of the fruits of his labour. Picked out of the rock were sizeable piles of iron and a smaller one of nickel that Derrick had neatly stacked off to one side.

"We've invested too much to go broke now," Derrick told him. His enviro-suit was filthy from the labour.

Rod jumped off the drilling platform and inspected the metals, smiling, before turning to Derrick. "So you listened to me, eh?"

"Yeah, I thought about what you said. Better to hedge our bets. There's some magnetite and goethite here."

"Don't worry, we'll reach that lunastone tomorrow," Rod said. He could almost hear the hunger in his voice and was surprised that it was now he who was spurring the effort.

They ate and retired to their cabins on the ship. Rod closed his eyes, imagining signing a contract with a big mining company, smiling at the thought of living in comfort for the first time in his life.

ROD FOUND DERRICK AWAKE first. The younger man sat at the table in the ship's galley, nibbling on some toast. He said nothing, and Rod saw no reason to coax him into conversation—he was in one of his moods.

While Rod made his breakfast, he could feel Derrick's eyes staring at his back. He poured milk on his cereal and turned around to see Derrick's bloodshot eyes looking up at him.

"Didn't you sleep?" Rod asked.

The sound of Rod's voice seemed to snap him out of a trance. "Huh?"

"Didn't you sleep?"

"I slept."

Rod sighed and sat at opposite his business partner, content to just eat his cereal and get to work. But every time he looked up, he saw Derrick staring right back at him.

"What?" Rod asked, trying to hide the frustration in his voice.

"What?" Derrick replied without blinking.

"You're gawking at me like a vulture. What is it?"

"Nothing. I'm just thinking." Finally, he peeled his eyes away and stared into his coffee mug. "We're close to that lunastone, you know."

"Yeah, that's what I said yesterday. We'll reach it today."

Rod picked up his empty bowl and took it to the galley sink, glad to have finished. There was an unnerving silence between them while Rod cleaned his bowl. He wondered what had gotten into the younger man. Did he stay up all night wondering if the lunastone was even there? Or was he worried they'd get ripped off by one of the big mining companies? Well, they wouldn't if they stood their ground. He turned around and leaned against the galley bench.

"The sooner we get off this rock, the better," Rod said.

One side of Derrick's mouth stretched into a smile. "Agreed."

THEY DUG FOR HOUR after hour, burrowing through rock like super ants. Rod didn't care how much iron or nickel they turned up. He imagined the conical piles of unwanted raw material Derrick made as he emptied each skip outside, and how they'd be a good back-up. But that thought didn't last long. He had the scent now. His miner's intuition told him he was close. So close.

Suddenly, the platform stopped shaking. Dust filled the tunnel. Rod stopped the machine.

"We got it!"

"I know," Derrick replied excitedly. "I saw some of it in the skip." He climbed atop the platform to get a better view, scanning it with his hand-held sampler. "Lunastone! Definitely lunastone!"

A sigh of relief escaped Rod's strained lungs. He slumped victoriously and tiredly in his seat, enjoying Derrick's jubilation.

"Let's not waste any more time," Derrick called. "We've got a sample to collect."

With that, Rod eagerly reversed the platform out for the last time, leaving it near the ship. This next phase of the operation required some hand-held power tools. Derrick fetched four trusty pulse cutters and two heavy-duty drills from a toolbox and beckoned Rod to follow. He moved as fast as his suit allowed in low gravity, but it was fast enough that Rod struggled to keep up.

Damn him, Rod thought while he wheezed from the effort. He slowed to a more practical pace. I'm not running for seventy metres in low-grav.

Derrick waited for him at the end of the tunnel, wall lights illuminating the workspace. He handed Rod two pulse cutters and they set to work on precise measurements, marking the lunastone wall in front of them with special pencils. The mining companies required a specific size for their samples, but Rod and Derrick were fortunate to have the right tools, knowledge, and experience for that. They double-checked their calculations.

"Don't want to go overboard and give them too much, do we?" Derrick asked with a grin.

Rod laughed. "No. But we don't want to undercut ourselves either."

If they had their numbers right, which Rod was absolutely sure they were, then they would cut a five-hundred millimetre-cubed lunastone sample block.

"Right, let's do this," Derrick said.

Rod picked up his drill and planted the long, narrow bit against one of the marks he'd made. The diamond-tipped blade made short work, drilling a hole a bit more than half-a-metre deep. Once all four holes were drilled, Rod and Derrick slipped in their pulse cutters, careful to twist them so that they were perfectly lined up. Then Derrick started cutting.

Rod heard nothing with his head sealed up in the helmet and with no atmosphere on the asteroid, but he saw the bright red flashes of super-heated plasma beams spread in a straight line between the top cutters. They blinked several times a second, shaping the top face of the lunastone block, slicing the depth of the cube. Then they lit up again between the left pair. Each face was cut this way.

"Ain't she a beauty?" Rod quipped.

"Sure is." Derrick gripped the two cutters on his side. "Come on, let's pull it out."

Rod held his cutters and they pulled the block out of its niche. Rod knew it weighed over a hundred kilograms, but it was easy to pull in low gravity. It was still enough to strain his lungs, though.

"Oh, wait," Derrick said, stopping. "You know what? I forgot the grav trolley."

"Yeah, true, we should use it." Rod didn't want to carry the block all the way back to the ship. It wouldn't be too heavy for them, just awkward. "You came down here in a hurry."

"I was excited." Derrick darted away, leaving Rod with the lunastone block half pulled out of the tunnel wall. He ran wet eyes over it and caressed it with a gloved hand. It was just a cube, but it was the most beautiful object he had ever seen. It meant an end to his rough life, and he owed it all to Derrick's enthusiasm and drive. The young fellow had given Rod a nice retirement package, and for that, he was eternally thankful.

Rod's daydreaming about retirement ended when he saw Derrick in the corner of his vision. The younger man had returned, put the grav trolley aside, and was standing with his hands clasped behind his back, looking smart and out-of-place. With that posture, Rod figured he looked like one of the many company executives who used to inspect the various mines he'd worked for.

"What time is it?" Rod asked. But Derrick didn't reply. Rod thought maybe his helmet mic didn't work, so he asked again.

"It's time we discussed your role in our business," Derrick replied. He put his arms to his sides and Rod saw a pistol in one hand.

"What the hell are you doing?" Rod backed up, brushing against the lunastone sample.

Derrick kept his eyes on Rod. "Well, I got to thinking the other day: once we find the lunastone, you will have spent your usefulness." He raised the pistol, pointing it at Rod's chest.

"Hey, we're partners. Equals! My usefulness helped us find this stuff."

Derrick shook his head. "You were an investment. One man couldn't do this alone. Besides, you're sick, dying. You'll get your millions and then die a few years later. No amount of money can save you from your illness."

Rod's shoulders sagged. He knew this to be true. His coughing grew steadily worse every year, but he had clung to the hope of a quiet and peaceful retirement. "I could live out my dying years in comfort, at least."

"A waste," Derrick said softly. "Better if I get it all … and speed up your death now by putting a few bullets into those rotting lungs of yours."

"Not if I can help it."

Rod jumped to one side, saw the flash from Derrick's pistol, felt the chemical bullet tear through skin and bone, felt the suction of his suit quickly sealing the entry hole in the fabric. But he ignored the pain for a split second, enough to launch himself forward and crash into Derrick. He heard the younger man grunt over the radio as they fell against the tunnel wall.

With a searing pain in his gut, Rod threw Derrick to the ground, using his bigger frame to overpower his associate. Derrick dropped the pistol, but used his foot to stop Rod's advance. The foot caught Rod in the knee, jarring his movement and bringing him down. He fell next to Derrick in the slower motion of low gravity, but wasn't quick enough to shield his helmet from the tunnel ground. He fell face first, scratching his visor on the rough surface.

With his vision now impaired, Rod thrashed wildly at Derrick, keeping the Derrick's hand from retrieving the pistol. He felt his fists connect with Derrick's torso, but wasn't sure how effective his attacks were.

Derrick finally grabbed the pistol.

Rod used both hands to stop Derrick's arm from folding back and killing him once and for all. Against the stupid boy's inferior strength, Rod easily kept the pistol pointed away.

"You're going to die, old man," Derrick taunted.

Rod ignored him—and ignored the pain in his rib where the chemical bullet was doing its work. He could feel the blood spreading under his suit.

Derrick squeezed off a shot at the tunnel's ceiling. It was uncanny not being able to hear it and only seeing the muzzle flash. Maybe that's what gave Rod the courage to keep fighting. He forced Derrick's elbow and wrist to bend in his favour, slowly bringing the pistol to point at Derrick's head.

Derrick fought it. With his free hand, he reached out and punched Rod's wound. The older man shrieked and used his renewed anger to complete his objective. With the pistol finally pointing at Derrick, Rod took one last look at Derrick's pale, wide-eyed face before regretfully pulling the trigger.

The muzzle flash momentarily blinded Rod, but he felt Derrick go lifeless almost instantly.

Rod rolled onto his back, breathing heavily and shouting in pain and misery. He looked at Derrick's body, but couldn't bring himself to look at his face. He thought about all the laughs and beers they'd shared. He remembered their first meeting in a mineshaft, how Rod had mentored the then sixteen-year-old boy and taught him the ins and outs of the job. And now he'd killed him … his business partner, his only friend. He sobbed—just laid there and sobbed. The helmet prevented him from wiping his tears. They stung his eyes.

He put a hand over the sealed entry wound and brought himself back to reality. He had to get back to the ship and clean the wound and dress it before the chemical bullet infected him. Sure, he was already dying, but he'd rather live at least a bit longer and enjoy the money that was now his alone. He choked back a tear at that last thought, then sobbed as he took one last glance at Derrick's body before crawling back to the ship.

He hoped he could make it. The tunnel seemed much longer now that he was wounded. But if he didn't make it, then he'd perish along with his friend—alone, poor, and all the work already done for the next people to land on this rock. That thought kept him going with each step—each painful, weakening step until he made it out of the tunnel.

A sad smile crept up on him on seeing the ship. It looked like he would make it after all. But he knew he couldn't have that peaceful retirement he'd chased for so long—not now that he'd paid such a high price for finally achieving his dream.

ABOUT THE STORY

"A MINER'S DREAM" WAS the first story I ever wrote. It probably shows too. The inspiration came to me while shovelling cement into a mixer. I paused and reflected on how fine the cement was.—so powdery! It made me think of moondust. As I continued to add cement, lime, sand, and water into the mixer, over and over again to create an endless supply of mortar for a brick and sandstone wall, my overactive mind outlined a story.

What resources could be mined from the moon? Could we make concrete and mortar from moondust? What about aggregate from moonrock? I knew that lunar regolith had already been considered in applications termed lunacrete, mooncrete, or Astro-Crete, so I didn't want to go that basic. I also knew that moondust had some negative properties, such as being abrasive and possibly causing respiratory problems. But I wanted to think past that. I wanted something a bit fantastical. Hence, *lunastone* was born!

I'd like to say I did my homework, but anyone would agree that the industrial application of lunastone in "A Miner's Dream" is pretty bogus. Well, I had the *what* and some of the *why*. Lunastone is a highly valued raw material, enough for two hungry miners to hunt for it. That was the *who*. With these basics, the details of the story naturally took shape.

Conflict is a major element of stories. The central conflict in "A Miner's Dream" is the differences in age, personality, and goals of the two protagonists. From the earliest draft, the resolution of that conflict was always the same: Derrick would betray Rod, there would be a scuffle, and Derrick would be fatally shot.

Aside from the character conflict, there was a key element in the first version of the story that gave the ending a much darker tone. I weaved in a species of mythical, aggressive asteroid-inhabiting aliens called Phantoms. In doing so, I had inadvertently added a horror element to my story, because these beings preyed on any traveller or miner who was foolish enough to wander into their territory. After Derrick is killed, a wounded Rod stumbles out of the tunnel and heads for the ship. He is emotionally shattered, desperate for medical help, and wants to leave the infernal rock and never return. But he never reaches the ship. A pack of lanky, translucent Phantoms are waiting for him at the tunnel's entrance, and that is where he meets his grizzly end.

It was an amateurish ending for a story, but it was my first one, after all. There was much to improve. A critique from *The Magazine of Fantasy & Science Fiction* stated that the story needed stronger characterisation and a better ending, but praised the action sequences. Slush readers from *Aurealis* were even more specific, noting that there was too much exposition in the dialogue, and, true to my long-form leanings, the world was too ambitious for the short story format. *Andromeda Spaceways Magazine* criticised my choppy pacing and mentioned that the Phantoms could have been featured earlier. Clearly, this first attempt at a short story fell way below the mark. Nevertheless, I was not put off by the rejections.

The next version of the story removed the Phantoms altogether, added more conflict, boosted the characterisation, replaced exposition with the show-don't-tell approach, and added an emotional twist to the ending. I couldn't do much about the scope of the world. My characters needed a motive, and our motives are often fuelled by a complex fusion of internal and external factors. The lure of lunastone was a big external factor.

I began resubmitting the story. By this time, "Pilgrimage to Earth" and my novella *Fire Over Troubled Water* had been published. I'd started a newsletter and needed a free story to offer new subscribers, so I pulled "A Miner's Dream" from the submission cycle and self-published it. Despite the good advice of not offering your first story as a newsletter reader magnet, the story remained exactly that for several years. It has been slightly improved in this collection.

DIRECTOR'S CUT

ELO ENTERED THE BRIGHTLY lit room and felt the air thick with body heat. Too many people crammed into the small room with a broken air conditioning unit. He nodded to the waiting casting crew and put his duffel bag out of the way. One of the casting crew at the table pointed to a small red cross taped on the floor. Elo dutifully stood on it, knowing the procedure. He gave one final look at his ultra-shiny shoes, hoping they would give him good luck yet again.

"Slate," the director grunted. She was a middle-aged human, a legend in galactic cinema—Anna Perón.

Elo cleared his throat and focused on the little camera filming the audition. "Elo Tubani, Interstellar Talent Management."

The man next to Perón, who thus far had not looked up from his notes, lifted his head when Elo spoke and raised an eyebrow.

Good, Elo thought. *Maybe my blue skin is a plus.*

"Start," Perón said with a wave.

Elo lifted the screenplay and read from his assigned monologue.

"'What?'" He grumbled the question, drawing it out with enough force to set the tone for his audition. "'What did you say? How *dare* you speak down to me!'"

His arm swung out, one of his three fingers extended, pointing at the imaginary recipient of his angry monologue. He avoided Perón's gaze, tried not to get nervous at her stillness as she studied his performance.

"'We are equals on this ship. I will not put up with your insults anymore! Do you know what I'm capable of? Do you even know why I was chosen for this mission? With my bare hands, I could—'"

"That's enough," Perón interjected, holding up a hand. "Thank you for your efforts, but you're not what we're looking for."

As an actor, Elo had been rejected before. But this was Anna Perón, the greatest human film director in the galaxy! His two hearts beat out of sync momentarily, but he recovered quickly and remembered to be polite and respectful, thanking her for her time. He bowed his head before backing out of the audition room, picking up his duffel bag as he went. Even before he reached the door, the man who had pointed him to the red cross on the floor shouted for the next actor to come inside.

Out in the hallway, a line of waiting actors fidgeted and rehearsed. They were all aliens. The role called for a two-armed biped male of any alien species. He'd watched some of them leave the audition room dejected. Now, those still waiting perspired and re-read their lines nervously. Elo licked his lips and went straight to the nearby restroom.

Some actors were using the amenities. Perhaps their nerves had an overpowering influence over their bladders, if their biological makeup was that way inclined. Elo made sure nobody saw him enter the room and then found an empty stall and locked himself in.

Then he hurried. Time was of the essence. He took off all his clothes and stood barefoot on the cold tiles.

Then he willed it to happen.

Silently, Elo changed. He watched himself in the mirror on the toilet door. First, it was his skin pigment. It went through the colour spectrum until he was deep purple. His bald head grew black hair, and his eyes also changed from blue to black. Muscles became more defined, and his facial structure remoulded itself into a face completely different from the first. He even grew slightly taller. He whispered a few of his lines, happy with the adjustment of his voice. After this, he donned a new pair of clothes from his duffel bag, stuffing the old ones away. His feet hadn't changed, so he re-tied his lucky shoes—maybe second time lucky.

Just like that, Elo Tubani, the shapeshifting actor from Promixa 12, became someone else.

Take two, Elo said to himself as he exited the restroom.

Elo drummed rhythmically on his duffel bag, rehearsing his monologue in his head. Anna Perón obviously didn't like his first performance, so he worked on a slightly different presentation. That, he figured, was the advantage he had over the other auditioning actors.

At last, they called him in, this time using the alternate name he'd given the secretary: Pular Katish. As he stood, he remembered his duffel bag. *I can't take this in again*, he thought worriedly. His eyes darted around, looking for a safe place to put it. The full length of the hallway was crowded with actors busily reading scripts or staring at the opposite wall in some personal, trance-like, pre-performance nerve-loosening exercise.

He picked the closest actor and held out his bag. "May you please watch this?"

The young androgynous Yismerulan snapped his head up at Elo. "Huh? Yeah, yeah." He waved Elo away, returning to a script.

Elo took a deep breath as he entered the audition room, worried that those precious seconds wasted in the hallway would adversely affect his performance. Anna Perón was notoriously impatient. He gave the best smile his new purple face could muster, greeting the crew inside. Again, the same individual directed Elo to the red cross crudely marking Elo's spot in the room.

Anna Perón regarded him with a frown. She had a half-eaten sandwich in front of her, its wrapper crumpled on the floor under her table.

"Slate," she said.

"Pular Katish, Centaurus Talent Agency," Elo said. He thought he sounded confident.

Perón nodded. "Start."

This time, with a deeper voice, Elo began his monologue more forcefully. "'What?'" he roared, his voice much louder than before. For a millisecond, he feared it might be too loud, for the crew at the table jolted to attention. That could be good or bad. "'What did you say? How *dare* you speak down to me!'" To finish that sentence, he'd quietened his voice, but kept the tone vicious. "'We are equals—'"

"Wait," Perón called.

Elo held his breath, not daring to look at her for more than a second at a time.

"You started too loudly," Perón said, "but I liked the way you kept the anger going with the lower volume. For those three sentences, could you start loud—but perhaps not as loud as before—soften the second question, and then use the same anger for the statement, but raise your voice a bit this time? Be sure to emphasise the *'dare'*."

Elo nodded and gulped. If she was willing to give him directions, maybe he wasn't doing too bad.

He started again with the angry, threatening question, then spoke the second with quiet malice. "'What? What did you say?'" Then, he put his whole body into the statement, pumping out his chest and stepping forward with one foot. "'How *dare* you speak down to me!'"

"Good, good," Perón started, "but this time, don't *act* so aggressively. Not yet, anyway. That comes on the next page. Say that last statement again, but with less movement. And remember the *'dare'*."

"Okay," Elo said, then returned to the cross. His mind raced, filtering through ideas on how to minimally act the spoken sentence to give it added force. He breathed to settle himself, and then launched into it again. "'How *dare* you speak down to me!'" He had flexed his biceps at the all-important second word, feeling the muscles stretch his shirt sleeves. In action movies, it was always good to show off a little muscle.

But Perón shook her head. "No, what you did there—don't do it. We don't want to unbalance the physical power dynamic between your character and the lead. Try again."

Minor panic flushed through Elo, but he ignored it because the crew waited for him. He spoke the statement again, this time only opening his eyes wider while standing still. But it felt so unnatural, and he knew he'd made another mistake.

Perón's frown returned, confirming his suspicion. "No, sorry. Thank you for your time, but you're not what we need."

Elo tried not to let it upset him. "Thank you," he said, but Perón's eyes were already down at her notes.

"Next!"

Elo quickly left the room, squeezing past the next actor to come into the dragon's lair. He grabbed his duffel bag, mumbling a word of thanks to the actor who'd minded it, and went straight for the restroom.

"SLATE."

"Vandon A. Maklyon, Supernova Management." Elo suppressed a wince at how high-pitched his voice sounded. But he cleared his throat, hoping that would explain why his next words would sound a little deeper.

"Start."

Elo cleared his throat again and tensed slightly. His mouth went tight and his eyes burned as he spoke. "What? What did you say? How—'"

"No," Perón called, waving her hand and shaking her head. "Your voice is too weak for the role. Next!"

Elo felt his hand clench, imagined himself roaring in his natural voice, letting his frustration out on the assembled panel of film greats. *Then you'll see the power of my voice!* Instead, he bowed respectfully and left without taking up more of their precious time.

For he was also getting time-poor.

"Sʟᴀᴛᴇ."

"Suanum Lithul, GalCore Talent."

Perón's head snapped up. "What?" She looked at her people. "How did he get in here? You know I don't work with GalCore!"

"I don't know," one of the crew said. "I—"

"Get out," Perón told Elo with icy venom. "I'd rather not waste your time."

Elo scurried along to the door.

"And I'd advise you to change talent agencies," Perón suggested as he was leaving, though her voice still reeked with contempt.

Oh, don't worry, I will, Elo thought, glad to have learnt something new about the famous director—something he should have known already. But he swallowed screams at losing another chance so quickly.

Aʟᴀs, ғᴏᴜʀ ᴍᴏʀᴇ ᴛʀᴀɴsғᴏʀᴍᴀᴛɪᴏɴs still did not secure Elo the role he so desperately desired. The hours dragged on and the line of auditioning actors grew short, as did Perón's temperament. And so Elo found himself the last actor waiting in the hallway. The tired assistant did her best to avoid eye contact, and Elo was glad for it. He was certain just one look from her would deflate his already low self-esteem.

Then came the call. He heard it bellowed from inside the audition room, and a downcast actor stepped into the hallway a second or two later. Elo gulped at the actor's sullen expression and entered the room, closing the door and standing on the red cross.

Perón looked exhausted, but smiled she looked him up and down.

She hasn't done that before, Elo thought.

"Slate."

Elo subconsciously glanced down at his shiny shoes—the ones he thought were lucky—and then he took a deep breath. An energy flowed through him as if he were back home on Proxima 12, performing in front of thousands at the State Theatre. "Jolli Fhain, Sol Talent Agency."

"Start."

Summoning a voice from the depths of his heart, Elo began. "'What? What did you say?'"

Perón leaned forward, planting her elbows on the table.

"'How *dare* you speak down to me!'"

Though he was looking just to the side of the famed director, Elo could see her lips curl upwards at the way he enunciated the word *dare*. It spurred him on.

"'We are equals on this ship.'" He continued. Then with his voice rising at every word, "'I will not put up with your insults anymore! Do you know what I'm capable of? Do you even know why I was chosen for this mission?'" He curled his fingers. "'With my bare hands, I could rip you to shreds. I could tackle the lot of you to the ground and crack some skulls while I'm at it.'" Then he settled, sighed, and spoke softer. "'I feel like doing that, but I won't. I'm here because the Tarathans are threatening my home-world, too! But just because we're on the same team, don't think I won't snap you in two if you push me hard enough. My people have suffered too much from our enemies. We don't need it from our allies!'"

Elo felt his hearts thumping. He stayed in character for the next few seconds, holding his exasperated expression to show he could also act nonverbally. When he brought his face to rest, he realised that this audition was the first time Perón let him say the full monologue.

And Perón just stared at him. One of the casting crew glanced over at the quiet director, cleared his throat, and then looked down at the table.

"At last, someone who gets it right," Perón said.

Elo didn't know whether to smile or breathe a sigh of relief. Fortunately, Perón broke his moment of thought with her next line of praise.

"What I particularly liked was your determination to get the monologue right. I mean, how many attempts did you make? Eight? Nine?"

The questions straightened Elo's back and he regarded Perón with fear, worrying that she had seen through his plot.

"Never have I had an actor come back and try again and again for the same role on the same day," she told him. She leaned back in her chair and folded her arms. "How are you doing it so fast? A shapeshifter? It has to be. You're too fast. No makeup artist can work that fast." She tapped a pen against her lips.

Elo swallowed hard and nodded. He tried to think of words to defend himself, but he didn't know if a defence was warranted, or even if it would be listened to. "How did you know?"

Perón sniffed a laugh and grinned. "Your shoes. You wore the same shoes to every audition."

This time, Elo managed a smile. "They're my lucky shoes."

"I don't think luck had anything to do with it … Jolli. If that is your name."

"Elo."

"Elo, okay. If you were lucky, I'd have given you the part on your first attempt. No, I don't believe in luck. Not in this business. Here, we rely on hard work, contacts, exposure, being in the right place at the right time. Some may call that luck, but it isn't. Not really. What you did was take a risk and work hard to get it right, and it paid off." She paused, rubbing her chin and sighing in thought. She looked weary. "I'd like you to be in my movie. We'll use the likeness and voice of Jolli Fhain for now. In later rehearsals, we'll experiment with other body shapes, but the voice and nonverbal language you used in this last audition was perfect."

Elo beamed at the news and her commendation. He felt like prostrating himself and thanking her in the traditional custom of his home planet, but human propriety stopped him before he went that far. "Thank you. Thank you so much for giving me a chance." He settled for a slight bow.

Perón smiled again and blushed at his humble acceptance. "Now, I'd like to see you in your original form and hear your slate. We need you on record."

"Change here?"

Perón nodded.

Elo had never changed his form in front of humans. But now that he had secured his role, he wasn't going to lose it by insisting on some privacy. Heck, he'd been filmed nude in some B-grade productions. He changed with his clothes on, trying to make it a comfortable viewing for Perón and her crew. Fortunately, changing back into his original form was always a smoother transition, and the humans in the room seemed not to be horrified or embarrassed in the least. He felt the threads in his shirt sleeves pull as his real muscles returned to their original size, and his belt needed loosening to account for his stockier waist, but apart from that, Elo was now his old self—a tall, muscular, blue-skinned, bald alien with sparkling blue eyes and a smile made for a movie poster.

"Slate."

Elo looked into the camera, like he was born to do. He grinned. "Elo Tubani, Interstellar Talent Management."

ABOUT THE STORY

Back in 2019, Kevin J. Anderson's own Wordfire Press made a short story submissions call for an upcoming anthology called *Monsters, Movies, & Mayhem*. It was a publishing project with graduate students at Western Colorado University, where Anderson teaches. Stories had to tie a monster-like character into a movie-themed story, and it had to involve some kind of mayhem. As you have read in "Director's Cut", I opted for a shapeshifting alien who causes confusion in an audition by pretending to be many different actors.

Ultimately, "Director's Cut" was not chosen, though it was well received. Here is the personalised rejection letter emailed to me by the editors:

> Thank you for submitting your story, "The Director's Cut," to *Monsters, Movies, & Mayhem*. Yours was a unique approach to the theme, and the member of our team with theater/acting experience particularly enjoyed the insight the character and story showed to the audition process. In addition, the approach to creating a "monster" in your protagonist was exceptionally creative and very well-communicated for a new-to-your-story being.
>
> We received over 400 stories, and more than 300 were dropped in the first round. The editorial team kept your story for a second round of consideration, and we enjoyed the chance for another look, but unfortunately it did not make the final round. Best of luck placing it elsewhere.—THE EDITORS

Naturally, I was overjoyed to receive such a lovely rejection letter. When the anthology was published, I completely understood why my story was rejected. The anthology definitely had a darker theme.

"Director's Cut" was rejected a further eight times after that. It went to the highest round in the slush pile at *Fireside Quarterly* and received glowing comments from first readers at *Cosmic Roots & Eldritch Shores*, and even received a Silver Honorable Mention for the Writers of the Future 3rd Quarter 2020 contest.

Finally, in 2021, *Space & Time Magazine* published it in Issue #140. They described it as "a perfect bit of brilliant humour" and "just what we needed". This really shows the high level of subjectivity and time sensitivity in the short fiction market. "Director's Cut" just happened to be the right fit for the right issue for *Space & Time Magazine*.

BIG GAME

Mick heard the roar—low, rumbling, far off. It penetrated his mind, weaving its way into his subconscious as he spoke pointless words to a faceless person. He woke from his slumber. The roar persisted, echoing now like the final blast of a horn section in a cavernous theatre. His mind started to put meaning to the noise, and his heart thumped as his mind connected the dots.

A breeze from the open bedroom window cooled his face. Through it came the end of that terrifying, ominous sound from the mountains north of the settlement. The sound carried in the night's cool air, finally petering out as he sat up in bed.

That was a long one, he thought. He knew that roar, knew the vile creature it belonged to. But most importantly, he knew what it meant.

Mick took a deep breath and quietly turned away from the window to look at his wife. He shook his head and stifled a chuckle. How she always managed to sleep through Caruso's roar continued to baffle him. But that was probably for the best. Come sunrise, people would be out and about and there would be enough anxiety then, if it hadn't already started.

He sat in bed staring at the ceiling, hoping Caruso wouldn't roar again, but knowing that one roar was enough.

The next day in the butcher's shop, Mick tried to go about his business. He toiled at the presentation of his meats in their cold displays, waiting for his assistant, Sam, to return from the cool rooms out back.

She stepped into the shop again. "We're low on pterus meat," she said flatly.

Mick whipped his head around and held her gaze, then swallowed and nodded. "I know."

She moved next to him and helped with the meats on display, lowering her voice. "You heard it last night?"

He nodded.

She sighed and opened her mouth to speak again, but the opening hiss of the shop door distracted her.

"Ms Dawson!" Mick said. He smiled broadly and looked down at Sam to do the same—the first customer of the day was here. "What are we looking for today?"

But Ms Dawson didn't smile back, nor did she respond immediately. She walked stiffly up to the counter, her eyes resolutely on Mick. "How much pterus meat do you have, Mick?"

Mick cleared his throat, hearing the question behind the question. "Not much, but there's enough for you if you want it. I hope to replenish the stock soon."

She stared at him wide-eyed. "Good. Yes, good, I hope so." Then she backed up and left the shop in a hurry.

Mick smacked his counter top. "The whole settlement is on edge today," he told Sam. "What was it like on your way here?" He lived above his shop, but Sam had to walk a few blocks.

"It was quiet," she said. "People whispered. They avoided me."

"They expect us to do something about it."

Sam said nothing, which was probably all she could do, given the circumstances. For years, the pterus problem had been put on Mick's shoulders. Broad as they were, figuratively speaking, he'd always felt the pressure of being the one to sort it out every season. Pterus meat was a tasty, healthy delicacy and a great financial boon for his business, but obtaining came at a cost. Oh, the cost!

The shop door hissed open again, and this time the settlement's security chief marched in.

"Joey," Mick said. "You okay?"

Joey stopped in the middle of the shop floor. His face was pale, his breathing clipped and shallow. "You have to do something, Mick. The Mayor's been breathing down my neck since he heard it last night."

"I always do something, don't I?"

"Yes, I know, but this time it's different." He stepped forward and glanced back at the closed door. "We have no … payment. What are you going to do?"

"Leave it with me."

"What are you going to do, Mick?" Joey asked again.

"I said to leave it with me," Mick replied more forcefully. He balled his fist, hiding it behind the counter.

Joey huffed and stepped up to the counter, eyeing the selection of pork delicacies. "Give me some cabanossi."

Mick frowned and cut him one slightly longer than the usual length. He knew Joey liked his cabanossi, and the security chief did an admirable job in the rough and tough colony. They deserved a little treat now and then. Joey took a bite and let off a troublesome sigh before waving the meat at Mick.

"Do something soon," Joey said, "or the Mayor himself will come down here."

Joey shoved the rest of the cabanossi into his mouth and left.

Sam raised her eyebrows. "He sure was insistent."

"He has to be. If we don't sort this out, you know what might happen."

As butcher and assistant brainstormed, the shop door again hissed open to admit an off-worlder. He stumbled in with his eyes closed, clutching his head. Mick didn't know his name, but he'd seen him around over the last few weeks. Fancied himself as a bit of a mercenary, taking odd jobs to stay afloat. But to Mick, he was nothing but a troublemaker through and through.

The off-worlder grunted and burped as he approached the counter. Sam scoffed and walked away, leaving Mick to deal with it.

The butcher cleared his throat. "You know, I don't believe we've met."

"Cole," the off-worlder said. He blinked bloodshot eyes, and the odour of some powerful liquor wafted across the counter.

Mick liked what he saw. It gave him an idea. "I'm Mick. You had a hard night?"

"Nah, just the usual." Cole leaned on the counter and surveyed the meats in front of him.

"Looking for anything in particular?" Mick asked him. He bit his lower lip, wondering how to approach the topic on his mind.

"No, no, I don't have enough money. Spent it all on drinks last night."

"I see." Mick tried desperately to hide his smile. "How would you like to make some money? I have a job for you, if you're interested."

Cole straightened his back and raised an eyebrow. "What kind of job?"

"Are you much of a hunter? Big game?"

"I've done some hunting, sure. Not here, though."

"You got a rifle?"

Cole chuckled and nodded. "Yeah. Yeah, it's in the SUV."

This time, Mick let himself smile—a big, toothy smile that seemed to put Cole at ease. "Listen, did you hear the roar last night?"

"Nah, I was out to the world last night. But people have been talking about it this morning. What's the story?"

"Well, you probably haven't seen one of them yet because they're in hibernation. But last night's roar came from a pterus up in the mountains. They're a dangerous animal. They kill our herds and kill anyone unlucky enough to be walking around undefended. But we hunt them for their meat."

Mick picked up a thin slice of salted pterus meat and gave it to Cole. "Here, on the house. Taste good, eh?"

Cole nodded as he chewed. "I can see why you hunt them."

"Yeah, well, we're running low on our stock of pterus meat. But we're just in time for the hunting season. That's where you come in. That pterus up in the mountain woke last night. In a few days, it'll be up in the sky looking for food. We don't want it to come to this settlement, do we?"

"No. No, I don't suppose you do. So let me get this straight. You want me to go up the mountain and shoot this thing? That's all?"

"That's all," Mick assured him. "And I'll pay you a thousand korins for the job."

Cole whistled. "A thousand korins just for killing one animal? I don't have to cut it up or skin it or anything like that?"

"No, I'm the butcher. That's my job. All you have to do is find it and kill it."

"Huh." Cole scratched his head and then put his hands on his hips. "I think we have a deal."

"Good." Mick reached over the counter to shake the mercenary's hand. "My assistant and I will come with you. We'll cut it up then and there."

"So why don't you kill it? Look, I'm not complaining. I need the money. But why pay someone *a thousand korins* when you could do the job yourself?"

Mick grinned. "I forget you haven't seen one. I'm an important asset in this settlement, so I can't afford to get hurt. But you, you're made for this sort of thing, I can tell."

"How bad can it be?" Cole asked. His mouth twisted into a smug smile.

"A pterus is a large carnivorous bird with sharp claws. It spits acid, and its feathers are like hard scales. You've seen the spikes and spires on the rooftops?"

Cole nodded and gulped.

"We built them so no pterus could land here, because they used to attack the settlement. Make no mistake, they're a dangerous animal and a tough bird to kill. But a clean shot between the eyes will do the trick. It's a spot with a little V-shaped indentation where there are no feathers and the skull is quite thin." Mick worried that giving Cole fair warning on the dangers of pterus hunting might scare the mercenary off. So he played to his ego. "You *are* a good shot, aren't you?"

"Of course I am!" Cole said. He looked offended. "I reckon I'll only need two shots. One to test the bird's reflexes, and the second to kill it."

One side of Mick's mouth curled into a smile. "Good, because this settlement can't survive without its pterus meat. It's our biggest export. We leave after lunch."

LUNCH WAS NORMALLY AN enjoyable affair for Mick, but on what he informally designated Pterus Day, he could never savour his meals. Sam, on the other hand, gulped down her lunch nervously and then complained of indigestion like she always did.

"At least you eat meat," he said with a smirk. His wife didn't.

Mick packed his knives and saws into his delivery truck. Cole was late, as expected, so Mick and Sam waited outside their shop. It wasn't long before they had someone else to talk to besides each other.

"I see you have your truck ready," noted Mayor Wilson, startling Mick. "Wouldn't be skipping town, would you?"

"What? Running away with my assistant?" Mick scoffed. "Wouldn't dream of it. I mean, she's a nice girl and all, but she's too young for me." He nudged her and chuckled. "And besides, I'm already happily married to a wonderful woman."

"You know what I mean," the Mayor retorted. He stepped up next to Mick and spoke softly. "What are you going to do about our pterus problem?"

"I'm sorry, I forgot to tell you. That mercenary hovering around town has ... accepted the responsibility."

Wilson shifted uneasily on his feet. "You mean he knows what he's up against and he still wants to do it?"

"In a roundabout way, yes," Mick said. "Oh, look, here he is now." Mick tapped his watch as Cole parked across the road.

"I know," Cole said through the driver's window. "But I won't apologise. You need me, after all."

Mick grinned and glanced at the Mayor. "So we do. Before we head out, I'd like you to meet Mayor Wilson."

Cole waved.

"You're doing a great service for Wolverton," Mayor Wilson said. "We'll remember it for years to come."

"It's just a bird," Cole said.

Wilson lost his smile, looked at Mick. "This guy has no fear?"

"I can handle myself," Cole said more strongly. "I carry a gun for a reason."

The Mayor nodded slowly, obviously smart not to press the topic further. "I look forward to sampling the new stock of pterus meat."

"We'll get it," Mick assured him.

With that, Mick and Sam hopped into their truck and led Cole out of the settlement. The spiked rooftops reminded him of the first pterus attack years ago. A single bird had killed four people and permanently disabled several more with its acid spray. Only the concerted efforts of many armed colonists had shooed it away.

"You remember that one?" Mick asked, pointing to the remains of a farmhouse in one of the outlying fields.

"Yeah," was all Sam said.

That particular pterus attack had destroyed half the building with acid alone. But the colony had been safe ever since Mick concocted an ingenious plan a couple of years ago; however, it was now his responsibility to see it through every season. And every season he suffered the terrible worries of failure.

The roads of the recently colonised planet were rough and rugged. Mick expertly navigated the ruts, lumps of earth, and muddy bogs all the way to the base of the mountain. He pulled up and waved at Cole to park next to him.

"This track will take you to the summit," he told the young mercenary. "Stay on it, or else you'll get stuck."

"I won't get stuck."

"Listen to me, damn it!" Mick snapped. "You *will* get stuck, and if you do, that pterus will hunt you down. You're on his turf now."

Cole swallowed, nodded. "I guess I'll stay on the path."

"It's nearly an hour's drive to the top. That's where the things nest during the cold months. I advise you to leave your car and walk quietly the last hundred metres or so and keep your rifle ready. Stay under the trees and don't let it fly. It'll be easier to kill on the ground."

"What if it flies away?"

Mick grinned. "It won't fly *away*. But it might fly to reposition itself. It'll stay and fight until one of you is dead."

Cole digested that information. Mick studied him. Was it fear on the young man's face? What happened to the youthful gung-ho attitude? The mercenary glared as the full realisation of his contract washed over him.

"This feels like it's worth more than a thousand korins."

Mick pointed at him. "Now you listen to me—a thousand is more than you'll ever get for any job in this colony. You already agreed to it, and we're here now. There's no backing out."

"I don't know—"

The mountain rumbled like distant thunder. Cole looked up at the foggy summit.

Mick stared at him. "If you back out now, I'll make sure everyone hears about it. You'll never get another job on this planet, so help me God." Cole frowned and glanced at him. "And if you take down this bird, you'll be a legend—the biggest hunter to walk this planet."

Cole squared his jaw. "Fine. Can I go now?"

"By all means," Mick replied. He gestured up the mountain track. "Call me when you've killed the beast. I can taste the meat already."

Cole drove up the mountain like a madman, splashing mud and flattening low-lying shrubs. He'd never driven through such a thick mess of vegetation. The humidity nearly choked him. But at least the air was clean. Not like Earth. No, he was happy to have left Earth for good.

That trumped-up butcher didn't know how much money he was throwing away. A thousand korins just to kill a dumb bird! It would be the easiest money he'd ever made. The quickest too. His plan was simple: get in, shoot the damn thing, get back, and collect his money. He thought about demanding a higher reward a bit more aggressively, but waved the thought away. Maybe the butcher would use him again. No sense upsetting a potential business partner.

He stopped his SUV in some low brush off the barely discernible track and studied his map. It was a crude hard copy. The colony had no GPS satellites yet, so he was doing it old-school. If he'd followed the map correctly, he should be roughly two hundred metres from the summit. It was a steep, winding path.

"Might as well get a little dirty for my pay," Cole said to himself. He reached for his rifle and resumed the ascent on foot.

All manner of life chirped, creaked, and sung, but none of it could be seen. He breathed quickly, frustrated by the amount of noise. It was hard to focus on potential threats when every sound was new to him. The butcher hadn't mentioned any other animals of concern. But nothing jumped out at him. The sounds of insects and other lifeforms were just ambient noise.

That is, until he heard the low rumble up ahead.

He crouched, eyes wide open, rifle at the ready. Was that a pterus? His mind attacked him with eroding thoughts. *How am I supposed to hunt an animal I've never seen before? What if it burns half my body with acid? What if it actually does fly away?* He'd be damned if he'd let a thousand korins escape his grasp. He gripped his rifle tighter and crept in to get sights on the bird.

His heart beat faster than a jazz drummer, his chest rising and falling in quick succession. But he kept his mouth closed and his eyelids open, inching forward like a cat stalking its prey. The thought made him smirk.

That's what I am, he mused wickedly. *I'm a cat, and I'll get my bird. Cats love to kill birds.*

The low-pitched growl froze him in place. His eyes darted around in their sockets. That growl was close.

There! He saw movement through the trees. His eyes opened wider. All he saw was a leg and a scaly body.

How big is this thing?

He swallowed the saliva that pooled around his tongue and slipped sideways into the heavier scrub of the mountainside, taking shelter behind a downed tree trunk. He rested his rifle on the dead wood, aiming at the moving bird.

Doesn't even look like a bird, he grovelled.

The beast turned, walking further away. Cole squeezed his hand into a fist and climbed over the tree trunk. He checked his watch. He didn't want to be on the mountain all damned afternoon. Only a few hours remained until sundown. He made a snap decision.

He gripped his rifle at the ready and moved briskly through the scrub, hoping the ambient noise would mask his steps. The pterus was still moving away. Its scaly back reflected the afternoon sunlight as it moved towards the middle of a large clearing. It looked very much like where an animal of that size would rest.

Then Cole stepped on a thin branch, snapping it under his foot.

The beast spun around, stomping one long-clawed foot onto the soft ground. It roared upon seeing him exposed, but he was fast. He raised his rifle and squeezed the trigger.

MICK HEARD THE CRACK of the rifle. He stopped chewing and studied the mountain before him, trying to imagine what had happened. Then he looked over at Sam, who was still eating her sandwich. He raised an eyebrow. All she did was nod and take another bite.

One shot to test its reflexes, the second to kill it, Mick recalled the mercenary saying. But there was no second shot. Was he dead already? Did he get lucky with his first shot? Or had the bird taken flight?

The rifle cracked again.

THE FIRST SHOT STRUCK the bird's cheek, ricocheting off into a tree. Cole swore and started to chamber the next round, but his hand, slick with humid sweat, slipped and he failed the bolt action. The pterus eyed him, readying to pounce. He swore again, grabbing the bolt handle tighter and clicking the next bullet into place. The pterus stomped and spread its wings. He aimed and fired again, this time missing completely.

The bird swooshed its wings and took off into the air without even a run-up. It spat acid at Cole, who ducked sideways just in time. The steaming liquid hit a tree and instantly burned a hole through to the core. Cole aimed for a third time, but it was pointless. The pterus had vanished above the forest canopy.

That damned butcher said the bird wouldn't fly! Cole panicked. He scanned the sky—what he could see of it.

The sound of rushing wind came from his left. He swung his rifle and saw the pterus swoop down and swipe at him with a clawed foot. The force of it pushed him aside. One of the bird's claws tore at flesh. He screamed at the searing pain, dropping his rifle and falling on one knee. He heard the pterus growl again. It somehow sounded victorious, almost mockingly so. It flew up and came back in a sharp arc, dropping to the clearing with ferocious speed.

This was Cole's chance. He pulled at his rifle, dragging it through the muddy ground until he'd hefted it up to his shoulder. He lay on his back, cocked it, and used the hand of his wounded arm to pull the trigger. Firing with his non-dominant shoulder had the expected effect—the shot was nowhere near where he wanted it to go. It bounced harmlessly off the bird's scaly breast.

The pterus landed in front of him, roaring its loudest yet, then launched itself at the wounded human.

Cole screamed and fired once more.

Mick hated the waiting game. The roars and gunshots made him pace back and forth next to his truck. He couldn't sit still, not knowing what was happening up there. There had never been so much commotion at the mountaintop, and he was sweating over it.

"Why don't you sit in the car?" Sam asked.

"Can't. Don't ask me again." He breathed heavily, silently apologising for being so snappy.

Then he heard the whooshing of wings against wind and he tensed. Caruso was coming.

The pterus circled above them. Mick stood still and watched the beast, leaning against his truck with one hand. Was this it? Was this the day he'd die, all his seasons of hard work and careful planning for nothing?

Caruso landed before them and locked eyes with Mick. Those bird eyes were the menacing, cloudy windows into a local lifeform that nobody had dared study too closely. But Mick had known Caruso long enough to guess what was on the bird's mind.

Red blood glinted on its shallow beak. It carried a muddy rifle in its clawed foot, which it dropped in front of the butcher. Caruso growled, and the hairs stood on Mick's neck. That growl gave him goosebumps, made his heart flutter. Caruso was not happy.

"I didn't have any unarmed inmates for tribute this time," Mick said desperately. He didn't know if Caruso understood him, but the bird usually responded well to his words. "That mercenary was all we could find. You woke much earlier than usual. We were unprepared." Mick saw the blackened marks of where the bullets grazed Caruso's scaly feathers. He breathed fast, fearing the situation was lost. "I'm sorry."

Caruso stood at full height—easily five times taller than a man—growled softly again, and then stretched his wings out. The King of the Mountain truly was an impressive beast in Mick's mind. He had the utmost fear and respect for Caruso and all of its kind, though he understood little of their motivations or intelligence. The pterus exhaled deeply, smothering Mick and Sam in hot, acrid breath.

Caruso brought his wings down in a huff, lifting off and flying away, leaving a wake of swirling air around the butcher and his assistant. Mick breathed out shakily, sure that his face was pale.

"Where do you think he's going?" Sam asked.

Mick stared after the magnificent beast, watched it glide away towards a known pterus roost atop a distant mountain range. Would Caruso live up to his end of the bargain? Or was he going to rouse others of his kind for retaliation? Mick hoped it was the former, as it had been for several years—one human for one pterus, food for food. Sacrificing the settlement's criminals bought Caruso's protection. In exchange for the delicacy that was human flesh, he would keep the settlement safe from pterus attacks and ensure a supply of its most valuable commodity—pterus meat from the carcasses of other birds that were inching too close to his roost.

Mick turned to Sam. "He's fetching us a pterus," he whispered, hoping the status quo had been maintained—as if saying it aloud would make it true.

ABOUT THE STORY

In 2019, I found a submission call from Joshua Palmatier's Zombies Need Brains (ZNB), a publisher of science fiction and fantasy anthologies. They release anthologies every year, and this time they had a call for three at once, one of which was called *Galactic Stew*. It called for a food-based story with some kind of speculative element.

I always wanted to write a story about a dragon, but dragons are fantasy creatures. As a science fiction writer, I didn't want to step into another genre—I wanted to maintain my brand. This challenge formed the basis of "Big Game". How do I include a dragon-like creature in a science fiction setting?

My solution was the pterus, pronounced with a silent *p*. The word is derived from *Pterodactylus*, an extinct winged reptile. In writing this behind-the-scenes article, I have just discovered that a Pterodactylus is not considered a dinosaur, even though it lived in the same time period. Random fact aside, I felt the pterus satisfied my goal of having a dragon-like creature in my story. I then need a plausible reason for their existence, which led to some worldbuilding.

The story of "Big Game" takes place on a colony world reminiscent of the Wild West. A young agricultural town must face the aggressive native pterus population that prey on livestock and humans alike. I then had to build the food requirement into the world, and it seemed like a no-brainer to have the food sourced from the most dangerous animal on the planet.

My idea was to have a butcher who sells the expensive and tasty pterus meat. I had known a guy named Michael who was a butcher and meat inspector, so I named the main character Mick. This butcher would be the only human on the planet who sells pterus. But I needed a way for Mick to source his meat *and* keep the colony safe at the same time. To do this, I leaned on some old fantasy tropes for dragons, namely: 1) that the pterus has a lair; 2) that it will emerge from a period of hibernation; and 3) that Mick would have a pact or agreement with it.

The first two tropes were easy. The pterus (named after Enrico Caruso, the powerful Italian opera singer) lives in a mountain-top lair close to the colony. Caruso would wake from one of his regular slumbers and be extremely hungry, as expected. That would prompt the main conflict of the story: a hungry, angry pterus has awakened, and the colony has no tribute. This set up the third trope well.

Mick's pact with Caruso is very simple: a human life given to Caruso every hibernation cycle for protecting the colony and for free pterus meat. In effect, it is food for food. Caruso would then defend the colony from others of its kind, exerting its dominance over its territory. Any pterus Caruso kills would be brought back to the colony, hence the free pterus meat. But this transaction is too clean. I needed another challenge. What would happen if there were no criminals to sacrifice to Caruso?

Now we have a moral dilemma. Does Mick let the colony die because there was no sacrificial lamb? Or does he choose someone not deserving of capital punishment to save the lives of many? To show a dark side of Mick and make the reader question whether he is a good man, I created Cole, a drifting hunter who is causing problems for the colony. In Cole, Mick sees an opportunity, but it is one of desperation: feed Cole to Caruso, thereby satiating the pterus' hunger, upholding his end of the bargain, and ridding the colony of a dangerous man. The catch is that Cole is tricked into being the sacrifice.

Now Cole has a mission to hunt Caruso, which creates another dilemma. If Cole succeeds, the colony no longer needs to sacrifice a human to Caruso every hibernation cycle. But it also means the colony will be unprotected. And if Cole fails, how would Caruso respond? I purposefully left the ending ambiguous. When Caruso flies away, is it going to bring Mick some meat, is it finding another lair, or is it going to find other pterus' and return for some retaliation? Sometimes ending the story with a question works very well.

Unfortunately, "Big Game" was not accepted for the *Galactic Stew* anthology. First readers at *Speculative North Magazine* said they liked the concept and twist of the sacrifice to the dragon trope, but it needed more characterisation. One reader at *Speculative North* unfortunately missed the twist of Mick's arrangement with Caruso. *Escape Pod* stated that while the story was well written, they felt the information-hiding structure of the story didn't work for them. These comments informed further edits of the story, the final version of which is in this collection.

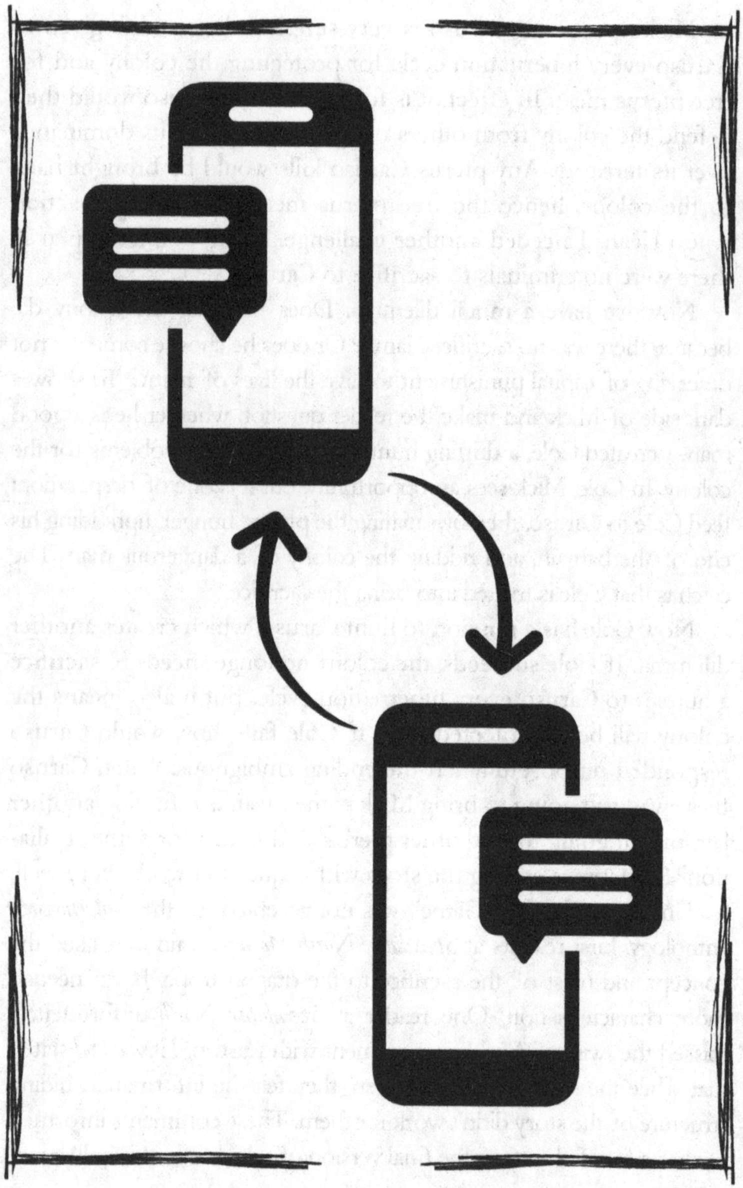

WHAT'S YOUR OTI?

THE SINGLE, HIGH-PITCHED NOTE hung in the air, breaking the silence as it always did. Hannah averted her eyes from her psychology textbook and stared at the phone. That noise aroused in her a mild frustration at the interruption, but also the unstoppable urge to pause her studies and check the notification. Well, procrastination was one of her virtues, as her father often quipped.

The notification came from one of her social media apps. Since moving away from family to stay on campus, she'd used social media more and more to keep in contact with her relatives and to associate with fellow students without actually having to speak to them face-to-face. She preferred the physical isolation.

The app in question was SpeakNet, a broad, worldwide medium for both serious discussions and pointless banter. Hannah navigated to her notifications list and read what it was all about. A high school student on the other side of the country had posted a general message that Hannah's profile had flagged:

> **ChelseaBoo(56)—**I just feel so depressed today. Nobody understands the pain I feel. I haven't gone to school all week. Can't even get out of bed. The school counsellor doesn't take me seriously, and my parents are too busy to notice. Sometimes I think they don't even care about me. I hate my life.

Hannah's heart went out to this girl. She knew well enough how bad Chelsea was feeling—she'd been through it herself. That was why she'd set up SpeakNet to flag posts with "depression", "sad", "suicidal", or other similar words.

Hannah wanted to write something encouraging for this girl, because that was what she found had helped her in the past. She tapped on the notification and it brought her to the original thread. That was when her heart sank.

> **AdRiAn(142)**—Just suck it up and keep going. Nobody cares about your problems. The sooner you realise that, the better.
>
> **GoldenHair(187)**—Hun, you're just one of the millions who have to go through crap every day. Grow up and deal with it.
>
> **Mister_Bull(190)**—Oh look another one seeking attention.

Hannah's blood boiled. Trolls! There were more, but those were just the first three she read before looking away in disgust. She opened each of their profiles. She checked the trends in their Online Toxicity Index, their OTI. Their graphs showed a long-term upwards trend, but all three were in the Green Band—between 0 and 199. Low-level trolls, but harmful nonetheless.

She cursed softly at the horrible responses ChelseaBoo was receiving.

"Did you say something?"

Hannah glanced over at Melanie, her dormitory roommate. "Nothing."

Melanie grinned and carried a basket of clothes out of the room. But Hannah's mind spun over the SpeakNet exchange. She wanted to do something about it.

> **HannahannaH(21)**—Hey @ChelseaBoo, don't listen to these scumbags. They don't know what it's like to suffer. I've been where you are. Still there sometimes. The world would be easier

> for everyone without jerks like the ones in this
> thread. Be strong. I'm here for you. DM me if you
> ever want to talk.

Hannah's OTI increased by two points because of her mildly aggressive retort to the SpeakNet trolls. But she didn't care. She was safely in the green zone where she had been her whole life. She could afford a small increase if it meant standing up for a psychologically vulnerable high schooler.

> **ChelseaBoo(56)—**ty.

That made Hannah smile. Just a small comment to know she had made a good impact was enough to lift her spirits. She hoped ChelseaBoo was feeling better.

Then came the trolls.

> **GamerDude(306)—**Stop babying her. She needs to learn how to live or she'll never survive in the real world.

> **JessicaPrincess(112)—**You her mother or something, @HannahannaH? Why don't you stay out of this?

Hannah ground her teeth and squinted at each new message that came her way. ChelseaBoo had written nothing other than the original message and her thanks to Hannah. But it seemed nobody was talking to ChelseaBoo anymore. Most were aiming their taunts directly at Hannah now.

> **SoccerBallJoe(177)—**You're all idiots for even contributing to this thread. **@ChelseaBoo** and **@HannahannaH**, you both need help. Get off my screen.

Hannah threw her phone against the desk and huffed. This was cyberbullying, pure and simple. How dare these people write such rubbish online! The rudeness and impulsiveness directed at her made her stomach feel hollow.

> **HannahannaH(23)**—These comments are horrible.
> Depression is a serious issue in today's society.
> You deadbeats need to show some respect.

AdRiAn(144)—OK boomer.

With an exasperated shout, Hannah put her phone aside and stared out the window next to her desk. She forced herself to look at the green grass and admire the different shades and colours of vegetation on the university grounds. It was a calming strategy.

She shook her head. *I'm not even a boomer,* she thought. *I'm just a girl who tries to respect others.* Was it wrong to try to have a logical, peaceful conversation with others about a serious issue? Why couldn't people respect each other online? She shook her head again. *I guess that's one reason why I'm studying psychology—to understand everyone.*

Sometimes trying to understand the people around her made her blood boil. She'd have to work on that if she was going to be a psychologist someday.

AFTER A LONG DAY of lectures, reading, writing, and generally avoiding people, Hannah retired to bed. Too late, as usual, but she was accepting the necessity of late nights. Sometimes, it felt like her mind was drowning, her head spinning on the currents of all the newfound knowledge she was ingesting.

Despite being tired, Hannah always found it hard to fall asleep at night. Maybe it was because at night in bed, when there were no books to read or professors to listen to, her mind free-dived into the darkest pits of her warped sense of reality.

I'm an ugly, boring girl, she thought sadly as she tucked herself in bed. The warm embrace of the blankets did nothing to comfort her. *I'm going to end up alone and unloved. Maybe that's how it should be ...*

She sighed and stared at the ceiling, willing the thoughts to stop, but knowing it was pointless to think they would. The only way to stop them was to distract herself until she was too tired to stay awake.

Her hand slid up from under the covers and reached for her phone. The screen's light momentarily blinded her in the darkness. She blinked until the light was comfortable. Her finger habitually went to the SpeakNet app symbol, but she stopped over it as her brain caught up to what she was doing. She remembered the online argument earlier in the day and wondered if she should risk looking at it again. But the budding psychologist in her pushed that thought aside.

SpeakNet flashed open and she immediately checked her OTI. It now sat at 151, in the upper green band, a whole 128 points higher than what it was earlier in the day. Hannah mouthed a question at the abrupt change and soon found out why. The notification panel was filled with reactions and replies to her comments about ChelseaBoo's depression post. Most were negative reactions, the kind that bumped an OTI upwards. Hannah couldn't resist investigating further.

> **AniseHorvath06(97)—**The last thing I want is some self-righteous college student telling me how I should feel.
>
> **Gr8M8(469)—**This is what happens when we live in a care-bear nanny state. People don't learn to toughen up. The world is what the world is. Now we have an idiot psych student thinking she can change the world by making a few comments online. It's gonna take a lot more than that, and even then you'll fail.
>
> **JohnnyTwoThumbs(229)—@Gr8M8**, it's survival of the fittest.

Hannah knew every person who made a horrible comment would have their own OTI increased algorithmically. It's just how the system worked. But she had a lot of downvotes recorded against her. These people were doing more damage to her than they were to themselves. She had to set the matter straight.

> **HannahannaH(151)**—We don't live in a nanny state. We live in a world where depression, anxiety, and suicide is rampant. More needs to be done to help people suffering from mental health conditions. It takes a lot of courage to reach out like **@ChelseaBoo** did, and she doesn't deserve to be blasted like this. I'm calling for the **@AOTI** to take action on these people making such horrible comments. It's people like you who are causing so much pain and suffering, and you need to be punished.

She regretted it the moment she tapped POST. The message was written so fast, her thumbs moving with such agility that before she knew it, the words were down and she hadn't bothered to read through it before sending. Reading it after the fact, several words and phrases brought up red flags in her mind. Then the responses flooded in.

> **JohnSmith2937(242)**—You're asking the AOTI to get involved in this. Are you crazy? It's our right to speak our mind here.

> **3L3V3N(350)**—Somebody get this bitch a Xanax.

> **RightHonorableHeathen(378)**—I seriously doubt the AOTI will listen to a whining little tramp like you, @HannahannaH. Leave public policy to those who know what they're doing.

Her phone buzzed at the receipt of an email. She pulled down the preview tab and saw it was from the AOTI. Amazed that they would respond so fast and wanting to peel her eyes away from the online onslaught, she quickly opened the email. It looked like these trolls would get what's coming to them after all.

But it was not to be. Her eyes went wide at the email's brief message:

Dear Hannah Grove,

It has come to our attention that the SpeakNet social media account, HannahannaH, to which you are connected, has reached and/or surpassed OTI Level 200. This means you are now in the Yellow Band. You may consider this a formal warning. A further warning will be issued at OTI Level 300.

Regards,

Benjamin Holmes, Director
Agency of the Online Toxicity Index

Hannah stared at the screen. Level 200? But it was only 151 a moment ago! She checked her SpeakNet profile. Her OTI was at 229. In the few seconds of staring at it in disbelief, that number increased to 235. Her online comments were inciting people to angry responses, fuelling a fire that could easily get out of control.

> **BethanyOBrien(81)**—I agree with you, **@HannahannaH**. This world needs to change. We need more psychological awareness. Keep up the good work.

Hannah's eyes grew wet at the latest tagged post. So there were still people out there who shared her thoughts? She checked BethanyOBrien's profile. A middle-aged woman, subjectively judging by her profile photo. She was married, from England, living in Canada, working as a paralegal at a law firm called Johnston Tremblay & Martin. Just an average person, like Hannah, working through life as best she could.

Hannah upvoted BethanyOBrien's comment, feeling a surge of courage pulse through her veins.

HannahannaH(246)—I'm glad there are still some people out there who understand the plight of those who suffer in silence and those who find the courage to speak up. We do so because we feel uncomfortable voicing our feelings. We feel uncomfortable because this system is geared against us. Too many people either don't understand the situation, are ill-equipped to give support, or simply don't care. This is the biggest health concern of the modern world. Something needs to be done about it!

This time, Hannah took the time to read through her words before pushing POST. BethanyOBrien and ChelseaBoo were among the first to upvote it. *Good*, Hannah thought. It showed they were following the discussion and lending their support. But there were still some people reacting and commenting negatively to her previous posts, so she wrote more.

HannahannaH(253)—We have the OTI laws to discourage toxic online communication. Do they work? Maybe. They may punish those who step on the depressed, the anxious, or the suicidal. But that is as far as they go. They don't help the ones who really need help. They only try to lessen negative communication (which isn't working, btw). What we really need are laws that give focused and immediate assistance to those with mental health issues who reach out.

AhmedTheGuy(101)—@HannahannaH, if only!

BethanyOBrien(83)—@HannahannaH, amen to that.

ColinFromEarth(187)—Y'all need to see a shrink!

Stan_the_Man(230)—Ain't nothing wrong with the system, just with you.

HannahannaH(259)—Too many people who need psychological help cannot afford it. The system is at fault.

ElsaMcGee(768)—Nah, it's just whiny brats like you who think the system needs a change. Most people live just fine in this world. It's those who can't handle it that complain the system is broken. The way I see it, that's just the natural order. If you cannot deal with the system, that's nature's way of saying you're weak and you should move aside for the stronger ones. So stop trying to change the world, girlie, because it won't happen.

HannahannaH(262)—**@ElsaMcGee**, that's a horrible thing to say! You're the reason so many of us are trodden on! It's people like you who put up barriers, who divert funding. Do you realise how many suicides you're indirectly responsible for? It should be illegal to let people with mood disorders go untreated. It's tantamount to manslaughter!

ElsaMcGee(774)—**@HannahannaH**, I'm not the bad person here. I've dealt with my own struggles, and I've emerged stronger than before. If you can't do that, then what good are you? The world needs leaders, but it needs a heck of a lot more followers.

HannahannaH(270)—**@ElsaMcGee**, the world doesn't need followers, it *wants* them. The world is putting so much pressure on all of us, it's no wonder someone as young as ChelseaBoo is struggling. It's no wonder so many teenagers

> and adults lose the will to go on. The world is in
> a dark place, and we're all suffering, whether you
> feel it or not!

When Hannah checked the time, she saw how fast the hands had ticked by. She felt so riled up that there was no way she'd fall asleep anytime soon.

> **Frankfurter(309)**—You make a lot of talk,
> **@HannahannaH**, but I don't see you taking any
> action. Perhaps you're also the problem, because
> everywhere I look, I see everyone talking and
> nobody doing anything about it. So whether you
> realise it or not, you're actually a part of this
> system too. Welcome.

Hannah's OTI was now nudging towards 300. She groaned and shut down her phone, tossing it onto her bedside table and pulling the blankets over her head. She squared her jaw and fought back tears, wondering how the world had become so unloving.

It was one of those mornings that Hannah woke and stared at the ceiling with a frown. Her head throbbed and her vision was blurry. She swung her eyes down to glimpse at Melanie's bed across the room. It was empty, of course. The roommate probably crashed on someone's couch.

Hannah looked over at her phone and scowled at it—her little window into a world of hate. Her parents said that in the past phones could only make calls and send texts. Now they were the source of so many problems. She reached for it anyway. Sometimes it was hard to break a morning ritual.

She turned it on and soon had a flurry of app and email notifications. Knowing exactly what the SpeakNet ones would be about, she ignored them and went for her emails. She subscribed to a few psychology newsletters and clothing catalogues. As per custom, she'd lie in bed and read through some of them before rising for breakfast.

There were three emails from the AOTI. The latest was the one that troubled her most:

> *Dear Hannah Grove,*
>
> *It has come to our attention that the SpeakNet social media account, HannahhannaH, to which you are connected, has reached and/or surpassed OTI Level 500. This means you are now in the Orange Band and are hereby fined $350, payable in 14 days. Please be advised that every increase of 100 past this point will incur further fines, with fines above Level 700 (Red Band) being over $1,000. Continued increases in your OTI ranking or failure to pay your fines will lead to legal action taken against you and your social media account.*
>
> *Regards,*
>
> **Benjamin Holmes, Director**
> *Agency of the Online Toxicity Index*

Hannah's mind raced through the ramifications of the email. A fine? She hadn't been fined for anything in her life. How could this happen to her? Why was it happening? The questions forced her to open SpeakNet, where all the answers were bound to be.

Sure enough, after her socio-political rants before falling asleep, people had responded and reacted. Many people. People all over the world, it seemed. Her comments clearly divided those who felt the need to reply, with some offering words of support, while others posted vehement opposition. And during the hours of her sleep, her OTI had risen by over 200 points.

Over Level 500 and fined $350—not an expense a college

student needed. Her head sunk deeper into the pillow and she debated what to do next. Should she argue the fine? Was the fine really the issue here? Or was it the attitudes of other SpeakNet users? She shook her head and decided.

> **HannahannaH(535)**—I just want to say that I have been fined $350 by the wonderfully upright justice organisation known as the **@AOTI**. I hold society accountable for this unjust punishment. I have done nothing wrong. I have been judged by strangers who don't even know me, for comments that speak only the truth about an issue that is affecting millions of people worldwide. This is why I will not be paying the fine.

It was the wrong thing to say, but at the same time, she was right to say it. In her mind, how could it be an offence for someone to publicly highlight the shortcomings of society? Whatever happened to freedom of speech?

> **HeyItsJosh(209)**—I'm sorry, but that's the law. If you've been fined, it means you've done something wrong. You have to pay it.

> **TranNguyen(162)**—You're right, we are accountable for judging you. That's the law. We judge you because what you're saying is toxic.

> **Hunky_Dory(156)**—@TranNguyen, is she toxic or is it, or is it illegal? Is there a difference? It may be toxic to you, but is it toxic to someone else? If it's illegal, then it's wrong no matter what.

> **TranNguyen(164)**—@Hunky_Dory, nobody asked you.

> **EmilyTanaka(289)**—Pay the fine. Do the time. Stop now before you reach 1,000. I've been there.

> **AYDSGSTWYKBF(866)**—Nah, Level 5,000 is much worse. **@HannahannaH**, if you think $350 is bad, you got no idea. I dare you to keep complaining. Maybe you'll beat my record!

Those were just some comments that came through hard and fast. Even the AOTI had something to say.

> **AOTI_Public_Relations(X)**—The AOTI reminds all SpeakNet users that the OTI is a legal measure of online communication, subject to criminal charges if one's index surpasses the thresholds. In this case, **@HannahannaH** was fined in accordance with the law and will be required to pay said fine within the established time frame. Any refusal to pay AOTI fines will result in further criminal charges. We encourage all users to engage in online communication in a respectful, encouraging, and sensitive manner.

After that little message, Hannah received more negative responses. Her post was downvoted by even more users, and there were many calls for her to accept responsibility for her words and pay the fine.

The problem was, the negative publicity brought about by the AOTI nudged her ranking even higher. Before too long, she hit 600. Less than a minute later, she received another email, this time stating that she was being fined $500 in addition to the still outstanding $350 attached to her account.

Hannah closed her phone and cried. She just cried.

HANNAH DIDN'T GO TO her lecture that day. In fact, she didn't even get out of bed until nearly lunchtime. Not that she cared. The stress of online persecution made her weak. All she wanted to do was hide until it all blew over.

On TV was one of those midday talk shows where the hosts sit around a couch or table and give their thought on current events. Hannah never paid them much heed—the incessant blabber of unprofessional opinions frustrated her even in the best of times. But their topic of discussion caught her attention.

"We turn now to something that has caused a heated debate on SpeakNet," one host, a balding male, said. "Sparked by one user's plea for emotional support and understanding, the SpeakNet community replied disparagingly. When another user came to the original poster's rescue, they were also blasted. Your thoughts, Abigail?"

A blonde, middle-aged woman shifted in her seat and spoke up. "This is exactly why the OTI laws were written. It doesn't matter whether you're right or wrong online. Whatever arguments you put forth need to be written in a respectful way."

Hannah scoffed.

"Yeah, but don't you think that the issues being raised here are so overdue for action that they warrant the straightforward, blunt arguments we've been seeing?" the first host asked.

"No, I don't think that, Trevor," Abigail replied. "We live in a society that is supposed to be governed by the people. Well, the people have spoken. If this Hannah girl has made harsh comments, then she must pay the penalty. Part of that is social shaming, and the other part is a fine."

"But she was responding to harsh criticism aimed at the original poster in the thread," a third host said. Hannah brightened at her supportive words. "She was highlighting the negative trend of the replies."

"And being negative herself," Abigail replied.

"But is it illegal to be negative about the negativities of society?" Trevor asked. "The way I see it, we need people like Hannah to highlight problems like this. Otherwise, nothing will change."

"This country tried an all-encompassing mental health program," Abigail said, "and it failed. It was a major financial burden, and it was taxpayers who got stuck with the bill, including taxpayers who had no need for the program. I bet some of those taxpayers are the ones responding negatively to Chelsea and Hannah."

Hannah was old enough to remember the public backlash over the now-scrapped National Mental Health Scheme. Some said there was no problem with the already-existing health measures, while others complained the new scheme was too expensive. What few saw was just how much of a cost blowout it would be. Years later, the government was still trying to recoup its losses.

"We're going off-topic now," Trevor said. "Let's not open up old wounds. The main thing I want to discuss is whether Hannah's example should be criminalised. Under the current laws, she is already facing fines of nearly $1,000. Since when do good Samaritans get penalised?"

"When they break the law," Abigail said.

"But should it be illegal to come to someone's aid online?" Trevor pressed.

No, Hannah thought resolutely.

"Yes," Abigail said, "if they do so without calming the argument. Otherwise, they're only making matters worse."

"I personally don't see how Hannah helping Chelsea could have calmed the argument in the short term," the third host said. She paused as if to collect her thoughts. "It's like a big nation going to war to defend a smaller nation. There will be conflict until the conflict is resolved."

"Right," Trevor said, leaning forward. "And this is the point I'm trying to make—the fact that Hannah felt the need to jump in and defend Chelsea tells me that there is something fundamentally wrong with the OTI laws. Do you believe they work?"

"No," the third, as-yet-unnamed host said.

"Yes," Abigail replied.

"But it's clear in this situation that they don't work," Trevor continued. "Otherwise, Hannah would not have gotten involved. And for that reason, I don't think the penalties should apply to her. Look at how fast her index has risen! Have you ever seen anything like it before?"

"Only when celebrities make bad remarks," the third host said.

"And that, Trevor, says to me that the laws are working. They're an indication of the public's perception. They read Hannah's statements and they *know* she is wrong to say them. They—"

"Wrong to say them?" Trevor interjected. "Or wrong to say them as she said them?"

"Both, so—"

"I'm sorry, but I'll have to stop you there," Trevor said with his finger in the air. "What we have here is a conflict between freedom of speech and the OTI. The OTI is supposed to improve online behaviour and interaction. Freedom of speech is exactly that—freedom to speak one's mind, like we're doing now."

"Okay," Abigail said. "So she's wrong to say it like she said it—or wrote it. But if you're saying that—"

Hannah's eyes peeled away from the TV screen as her phone beeped to life. She opened it, saw that it was an email, and then promptly felt the sickness in her gut when she saw the sender.

The AOTI.

Dear Hannah Grove,

It has come to our attention that the SpeakNet social media account, HannahannaH, to which you are connected, has reached and/or surpassed OTI Level 700. This means you are now in the Red Band and are hereby fined $1,000, payable in 14 days. Our records show that you still have outstanding fines totalling $850, with 14 days left to pay. This leaves a total of $1,850. Failure to pay your fines will result in legal *action. Please be advised that every increase of your OTI past the 100-point thresholds will incur further fines, with penalties over Level 1,000 including legal action against you and your social media account.*

Regards,

Benjamin Holmes, Director
Agency of the Online Toxicity Index

The publicity was making it worse! In the time it took her to read the email, her OTI was already nudging past 750. She shook her head, but this time she felt no anger. The frustration that had previously sapped her composure had somehow magically disappeared, replaced by a feeling of stony resolve—a resolve to carry the fight to the end. If her OTI was going to rise anyway, she might as well argue her case, and argue it well. People needed to hear what she had to say.

So, while the talk show hosts debated amongst themselves, Hannah opened SpeakNet, ignoring the other comments that had piled in overnight, and drafted a message. She put thought into it this time, planned her response, read through it several times, adjusted it, read it aloud. Satisfied that she could improve it no more, she pushed POST.

HannahhannaH(759)—In light of the recent public discussions about this thread, and to promote free online dialogue of mental health issues, I have decided to make it my mission to reform the OTI laws. It is clear that some people know how unstable the OTI system is. And it is also clear that some people do not understand the basic principles the OTI laws are trying to uphold. The OTI laws do not work. They are righteous in principle, but not in practice. They are like a huge dragnet catching the bad fish and the good fish at the same time. I have been called a Good Samaritan by some. Others have called me names I do not wish to repeat. According to the OTI language algorithm, I am a bad fish. According to that same algorithm and the opinions of other SpeakNet users, **@ChelseaBoo** is a bad fish. But I am glad that I came to her rescue, because now I am bearing the brunt of the online attack instead of her. I will take this matter as high as it can go, and I will not stop until changes are made. My first act of defiance will be my refusal to pay my AOTI fines. I am happy to do this alone, but if you want change too, then join me. Together, we can reform the OTI laws so innocent people no longer have to be the government's cash trees, and so that people who are barely holding on to life can have the support they need to keep going. My fight starts today.

Then she turned her phone off, determined not to be interrupted by the situation for at least the rest of the day. She felt good about herself, felt like she was on the cusp of making a difference.

A THUMPING ON THE DOOR jolted Hannah awake. She sat up in her bed and stared wide-eyed at Melanie, who was scrambling to put some pants on in the dim morning light.

"Who is it?" Melanie called. She had returned overnight.

"It's the police."

"Coming."

Hannah jumped out of her bed and threw a shirt at Melanie, then waited by the door until her carefree roommate was dressed. Two plainclothes police officers stood before her when she opened the door. They flashed identification.

"Are you Ms Hannah Grove?" one of them asked.

"Uh, yes …"

"I'm Detective Swanson, and this is Detective Cargill. We're here with a warrant for your arrest."

"On what grounds?"

"Your OTI has reached Level 1,000," Cargill said. "That means you must come with us and be processed before going to court."

Hannah stood silent for a moment. She dearly wanted to check her phone to see if the numbers added up. Could her OTI have organically risen from roughly 750 to 1,000 that fast? She played it safe.

"I know about my OTI and what it means," she said. "But why is my OTI so high?"

"Your SpeakNet posts were downvoted by other users and by the system's language algorithm," Swanson told her. "That's how it works."

"I know how it works," Hannah persisted. She folded her arms, surprised at her own defiance in front of the two imposing detectives. "But what I'm asking is: What did I do for it to rise so high?"

The detectives exchanged a glance, but it was the younger one, Cargill, who answered. "The report says that you ... that you defended a girl with depression, you argued for better mental health services, and you demanded reforms to the OTI laws." He averted his eyes from her, clearly embarrassed at the stupidity of the charge.

Hannah squared her jaw, letting those spoken facts hang in the air. Then she raised her wrists so the detectives could cuff her as the law stipulated.

The fight was just beginning.

ABOUT THE STORY

Back in 2019, I launched myself into a flurry of short story activity, and "What's Your OTI?" was one of those stories. Vernacular

Books put out a call for submissions for their upcoming anthology *The Way of the Laser: Future Crime Stories*, and I dreamed up "What's Your OTI?" as my interpretation of future crime. Vernacular allowed multiple submissions, so I also submitted "Just Deserts", which had recently been rejected for Flame Tree Publishing's *Detective Thrillers* anthology.

Shortly before writing "What's Your OTI?", I had watched an episode of Seth MacFarlane's *The Orville* called "Majority Rule" (S1 E07). In this episode, a humanoid society uses a form of social justice to publicly vote for criminal punishments. Being a criminology graduate, I found the whole concept fascinating and decided to invent my own form of social justice system.

"What's Your OTI?" evolved from two lines of thought. First, I had already grown despondent by the amount of toxic and aggressive behaviour in social media comments, and I wished users would have more manners and more maturity. Second, through my criminology studies, I appreciated Professor John Braithwaite's theory of *reintegrative shaming*, which states that when a community collectively views an action as shameful, and when such shame is communicated on a continuum of shame that encourages forgiveness and rehabilitation, there will be fewer instances of that action. For more information on Braithwaite's theory, I highly recommend any of the peer reviewed books or articles about it, including *Crime, Shaming and Reintegration*, his 1989 book, which introduced the theory.

So I had a problem I wanted to criminalise (toxic online behaviour) and a criminological theory I could apply to it (reintegrative shaming). For this to work, I had to invent a future society which was more proactive about cyberbullying, proper interpersonal communication, and general online interactions. Therefore, I invented SpeakNet, a social media platform that allowed me to experiment with my idea. I also needed a formal mechanism to criminalise and measure online toxicity, so that gave birth to the

Online Toxicity Index (OTI) and the Agency of the OTI (AOTI). In some tribal societies, shaming was an important means by which younger people learned how to speak and behave appropriately, and how such behaviour was maintained throughout adulthood. In a modern, globalised setting, I needed something on a larger scale. The OTI became the dynamic public shaming system, assisted by the kind of social media algorithm we have all come to despise.

Online toxicity and cyberbullying affect many people, but none more so than children and teenagers. This is not to say that adults do not behave immaturely online—in fact, in just a five-minute read of any social media thread, you are bound to find at least one adult purposefully insulting someone else. But young people are particularly susceptible to online bullying, so I created the catalyst for the story—a young person reaching out for support, a world that doesn't care, and a psychology student (Hannah) who cares a lot.

When Hannah passionately defends the young person and then bemoans the problems with society's attitude towards mental health, she is downvoted. I used that to highlight the imperfections in the OTI system. A social justice system based on shaming and electronic voting has the potential to criminalise actions and free speech that are intended for good. This is because everyone will have their own opinion of what constitutes toxic online behaviour. Thus, Hannah finds herself in an uncontrollable spiral as she continues to be downvoted. The SpeakNet algorithm ensures that the more people react to her replies, the more people see her comments, leading to more downvotes.

At this point, I realised that another theory finds an application in the story. Again, during my criminology studies, I learned about *labelling theory*, which is related to reintegrated shaming. Labelling theory was first discussed in the early 1900s, but it was applied to criminality and delinquency by Frank Tannenbaum in 1938 in his book *Crime and the Community*. The theory states that, initially, criminal behaviour is a matter of "good people doing bad things", but as time goes on, the definition of badness shifts from the bad act itself to the person doing the bad act. Those people then self-identify themselves as the problem, which contributes to ongoing criminal behaviour. This idea of criminal self-identification was developed further in 1951 in Edwin M. Lemert's *Social Pathology*. There is, of course, evidence against labelling theory, but I chose to use it in my story anyway.

Note how "What's Your OTI?" is structured. Every SpeakNet comment has an OTI rating after the username. Those with higher ratings are more toxic, almost as if they have accepted their online persona and happily continue to insult and bully others. Eventually, once Hannah's rating is high enough, law enforcement measures are taken against her, and she embraces her new label as a social media criminal. But rather than going full toxic on the world, Hannah decides not to back down, instead choosing to stand up for what is right. If that is what makes her a criminal by modern OTI laws, then so be it. She is content with being labelled as a criminal if it means shedding more light on the state of mental health and the effects of cyberbullying.

"What's Your OTI?" and "Just Deserts" were both rejected by the *Way of the Laser* anthology. One of the editors for Vernacular Books said that "What's Your OTI?" had "real positives" but that ultimately they could not use it. Soon after, the story became my first submission to the Writers of the Future Contest. I was over the moon when nearly four months later, I learned that the story was a semi-finalist, meaning it was placed in the top 18 of the thousands of stories submitted to the contest. This fantastic news was then followed up by a personalised critique from the then Writers of the Future Coordinating Judge and award-winning, best-selling author Dave Wolverton (also known as David Farland), which is excerpted here:

Congratulations on being a semi-finalist for the second quarter of the L. Ron Hubbard Writers of the Future Contest for 2020. This was the largest quarter of the contest ever, and so the competition was especially fierce. Your story was beautifully written and felt very timely. Ultimately, it almost didn't feel like science fiction … So, I kind of looked at the basic concept here and felt that perhaps it needed just a bit of a twist brought in, something to make the reader feel that it was a bit more futuristic. Otherwise, this is a very strong piece. I think you'll find a great publisher for this, and I hope to see more from you in the near future.

Contrary to Mr Farland's prediction, I could not find a publisher for the story. I submitted it five more times, all of which were unsuccessful. Then again, maybe he was right, because now "What's Your OTI?" is published by my very own imprint, Delta-V Press. I hope you enjoyed it as much as he did.

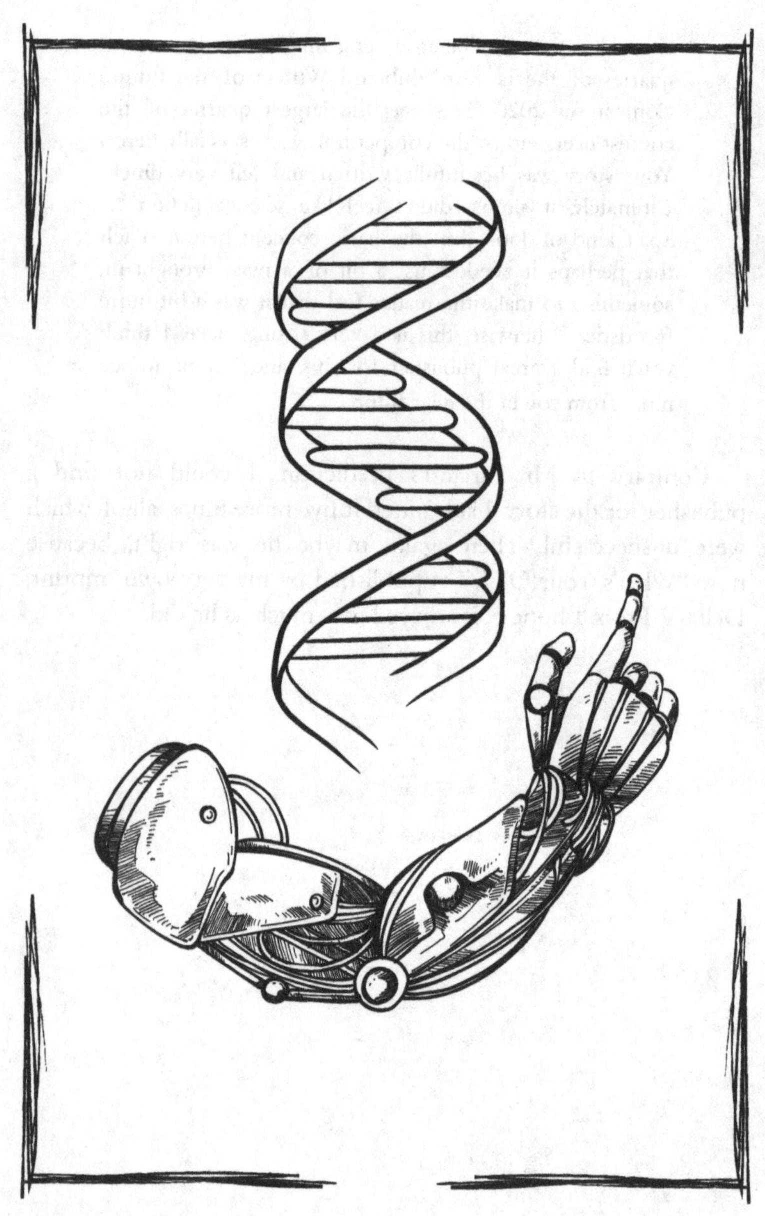

BRITTLE AND STRONG

Hans shifted his arm into the sunlight, his bones creaking with the movement. In the warmth of his apartment window, staring down at the city park below, he imagined being outside, enjoying all that the great outdoors offered. A frown crossed his fifty-something-year-old face. Those days might never happen again, not even for his kids. His grandkids, though—

"Your medication, Doctor Schreiber."

Hans turned slowly, deliberately, to face his Personal Robotic Servitor (PeRoS). "Just set it down there, Erwin. I'll walk to it."

"As you wish, *mein Herr.*" The gleaming white robot placed the small tray on a nearby table and faced its master. "Will you require assistance? You are not wearing your bracing weave."

"It's okay. Let's see if I can do it first."

The chair spun gingerly out from his desk and Hans readied himself for his first unaided walk of the day. He liked to set little challenges for himself, just to prove that he as an individual and a representative of the human race hadn't been defeated.

He braced himself on the armrests and slid forward, feeling the pressure on his bones already. But he suppressed a grumble and soldiered on. He'd stood up by himself before, and he'd be damned if he let a few creaks stop him this time. So he pushed on the armrests, letting out a sigh at the effort. His muscles weren't what they used to be. Erwin watched one step away.

Hans shakily balanced himself against the desk when he finally made it off the chair, and then quickly gestured for Erwin's help as he felt the strain on his legs. The robot dutifully stepped closer and helped its middle-aged master.

"Thank you," Hans said quietly. "Help me back down, would you please? And pass me the pill."

Erwin smoothly guided Hans back into the desk chair and reached for the medication. Hans shook his head ever so slightly. Little failures like what had just happened were a daily occurrence, but he stubbornly kept up his personal challenges. If his superior found out, however, then he'd be in big trouble. He was too important to be found broken and crumpled on the floor.

Erwin handed him the collagen pill, which Hans frowned at like he always did. Two pills a day, every day, for the rest of his life, unless the gene scientists performed a miracle. He rubbed it between thumb and forefinger before tossing it into his mouth and washing it down with water. The damn pharmaceutical companies were making a killing off collagen pills alone. Everyone needed them since the attack …

"I'll have that weave now, and my shock suit," Hans said.

"Of course, *mein Herr*," Erwin replied. The robot's head dipped slightly before it turned and left.

Hans had to sniff a laugh. Those PeRoS units were becoming increasingly more human-like with every newer model. But it was nice having the help and the company. His eyes moved to the photo of his wife, Helga, hanging on the wall above the desk. Her death had been premature—expected, but no less devastating. He blinked away tears as his mind replayed happy memories from times past. She was the whole reason he pressed on so stubbornly.

Erwin returned with the weave and shock suit draped over each arm. Then human and robot spent the necessary fifteen minutes getting Hans dressed so he could leave the apartment. Hans obeyed the robot's direction despite knowing the routine by heart. Raise one arm with Erwin's help, slip on the weave, raise the other, do the same, pull hands into gloves, collect around the waist, fit two legs, attach weave socks to feet.

"Test," Erwin said.

Hans raised both arms by himself, felt the weave's power compensating for and enhancing his weakened locomotive ability. Then he stretched his legs forward and back, bent slightly at the waist. The pain and risk of such movements were reduced considerably—another marvel of technology. Though the weave didn't give Hans total control of his body—for there were some movements and positions that were simply far too risky to attempt—it gave him much more mobility.

Next came the shock suit. With the weave already on, Hans could don the suit himself. Erwin passed the slightly puffy pants and equally puffy jacket as Hans needed them. He activated them and they immediately conformed to his figure, though they retained their puffy shape somewhat, for that was crucial to their design. Then Erwin gave Hans gloves and shoes, and with that, Hans was ready to go out in public.

"Thank you, Erwin," he said with a small smile. He silently appreciated modern technology every day, especially those produced out of necessity. "Please start the car. We're going to the lab."

"At once, Doctor Schreiber."

With the robot gone, Hans studied himself in the mirror. The drab colour of the shock suit made him look like something out of a science fiction movie from his childhood. Then he grinned. He supposed he was living in highly advanced times now, though everyone carried the scars of that journey. Gone were the days when he'd go to work in suits with different coloured shirts and ties. No, now he and everyone else had shock suits.

Shock suits, weaves, and collagen pills.

Hans always enjoyed the journey to the lab, especially because Erwin did the driving for him. It let him see just how well his part of the world had recovered from the attack. They drove on a smooth highway that had once been destroyed, through a clean and vibrant city that used to be nothing but rubble. Green trees dotted the cityscape. The pleasant scenery belied the true history of the area. It was much the same no matter where one went in the world.

They exited the highway, passing a cluster of office buildings still under construction. Shock-suited men and women hovered around the dirt and mud of the construction site, but it was the Worker Robotic Servitors (WoRoS) who scurried around with tools and machinery. Hans smiled sombrely at just how much the servitor models did for humans. Without them, Hans supposed the world would still be in ruins. And the future? He was thankful they could plan for the future now that the present had been rebuilt.

Their drive took them to the outskirts of the city, where a pine forest broke up the landscape. A single road peeled off from the major thoroughfare in that area, coming to a high fence with a guardhouse. A Military Robotic Servitor (MiRoS) approached the car, kneeling to look through the driver's window. Erwin gave it Hans' identification card.

"Welcome, Doctor Hans Schreiber," the MiRoS said. It paused ever so briefly, a glint of sunlight flashing on its black frame. "You may enter." It signalled to another MiRoS in the guardhouse and the sturdy gates opened.

Erwin took the car into the protected forest. Hans liked to look out the windows and try to count how many MiRoS units were patrolling the area.

"Do you ever wish you were a MiRoS instead of a PeRoS?" Hans asked.

"The answer to that question is not within my analytical parameters, *mein Herr*," Erwin replied matter-of-factly.

"Yes, I know." Of course he knew. He was on the PeRoS development team. "Are you happy being a personal servitor?"

"Happiness is not a matter that concerns me. I am built to serve."

Hans had to stifle a chuckle. Sometimes he quizzed Erwin with ridiculous questions, either for his own amusement or as serious—albeit informal—machine learning research. Then again, sometimes it was just nice to talk to someone who could give a straight, honest answer.

"Do you think you could take up arms to defend me if required?"

"That function is the domain of the MiRoS model."

"Suppose there are no MiRoS models nearby and I was in danger," Hans pressed. "Would you fight for me?"

"There are many variables influencing how I would respond to such a scenario."

This time, Hans did laugh. "Humour me."

"I would have to analyse the perceived threat to your safety. I cannot harm another human, nor can I assault another servitor unit or destroy private or public property without a direct command. If I determine that you are in danger and I can remove you from the situation without fighting, that would be my first action."

"But suppose you have to fight, and fight to kill. Suppose there is no other way to eliminate the threats to my safety."

Erwin remained silent for a few seconds. Hans could hear the whirring of fans in its core. "You would give me permission to attack a human or a servitor?"

"No," Hans replied quietly, "I don't anticipate threats from humans or servitors. There is another threat, one which you have never seen, but may return at any time. I would be limited in my ability to defend myself when that happens, despite my weave and shock suit."

"The Omegas?"

"The Omegas," Hans agreed solemnly.

"That sounds like the domain of the MiRoS model," Erwin responded quite rightly.

The forest opened up before them to a massive clearing, dominated by a tall, sleek, oval-shaped building that glistened in the spring sunlight. Off to the right was the forward part of a space-faring vessel that had plummeted to Earth during the life-changing invasion so many years ago. It was either a Russian or Chinese submarine that had shot it out of orbit with an intercontinental ballistic missile, kicking off the turning point in the First Contact War.

One more guardhouse and gate stopped them before they were allowed entry into the parking lot. Erwin parked the car in Hans' reserved space close to the building.

Before stepping out of the car, Hans turned to Erwin. "Thank you for your answers, Erwin. They have been most helpful."

IT WAS UNNECESSARY TO take Erwin into the Global Servitors AG research building. Hans stood in his office, reading through research notes from the previous night. The building operated twenty-four hours a day out of necessity. Every minute counted. He smiled gleefully at the progress his team was making. He was delighted to see evidence of improved efficiencies for the next PeRoS model. Every little bit helped.

Exhibits of past models lined one wall of his spacious office. Just looking at how much they had developed over the few years of their existence proved to him that humans were on the right path. Sure, nearly all of society was suffering from a debilitating physical illness, but progress in the robotics field was helping to alleviate that. Other responses to that problem were out of his control, however …

His office door opened and one of his longtime friends entered.

"Walther!" Hans said, closing the report on his computer. "Come in, please."

Walther Gruenburg was the company's military servitor division head and a proud proponent of everything the MiRoS model stood for. He powered across the office and greeted Hans, their weave-enhanced hands meeting in a strong grip.

"So, how did it go?" Walther asked. He sat opposite Hans.

"With Erwin? He couldn't comprehend the necessity of defending me in times of danger, much less helping a stranger. It seems there is a conflict in his code."

Walther cringed. "I thought that might happen. Our other tests have shown the same. Those PeRoS units you gave me failed the practical assessment. They either let their simulated human masters die due to indecision or were destroyed when assaulted."

A silence followed as each man digested the import of that news. "Are you really that concerned about the fighting ability of my PeRoS models?"

"It's not their *ability* I'm worried about," Walther sighed. "It's their lack of usefulness for when the Omegas return."

Hans resisted the urge to slump in his chair. "We're trying, Walther, believe me."

Walther nodded. "I know." Then he flashed a mischievous grin. "But I'm not the one that has to tell the boss."

THE BOSS WAS EMMA Kruger, a younger roboticist who spearheaded the entire research department at Global Servitors AG. Several key individuals met in her office to discuss weekly reports, and Hans and Walther were only a minute late. Emma checked the clock on the wall as they sat down.

"I have some bad news," she said, looking around the table. Hans leaned in and noted a few others who had stiffened. "The latest gene editing trials have not succeeded as hoped. So it's weaves and shock suits for a little while longer."

"What happened to the test subjects?" someone asked.

Emma swallowed hard. "Dead."

Hans closed his eyes amidst the outcry of sorrow and regret. Another failed gene experiment. For all the technological advancements made in the years since the invasion, his fellow human beings were having the most trouble solving the main symptom of their suffering. He dropped his eyes down to his shock suit. Osteogenesis imperfecta, more commonly known as brittle bone disease, hadn't stalled humanity's ability to advance, but if the effects of the gene weapon weren't reversed, it would spell the end of the human race.

While the scientists around him talked over each other, Hans thought about his wife. When the Omegas swept the world with their omnicidal gene-altering weapon, of course he and his wife had been affected. They persevered after the attack, but she died before the advent of weaves and shock suits. Now, encased in his protective and powered clothing, Hans felt just as helpless as when he hobbled after his broken wife while she tumbled to her death down a short flight of stairs. She was only thirty-seven. From then on, he was over-protective of his children. Now they were filling important roles in the development of defences for the expected Omega return.

Hans didn't know when the second wave of the Omegas would arrive. It had been nearly fifteen years since humanity blasted their ships out of space and gained a Pyrrhic victory. Maybe they were waiting for all humans to die out. Maybe it took a long time for news of defeat to return to the Omega homeworld. Maybe they were right now amassing an even larger attack force to ensure victory a second time around. Whatever the case, Hans knew he had to work harder to ensure humanity's survival, whether or not the Omegas came.

"Doctor Kruger?" Hans called above the voices of the others. When she put up a hand to quieten everyone, he continued. "I think the code for my PeRoS should be rewritten. If the gene experiments are failing, then servitors will be the bulk of our defence forces.

We should meet with the UN and decide soon—stockpile weapons for PeRoS units and rewrite their codes so that they can be used as reserve combatants when the Omegas come back."

There were heads nodding around the table. Emma Kruger studied everyone's faces, no doubt seeing agreement with the idea. "If we do that for PeRoS models, then we should do the same for the worker servitors too." She glanced over at Sofie Braun, the WoRoS research division head, and got a nod. "I'll pass it on to head office. Where the geneticists fail, the roboticists will pick up the slack."

Hans knew that comment held no malice for the work of the geneticists. They were doing their best. But the world hadn't recovered to where it stood today without the combined efforts of every speciality, profession, and trade. It was like a game of tug-of-war, except the humans were fighting time instead of some tangible opponent. Sooner or later, time would run out, and then the real enemy would resurface. He hoped they'd be ready for that.

"In the meantime," Emma continued, "get a head start on those codes. When the UN agrees with the idea, I want us to act as quickly as possible."

Hans and his WoRoS counterpart, Sofie Braun, accepted the order. Frankly, in Hans' opinion, he was happy to have a superior who understood the importance of time. She could boss him around all day if it meant humanity was better prepared.

At the end of the working day, Hans returned to his car. Erwin sat staring out the windscreen, powering up the moment Hans opened his door.

"Good afternoon, Doctor Schreiber," Erwin said as happily as a servitor could. "I hope your day has been productive."

"Oh, it was, Erwin. It was."

"Where shall I take you?"

"We'll go straight home tonight. There is much work to do."

With that, Erwin started the car and began on the winding drive through the forest. The sun was setting, casting its rays through the pine trees and sending shadows across the road. Sunlight flickered in the car as it drove through these shadows. Hans looked over at his PeRoS unit, but the servitor kept its eyes on the road.

Hans had owned "Erwin" since the first PeRoS models were produced. Every successive model brought better functions, but the memory data was transferred. Hans and Erwin had known each other nearly as long as Hans had been married to Helga. He supposed it was technically impossible to form such a bond, but Hans considered Erwin to be his friend. He smiled at the memories of how Erwin helped him with the daily difficulties of brittle bone disease.

"The gene experiments failed again," Hans said.

"I am sorry to hear that."

That made Hans chuckle. Could a servitor ever be truly sorry? He accepted the comment anyway. "Looks like you're still feeding me collagen pills."

"If they help you, then you must take them."

"What will you do if I don't want them anymore?"

"I will force you to take them."

"How?"

Erwin slowed for the first gate and remained silent as they were admitted through. "If I told you that, you would know how to avoid it."

Hans grinned. "How would you do it?"

Again, Erwin was quiet, as if forming the right words. "I do not know how." Then it spun its head sideways and gave Hans the typically expressionless look all servitors had.

Hans had to laugh. "Don't worry, I'll keep taking them."

"Thank you, *mein Herr.*"

"But it's nice to know you care about me. The whole human

race is in the same predicament, you know? But not all are fortunate to have a PeRoS unit to support them." He thought about isolated communities and governments that were still unsure about having robots in households.

"I am here to serve for as long as you need me."

Hans let that comment sink into him as they reached the outermost security checkpoint. By the time the MiRoS unit waved them through and the car entered the highway beyond the forest, Hans was fighting back tears. Erwin's comment had gouged into his heart a realisation of impending loss. Soon, the codes for the PeRoS and WoRoS units would be rewritten to include a conditional function to be enacted when the Omegas arrived. When that happened, Erwin would cease to be the servitor Hans had come to know and love. Erwin would leave Hans' employ, report to a military station, and be armed for combat, along with all the other non-military servitors.

Hans couldn't bring himself to carry on the conversation with Erwin. The chances were that he would never see Erwin again if the Omegas returned. The peaceful, friendly servitor would sacrifice his "life" to keep the rickety human race alive. And when it was all over—*if* humankind won again—they could go on rebuilding and undoing the effects of the Omegas gene-altering weapon.

Cars passed them on the highway. People were moving on in life, but their brittle bones were always with them. And yet, that had not stopped them. They kept going. The Omegas couldn't defeat humanity the first time, and Hans was sure they'd fail again. Out of their weakness, the human race had built strength.

Erwin's sacrifice would not be in vain.

ABOUT THE STORY

"BRITTLE AND STRONG" WAS written in response to a submission call from Twelfth Planet Press for their *Rebuilding Tomorrow* anthology.

The required theme was that the story had to have a disabled or chronically-ill character rebuilding society.

I focused on a world that had recovered from a huge alien invasion, but the repercussions were still being felt. The main character, Dr Hans Schreiber, suffers from a severe form of brittle bone disease. His condition is shared by everyone else on Earth because of a gene-altering bioweapon used against them by the invading aliens.

Being a science fiction writer, I looked to technology to help my character and the rest of humanity rebuild after the attack. Three key inventions were critical to their survival: shock suits, weaves, and robotic assistants. Additionally, the world began mass producing collagen pills.

I think I was overcome with creativity when I wrote "Brittle and Strong", because I fell into the worldbuilding trap again. I was creating too much of a backstory, too much history, and not enough immediate conflict. Still, the main element of the story—the relationship between Dr Schreiber and his robot assistant, Erwin—was well developed. This focus of the story meant I missed the mark for the anthology. The disabled character rebuilding the world became a background note in a more personal tale.

As expected, Twelfth Planet press rejected the story. I then submitted it to several magazines, all of whom rejected it, though some provided favourable comments, mostly praising the relationship between Dr Schreiber and Erwin. They also highlighted that the internal world was too big for the story.

Readers at *Cosmic Roots & Eldritch Shores* wrote that the story was "well-written, highly engaging, with gradual revelations of the world, a lovely relationship between Dr Schreiber and Erwin, plays to the heart", but that it felt "the piece is a gradual revelation of parts of a world, and does that effectively, but it does little more than tease at a larger narrative". Another reader noted the strong ways the story was written, such as: "The physicality of the piece is potent. We feel the cracking joints, the aching muscles, the tightening suits, squeezing everything into place. We feel the exhaustion of the protagonist." Yet another said: "The intimacy of the relationship between the protagonist and his servitor is interesting as well. Though it only really flares up towards the end, there are a lot of unique overtones to the way the two characters interact. Edwin feels partly like a live in nurse, partly like a son, partly like a rather simple butler who truly cares for his master. The revelation that the protagonist cares for Edwin, that he thinks of this servitor as more than a piece of equipment is a stunning little surprise at the end."

Escape Pod said, "we loved the relationship at this story's core", but they believed the first half of the story needed more context about brittle bone disease and the alien invasion. *Aurealis* echoed similar thoughts to the other magazines, that the story was well written, but that it lacked strength, the ending fizzled out, and that the protagonist faced no conflict, all of which I think is a product of it being just one part of a much larger story.

"Brittle and Strong" received an Honorable Mention for the Writers of the Future 3rd Quarter 2021 Contest.

I have thought about adapting the story into a novel, but I have too many other, more interesting long-form projects for now. Maybe at some point I will write a novel about a world of humans recovering from a gene-altering bioweapon and fighting back a second-round alien invasion with their robotic assistants, but for now I have plenty of other stories to occupy my time.

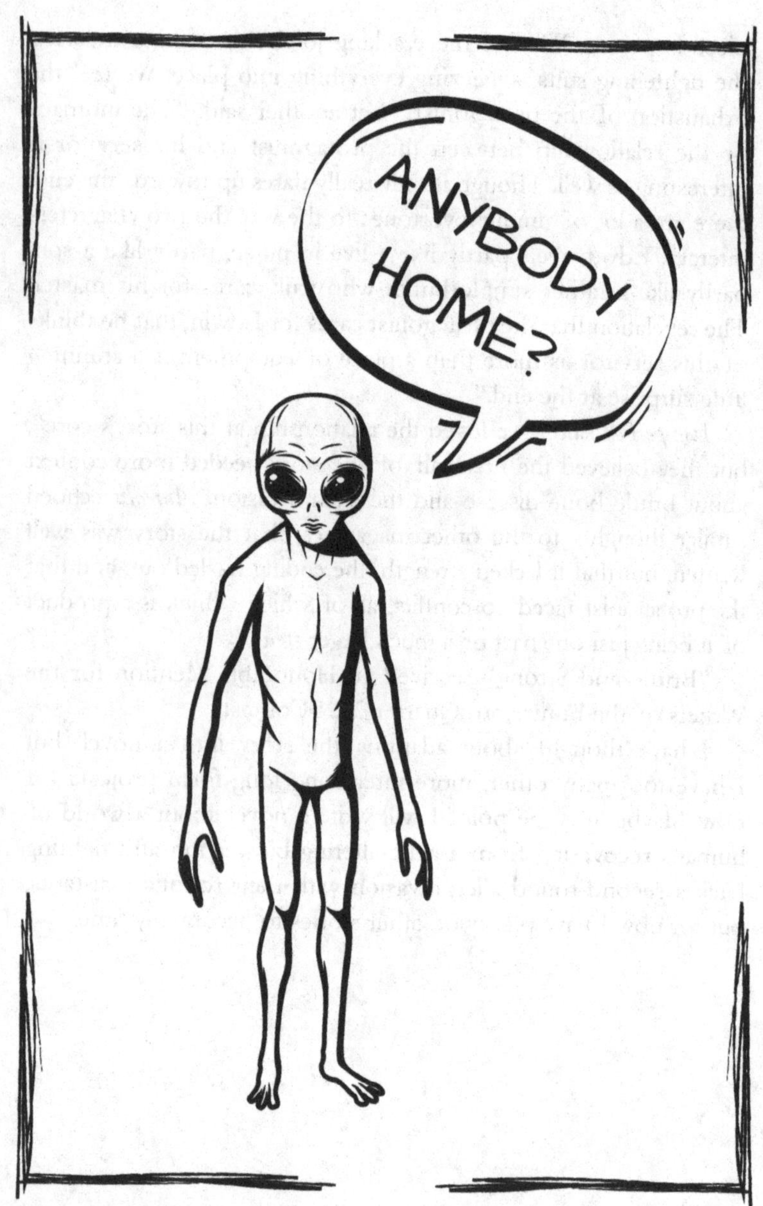

ANYBODY HOME?

GUIDELINES FOR SUCCESSFUL INTERACTION WITH FIRST CONTACT SPECIES

[VERSION 1.2]

THE FOLLOWING ARE GUIDELINES developed by a multi-national team from the United Nations Xenological Research Institute. For simplicity, the guidelines refer to a single extraterrestrial visitor, but they can apply to a group of any size. Observe these guidelines to the letter.

1. Do not say, "Greetings!" This is clichéd beyond the point of no return. However, if the extraterrestrial says "Greetings!" to you, try not to roll your eyes.

2. Observe the stipulated first greetings radius of between five and eight metres. This offers some opportunity for retreat should events turn sour, or if the extraterrestrial naturally emits a foul odour, in which case you might have to retreat anyway.

3. If the extraterrestrial has a noticeable feature
    on its face or body, do not stare at it.

4. Give the extraterrestrial your title and
    full name, but be wary of hypnotic or tele-
    pathic abilities that might reveal sensitive
    information, such as our planetary defence
    systems or knowledge of your embarrassing
    secrets.

5. Try to establish some form of communication
    and be sure to extend a warm welcome and
    emphasise your interest in peaceful rela-
    tions. However, if the extraterrestrial
    seems aggressive or hostile, adopt a frown
    to show you mean business.

6. Once communication is established, determine
    whether it is safe for them to exit their
    ship. Otherwise, you will be cleaning the
    mess when they explode/implode/melt/compress/
    etc. as a reaction to our atmosphere.

7. Avoid using common hand and facial
    gestures—what may be effective non-verbal
    communication methods may inadvertently be
    standard forms of communication for the
    extraterrestrial. We do not want you acci-
    dentally insulting them. Unless, of course,
    insults are an acceptable form of relation-
    ship-building on their world. But it is best
    to play it safe. This is why no individual
    from a cultural background of hand-talking
    will be allowed to interact with first
    contact extraterrestrials until a suitable
    relationship has been formed. The exception
    to the rule will be unless said individuals'

hands and arms are restrained or have been previously amputated.

8. Determine what position the extraterrestrial holds in their world. This will greatly assist administration personnel in allocating suitable accommodations for our visitor (i.e., luxurious penthouse versus three-star motel room).

9. Determine whether the extraterrestrial has come to destroy us, to help us, to ask for our help, is lost, or to simply make a rest stop as part of a longer journey. Either way, we want to be its friend. If its purpose is to destroy us, then we salute you for your courageous act as the first defender of Earth and will remember you for as long as the human race survives against the onslaught of a far superior alien menace.

10. If they are friendly, ask nicely if they may leave any weapons on their ship. If they don't comply, don't worry—there will be several heavily armed drones following your every move and waiting to bombard your position should the extraterrestrial turn hostile. Your family will be compensated for your loss through various financial and counselling options.

11. Ask if they will probe you—it would be nice to debunk a decades-old science fiction trope. However, if a probing will occur, enter your happy place and make this sacrifice for the benefit of humankind. You will

receive a cash payment for your services (should you survive and return from the procedure) of not more than $100,000 and access to free counselling and proctology services for the rest of your life.

12. Try to learn what planet the extraterrestrial has come from—there are several bets among Earth's space agencies that need to be resolved.

13. Try to find out if they have lawyers on their planet. If they do, we don't want them here. Bear in mind that a consensus on the formal and informal status of lawyers may be a point of common ground between their civilisation and ours.

14. At the earliest convenient time, learn about the extraterrestrial's gastronomical details. Chances are they will have brought their own food, but if for some reason they extend their stay on Earth, we will need to feed them. Not everyone likes coffee.

15. Try to balance our display of military power with that of economic strength. Money walks—or, in the case of our visitor, it might fly, levitate, crawl, or slither. If the extraterrestrial has no concept of money, alert the World Trade Organization immediately, because you've just discovered a gold mine.

16. Do not, under any circumstances, show them cats for an extended period. We do not want a repeat of cat worship like that experi-

enced in Ancient Egypt. The master-servant
relationship between cats and humans is
finally at a workable balance now, so there
is no need to ruin two millennia of pains-
taking reforms.

17.　Do not introduce them to films or literature
about humans destroying aliens. That is bad
publicity.

18.　State that we apologise if they intercepted
the 2008 Across the Universe interstellar
radio message. The Beatles, popular as
they were and still are, may not be to the
liking of our alien visitors. Best-case
scenario: it inspired an interest in 1960s
Earth pop culture. Worst-case scenario:
they prefer the Rolling Stones.

19.　Ascertain their interest in sports, as
this is often a point of common ground for
humans. If the extraterrestrial engages
in sports, show them an example of Earth
sports. Baseball will suffice, due to its link
with UFOs. If you must show them football,
make sure it's the real football (i.e.,
soccer), and never, under any circumstance,
show them an American team—the embarrassment
can only go so far.

20.　Try to learn about their technological
achievements and secure a deal to give us the
means of interstellar travel and colonisation. We really want to reach the stars, but,
frankly, it's taking too long doing it by
ourselves.

21. Assure the extraterrestrial that while our
     governmental systems may seem laughable to
     them, they actually are laughable to us as
     well. We will accept reasonable advice to
     improve this aspect of our civilisation.

Memorise these guidelines and check regularly for updates. We may only get one chance to form a friendly relationship with extraterrestrial life. The fate of Humanity counts on you! Good luck.

ABOUT THE STORY

"GUIDELINES" ISN'T REALLY A story. It's science fiction, certainly, but there is no story to it. However, I can imagine myself using it as the basis for a story, and one day I might just do that.

I've always struggled with writing *really* short fiction. There is an online magazine called *Daily Science Fiction* that only accepts stories between 100 and 1,500 words, and I wanted to submit to it. So it was a personal challenge.

I cheated when I wrote "Guidelines" for *Daily Science Fiction*. Yes, I wrote a story that wasn't a story. It is nothing more than a list with some context before and after. It was never intended to be a serious list, but I like to think that some of the guidelines are practical and life-saving, and elicit a laugh. This mild form of cheating is completely fine, though, because I had seen other list-like stories published on the *Daily Science Fiction* website.

Daily Science Fiction rejected it in 2020. I then submitted to *Flash Fiction Online*, and it was rejected there too. Finally, I sent it to *Uncanny Magazine*, who completed the trifecta of rejections. But I wasn't too fussed—I knew I wrote something funny, and that was good enough for me. There is still an aversion to humour in science fiction circles, but I try to provide some levity sometimes.

I ended up publishing "Guidelines" for free on my website because it was such a quick read. It stayed there for a few years before being lightly edited and included in this collection.

FALSEHOOD

Vorn examined the blue-and-white armoured soldiers in formation, sympathising with the discomfort they must have felt. They stood on parched ground in front of one of the Maker's temples, enduring the heat of the morning. Vorn squinted as the sun's rays reflected off their shiny armour. Their officers sat on horseback and had widely plumed helmets for shade, but Vorn knew from personal experience that the shade didn't count for much. The air itself was too hot for that.

Miserable bunch, Vorn thought.

The commander of the force, Lord Johl, dismounted and marched up to Vorn, bowing respectfully as all people did to the priestly class.

"Oh, Vorn, Keeper of the Living Force," Johl began with the usual pomp, loud enough for his troops to hear, "we come to you for sustenance and prayers, for we are to trek to the Wild Region."

"I have heard of your mission, my lord," Vorn replied. "You are right to seek guidance and the supply of that which keeps all beings alive. Your mission to the Wild Region is fraught with dangers, not least of which is the criminal you seek." Vorn was careful not to speak the criminal's name in public—he knew Johl had forbidden it throughout his entire province.

Johl raised his eyebrows ever so slightly at the priest's tactful words. "Then let us begin, for we have a long march ahead. Tasmania is a small land, but it's paths are ever touched by the burning sun."

"I shall delay you no longer than is necessary," the priest said with a solemn bow of the head.

With that, Johl motioned for the two horse-drawn wagons that had accompanied his force to be brought to the priest. They kicked up dust with every hoof that hit the ground. The wind sent the dust wisping through the air, through the ranks of the soldiers, but none stirred. Dust was a part of life and had been for centuries.

When the wagons were in position at the head of the assembled force, Vorn spoke up. "Let us approach the Maker." The soldiers bowed their heads in a cacophony of clinking metal chin guards on breastplate collars.

Vorn prayed to the Maker, thanking Her for life and a material world on which to live it. He thanked Her for the nightly reprieves of the heat and the provision of food and water to keep her subjects healthy. He noted that although their world was hot and dry, despite it being terribly hard to grow food and find enough water to drink, She always supplied them with enough water when they truly needed it. And so he prayed that in this instance She would provide water to fill the tanks on the wagons and that when the soldiers needed more and arrived at another of her temples, She would do the same again. Lord Johl was hunting a wanted man who had kidnapped Tasmania's only princess and was roaming the Wild Region with his lawless band of warriors. Vorn prayed that the Maker grant swift justice, and for the soldiers to return home safely. He closed his prayer with the customary hymn about the world's scarcest commodity—water, the Living Force.

When he raised his head and opened his eyes, Vorn turned to Johl. "Unhitch the wagons."

Johl repeated the order. While the wagon drivers obeyed, Vorn approached the Maker's temple. It was a square structure, two tiers high, with an immense central column atop the square base, rising to such a height that Vorn's neck hurt when he looked at its top.

The drivers pushed their wagons into position by the wide temple doors.

"I will now commune with the Maker on your behalf," Vorn said to Johl. "Have the eyes of your wagon drivers bound with the ceremonial cloths."

Strips of high-quality black cloth were tied around each drivers' head, rendering them blind. Only a Keeper of the Living Force was allowed to see the inside of a Maker's temple. Then Vorn faced the assembled troops, raised his hands high, and watched as the ranks dropped to their knees and bowed with their faces low to the ground. Their officers dismounted and humbled themselves in the same manner. Lord Johl frowned before joining his men. Vorn hid his knowing smirk.

Vorn unlocked the double doors to the temple while the armed force was prostrated. He beckoned the wagon drivers to push the wagons inside. Being a short, straight path and a task which they had performed many times past, it was no issue for them to do it blindfolded. Vorn kept a hand on the hilt of his priestly sword, just in case one of the drivers removed their blindfold. The punishment was always death for such an act.

Once the wagons were inside the temple, Vorn dismissed the drivers and locked himself in, plunging the interior into cold darkness. Vorn suppressed a shiver at the sudden change in temperature, drawing his clothes tighter to his chest. He moved by memory to the switch on the wall that somehow provided light to the cavernous room. Rectangular fixtures on the walls snapped to life, revealing just what a Maker's temple was all about.

Water tanks. Huge, voluminous water tanks, several times Vorn's height, arranged in a U-shape around the interior of the windowless room. Each tank had a durable hose with an automatic pumping mechanism. Knowing the soldiers and officers outside would be bowing until he returned, he quickly began filling the wagons with precious water.

Commune with the Maker! Vorn scoffed as he silently did his work.

He looked up at the spiralling metal staircase that climbed to the building's second level. He'd been up there before. All the temples were identical, and he had explored the second storey of every one he'd served in—pipes and smaller tanks with trickling water or rushing air, locked boxes that hummed and purred like animals, and strange artwork of changing numbers and lines plotted on a canvas of an unknown material. It wasn't glass, but when Vorn would look closely at the art he could see a reflection of his face if the interior lighting shone right. He had given up trying to understand the second storey.

What he did understand was the room with the water tanks and the massive central column that stretched high into the sky. He knew the water came from the column, but he could not fathom how that was possible without rain. There was, however, no shadow of a doubt that nobody—living or dead, material or spiritual—had anything to do with the supply of water. Of that much, Vorn was certain. Whenever Vorn had to enter his temple—or any of the other ones dotted around Tasmania—there was water to be taken. And he could remember times when he'd emptied a tank, only for it to somehow be filled again at a later date. These strange buildings that had been in existence for at least hundred generations were the only real water sources Vorn knew of.

As a priest, he was free to drink all the water he needed. The King had regular deliveries to his residence in Hobart, as did the provincial lords. But the people were on rations, and the land didn't get quite enough to produce full, healthy crops. Animals, especially horses and mules, were served comparatively more per day than their human masters, and soldiers had an increased ration. And to think that at one time there had been huge bodies of water separating entire nations!

Vorn shook his head at the current state of the world he lived in. He saw no room for improvement on the horizon, but he was content to fulfil his role as Keeper of the Living Force while other people collapsed from dehydration.

When the tanks were filled, Vorn cut off the strange light sources and rapped on the double doors. As per the custom, the leader of whatever group of people were assembled outside would ensure the wagon drivers had their blindfolds on when the doors opened to admit them. That task fell on Lord Johl this time, and Vorn soon heard the confident knocks in reply as the leader alerted the priest to the drivers' readiness.

With a hand on his sword hilt, Vorn opened the doors for the drivers and guided them to the wagons. Johl, he could see, had already re-prostrated himself to the hard, hot ground. Despite being significantly heavier, the wagons moved with a smooth easiness characteristic of Tasmanian-made wheeled vehicles. The drivers grunted only a few times as they pushed them out to the waiting horses.

The wagons out, and the communion complete, Vorn sealed up the Maker's temple and bid the men before him to rise. He spoke when everyone was upright and waiting for him.

"The Maker has granted you two full wagons of water for your journey!" Vorn announced. The officers and soldiers uttered in unison a holy word of thanks for the gift of the Living Force. "When you require more, petition one of my brother or sister priests at another temple, and they shall again commune with the Maker on your behalf." Despite facing the assembled troops while saying the last sentence, Vorn was speaking to Lord Johl.

Johl nodded unenthusiastically and fidgeted. Vorn could see he was eager to embark on his mission to hunt down the miscreant and sinner who was a threat to every Tasmanian. He nodded to the commander.

"Harness the horses," Johl said to the drivers. Then he turned to his officers. "Prepare the men to move out." While the disciplined soldiers kicked up dust as they formed into marching columns, Lord

Johl flashed Keeper Vorn a face of mutual understanding about his mission.

Vorn stepped closer to the provincial lord. He looked up to the sky and let the sun caress his face. "When you find this man who threatens our water, see that you spill from him every drop of blood that courses through his body. Teach him who the water *really* belongs to by being the one to take his life-giving essence from him."

"The king has demanded we bring him to Hobart for public execution."

"Then I shall see first-hand the death of the one who threatens my livelihood, and who denounces the king and his lords as liars and thieves."

"That we are …" Johl whispered, though the clopping of horseshoes and the slapping of sandalled soldiers dampened his words. "But his ramblings have done no more than stir the ire of those with the power to destroy him."

"That may be so, but other people have heard his ramblings and have acted on them. He now has a small band of warriors, as you yourself have stated time and again." Vorn sighed. "Let us hope he has perished in the heat already." *I hope, not pray, for there is no one to pray to.*

The soldiers finished their manoeuvre, the officers waited on horseback, and the water wagons were in position at the rear of the formation.

"And if he has not perished," Johl said, "then I shall capture him, see him executed at Hobart, and receive the king's daughter in marriage as a reward."

"You'll be the next King," Vorn said with one raised eyebrow and a crooked smile.

"And you, my dear Vorn, the Chief Keeper." Johl smiled. "With each passing generation, the world gets hotter and dryer. That dryness has given power to men and women like us, and you and I will keep it that way." He saluted by pumping his fist on his breastplate.

Vorn nodded, and with that Lord Johl departed, leading his troops into the depths of Tasmania, into the Wild Region, where the sting of the sun's heat was slightly tempered by the higher elevation, but where there were fewer sources of water, either natural or from a temple.

Temple, Vorn thought, looking up at the massive structure with it's strange, cylindrical centrepiece piercing the sky. *A temple filled with water, protected by me, a Keeper of the Lie.*

ABOUT THE STORY

"Depressing scenario with no hopeful future." That was how one slush reader from *Cosmic Roots & Eldritch Shores* described "Falsehood". Curiously, other slush readers from the same magazine stated that it was "well written, but seemed like only a beginning" and that it had "no real conflict, but interesting worldbuilding and a good start for a larger piece". How right they were.

You see, "Falsehood" was an experiment. It was my first creative foray into the world that became known as the Nahla Chronicles, the first book of which is *Nahla: Warrior of the North*. There is a lot of history behind this story, and it all starts with a germ of an idea attributed to Edgar Rice Burroughs. I've always loved Andrew Stanton's *John Carter*, the film adaptation of Edgar Rice Burroughs' Barsoom books. But it wasn't until I read the first Barsoom book, *A Princess of Mars*, that I got hooked on the idea of a far-future, post-apocalyptic, sword-and-planet story with an outsider for a hero.

It started as a joke in my family, naming characters after my parents and letting my dad have the '80s action hero body he always wanted. Think *Conan the Barbarian*. Sometime later, Flame

Tree Press put out a call for submissions for an anthology titled *A Dying Planet*. They requested the following:

> Resources running low, the population exploding, the planet is in danger: are we masters of our own destruction, or have we been invaded by aliens bent on mass extinction? Is this a pattern across the entire universe, or just our small sector of cosmic life? New stories needed to explore themes of a dying planet.

The anthology was perfect for my sword-and-planet idea, so I started writing an action-packed battle scene. Halfway through, I decided the battle was not the right story to tell for the anthology, so I switched to a slower, more ominous tale about the military force setting off *before* the battle. Even at this early stage, I knew the world was much larger than what could be contained in only a few thousand words. Really, "Falsehood" reads like one chapter of a novel. A few years later, I started writing that novel. However, the world was even larger that I'd thought—the scene I wrote in "Falsehood" could not fit in the first book, *Nahla Warrior of the North*.

At the time that this anthology is being prepared, the scene depicted in "Falsehood" has been completely reworked to match the more developed story arc in the Nahla Chronicles and is featured in Book Two, *Nahla: Enemy of the Kingdom*, which is currently in first draft.

"Falsehood" was rejected by six editors before I decided to pull it from the submission cycle and let the idea incubate into a novel. The experience taught me about the risk of writing a short story that has no business being a short story. It also taught me patience—if I really like an idea and want to write it, I should not rush into the wrong format; instead, I should take the time to write the full story in all its glory. And the story of *Nahla* truly is glorious.

ESCAPE VELOCITY

ACKNOWLEDGEMENTS

This collection was several years in the making. Originally, the intention was never to publish all my stories together. Therefore, each story was its own project. I am indebted to my family, who have voraciously read each story, even the ones that were never published.

As a former slush reader and magazine editor, I know how much time is involved in reading submissions, writing feedback, and sending replies to authors. Therefore, I am extremely grateful for the slush readers and editors who spent the time writing critiques for my submissions. Similarly, I thank the likes of Tom Dullemond, Shelly Nir, Samantha Ryder, Joel Schanke, Dirk Strasser, Stephen Higgins, Michael Pryor, Sheila Williams, Scott H. Andrews, Neil Clarke, Fran Eisemann, Michele-Lee Barasso, Jonathan Laden, Scot and Jane Noel, Mur Lafferty, Valerie Valdes, Aidan Wilson, Sheree Renée Thomas, Cavan Terrill, Lezli Robyn, Stephen Wright, W. Ward, Andy Cox, Gareth Jelley, John Joseph Adams, Angela Yuriko Smith, Tony C. Smith, Bennett North, Aimee Ogden, Gautam Bhatia, Lynne M. and Michael Damian Thomas, Jason Palmatier, Joni Labaqui, and many others for keeping the short fiction scene alive through magazines, anthologies, and podcasts.

Unfortunately, I have seen several magazines shut down even in the short time I have been writing. I thank all the readers who continue to support the publications that still remain, whether in print, digital, or audio format.

ABOUT THE AUTHOR

Nick Marone grew up in Sydney, Australia before eventually moving south towards Canberra. He developed an interest in science fiction in his teens and has been hooked ever since. His first book, the novella *Fire Over Troubled Water*, was released in 2019, which was followed by novels in the Space Trip Universe and the Nahla Chronicles. Over the years, he has worked for *Aurealis* and *Andromeda Spaceways Magazine*. You can follow Nick and subscribe to his free newsletter at **nickmarone.com**.

SPREAD THE WORD

If you liked *Escape Velocity*, please leave a rating and/or review on Goodreads. This helps other readers find the book. Word-of-mouth is also very helpful. If you think your friends, family, or social media followers would enjoy *Escape Velocity*, please tell them about it. I greatly appreciate your support.

THE GREEN REBELLION: A SPACE TRIP STORY

SPACE TRIP UNIVERSE: BOOK 0.1

Ichika Sato is an overworked and underpaid human resources officer. All she wants is a relaxing holiday enjoying the beaches and jungle walks of Paradise. The resort planet is touted as the hidden gem of the Centaurus Arm, and it is exactly what she needs to reset her mind.

When Ichika arrives at her long-awaited holiday destination, however, she finds a resort filled with people, contrary to the advertisements. But there is something more unsettling at play. The rough surf, the rustling trees, the rumbling wind—all speak to an impending disaster. Everyone sees the signs, but nobody knows what they mean.

Paradise is caught off guard. Instead of sunbathing peacefully on the beach, Ichika is trapped on the planet along with the rest of the tourists, at the mercy of Paradise's wrath. It's a fight for survival and a quest for understanding as Ichika teams up with tourists and resort workers to stop Paradise from destroying itself.

Scan with phone to go to
The Green Rebellion

SPACE TRIP

SPACE TRIP UNIVERSE: BOOK 1

Four friends—Dave, Eddie, Jimmy, and Chuck—are fed up with their boring lives. So when Eddie builds a personal interstellar spacecraft, the obvious thing is to go somewhere. Little do the guys know that simply going somewhere is never quite that easy. The galaxy is a big place, full of complex worlds, people of ill repute, and unexpected events popping up at the wrong time.

Join our woefully underprepared friends as they try desperately to get to the tourist world known as Paradise. Climb aboard *Liberty*, Eddie's oddly-shaped but perfectly functional ship, and share in their pains and joys as they press on to their goal and maybe learn a bit about themselves along the way. You deserve a break, too, and what better way to do so than to spend time with four misfits who clearly need help?

Chuck says to bring coffee when you meet them at the spaceport—don't forget!

Scan with phone to go to
Space Trip

SPACE TRIP II: THE JOURNEY TO FIND THE SECRET OF THE THING IN THE BOX

SPACE TRIP UNIVERSE: BOOK 2

Following their wild maiden voyage aboard *Liberty* and their impulsive purchase of an abandoned resort city, Dave, Eddie, Jimmy, and Chuck haphazardly embark on a new adventure.

Jimmy buys a mysterious box from a small, unassuming antique shop. When he finally gets it open, the secrets it contains will pull him and his friends into a galaxy-spanning hunt for answers and, hopefully, treasure. All Jimmy wants is a few pots of gold.

But the guys are not the only ones interested in the box and its mesmerising contents. A wealthy collector is on their tail—he cares less about treasure and wants more than just answers.

What's in the box? Why are four hopeless treasure hunters scouring the galaxy to unlock its secrets? Who is their pursuer, why is he after Jimmy's bargain box, and what tricks will he play to get what he wants?

Scan with phone to go to
Space Trip II

SPACE TRIP III: THE LOST CHAPTER

SPACE TRIP UNIVERSE: BOOK 3

Dave, Eddie, Jimmy, and Chuck are hard at work rebuilding the garden world of Paradise. All is well in their green slice of heaven. But their plans are rudely paused when a mysterious guest pulls them away from their projects.

The guys are given an impossible task: scour billions of planets to find one person hidden among the trillions who live in the galaxy. If they fail, they become mincemeat. Literally.

Their past has come back to haunt them, except they can't remember a thing. So they must clear the fog and finish the puzzle before it's too late. Once again, their journey takes them across the stars on Eddie's speedy ship, *Liberty*. Only this time, *Liberty* might not be fast enough to save them.

Scan with phone to go to
Space Trip III

NAHLA: WARRIOR OF THE NORTH

NAHLA CHRONICLES: BOOK 1

Old Earth is dying, but humanity endures despite the hardships of a far-future, post-apocalyptic world. Nahla, a disgraced and exiled veteran warrior from the Kingdom of Melbourne, treks across the Endless Land, ready to die for her failures.

Instead of succumbing to the barren wasteland, Nahla discovers a civilisation nobody knew existed——the Kingdom of Launceston. Here she finds a new king to serve and a new people to protect. But a dark secret and fiendish plots hang over this southern land, threatening to plunge the kingdom into war and chaos. Under the scorching sun and in the depths of shadows, Nahla contends with bandit clans, mercenaries, suspicious lords, murderous criminals, and hidden agendas.

With allies forged in unlikely places and enemies lurking in the shadows, she uncovers the threads that bind her destiny to the fate of the kingdom. In a world where the line between salvation and destruction is razor-thin, Nahla will fight not only for her own redemption, but for the future of a civilisation on the cusp of oblivion.

Scan with phone to go to
Nahla: Warrior of the North

NAHLA: ENEMY OF THE KINGDOM

NAHLA CHRONICLES: BOOK 2

The fight has just begun. Launceston is tearing itself apart. The King's Legion and provincial garrisons fight to contain a growing rebellion. King Eero struggles to maintain his iron hold on the populace. Faith in the Guardians of Life has been shaken, threatening to undo the status quo that has been so carefully nurtured for as long as recorded history. Nahla's legacy spreads far and wide, fuelling the discontent among the people.

Lord Johl, Governor of Launceston Province, has plans of his own, now made all the more difficult by the secrets uncovered by Nahla and Prince Myel. But he has the upper hand. His enemies are on the run, and he has overwhelming forces on his side, some of which have been kept in the shadows until now.

Pursued by Johl's army, Nahla's band of rebels flee until they can flee no more. Inevitably, they must face the cruel lord in one decisive battle. When that happens, it won't just be a battle for survival. Rather, it will be a monumental clash for the kingdom, a fight for truth and peace against the oppressive grip of lies and tyranny.

Scan with phone to go to
Nahla: Enemy of the Kingdom

www.ingramcontent.com/pod-product-compliance
Lightning Source LLC
Chambersburg PA
CBHW010300100726

47904CB00011B/2675